MURDER BY THE OLD MAINE STREAM

Bernadine Fagan

MURDER BY THE OLD MAINE STEAM

DEDICATION

This book is for my family

My husband Bill, who supports me always,
My daughter and my son, Kristen and Brian,
two people I am so proud of
My brother Francis who gave me my first computer
and told me I should write a book
My sister-in-law Bernadette who cheers me on
My daughter-in-law Gina who gives me feedback
Elizabeth, Paige and William, our three newest members, who are a
source of great joy

ACKNOWLEDGMENTS

Thanks to Nancy and Bob Young, first readers
who gave valuable input
Fellow writers Marilyn Levinson, Myra Platt,
and Marianne Tremmoroli who laughed in all the
right places and kept me going

ONE

The huge black SUV thundered to a stop close enough to Uncle JT's auto body shop to throw a spray of pebbles against the plate glass window of his office. I jumped back. Uncle JT never moved. He just stared, frozen, no expression on his face that I could figure.

My first thought was that we were isolated. Most everything in the Maine woods is isolated, of course. I never should have left New York City, no matter how desperate I was to get away, no matter how hurt, or how angry.

"Who is it?" I whispered to JT as a skinny guy bolted from the SUV and stormed our way. "He looks mad."

"Ay-uh," was all JT said.

Outside, a big guy sat statue-still in the passenger seat. I couldn't see him clearly. I tensed, thinking robbery, murder, maybe hostage-taking. Great-aunt Ida's ridiculous prediction about a coming murder raced through my head, and I slipped my hand into my purse and rummaged around for the mace I always carried.

As far as the family was concerned, I'd come here for the reading of Great-grandma Evie's will, and to get reacquainted with the extended family I hadn't seen since I was ten years old. I am now thirty years old. If I could find out the real reason we left Silver Stream in the first place that would be a bonus. No one knew what prompted me to leave the city in the first place. Some things are best kept secret.

Uncle JT puffed his cigar. Clouds of acrid smoke swirled and blended with the exhaust fumes and oily odors seeping under the garage door creating a toxic mix that would probably kill me.

"Don't worry, Nora. This is nothing much," JT assured me, his cigar-hand shaking. "Have a seat behind the counter. I'll handle this."

I wondered how many men he had working in this shop—I'd seen three when I drove up—and whether they'd come to our aid if needed. Would they hear a cry for help? The sound of a pneumatic drill rasped from one of three open bays beyond the office door, cutting into the harsh sounds of rap blasting from a boom box.

The office door burst open. "JT, we gotta talk. Now."

The guy had a narrow face, pointed almost, and wore an awful jacket, something brown and mustard-colored, a tweed, with imitation leather elbow patches that looked like they'd been pilfered from the set of an old movie.

Narrow Face ignored me. JT looked past him to the truck parked out front. "Percy with you?"

"Yeah."

"His wife's here, too," JT said slowly as he looked from the front to the side windows. "Don't know where she's gone and disappeared to. She just drove up a few minutes ago. Can't miss that red hair."

"This ain't got nothing to do with her," he fired back. His eyes narrowed as he finally looked at me, then down at my Diane von Furstenberg python print tote, which I'd selected especially for this trip. The rugged look had a woodsy quality that I thought went well with the surroundings, and with this outfit. Just in case he thought I had a gun in my rugged bag, I released the grip on the mace canister, eased my hand out and took a seat behind the counter.

"Outside, JT. We gotta talk." He jerked his narrow head toward the door.

JT hesitated, and I saw the ash fall off the end of his cigar as his hand trembled worse than before. Without a word or even a glance at me, he followed the guy outside.

Oh, God. What was going on here? I took the mace canister from my tote and slipped it into the pocket of my gray slacks for easy access.

The three men stood next to the SUV talking. I got up and inched closer to the door, but the noise from the open bay seemed louder and I couldn't hear a thing. I ambled around the room, trying to look casual, unconcerned. This was none of my business.

Suddenly the noise level dropped and I heard a different sound, a human sound.

"Pssst."

I tensed. Glanced around.

"Pssst. Over here."

The side door opened a crack and a hand, a skinny one, reached in and snatched my hand.

"Aaah."

"Shh. Nora. Nora Lassiter. It's me."

Without waiting for a reply, the owner of the brightest red hair on the east coast, looking like a live version of Raggedy Ann, tugged until I followed her behind a bushy evergreen with sharp needles. Since she had called me by name, I didn't yell for help, not that anyone would hear me or even care if I yelled. I guessed she was the woman JT had just mentioned.

"I'm Mary Fran Kendall. Do you remember me? We played together as kids? Of course, I wasn't Kendall then." She spoke rapidly and puffed as if she'd been running.

"Mary Fran." I shoved an evergreen branch away from my face. Yes, I remembered Mary Fran. Oh, did I. The memories came back in a rush, all of them bad. She was the only reason I was glad my family left Silver Stream years ago.

Lowering her voice, she leaned toward me and whispered, "What I have to say is urgent." She glanced at the SUV, then back at me.

She hunkered down in back of the bush, grabbed my hand and yanked me down beside her. Sharp branches from another bush poked me in the back, and lower. My irritation kept pace with my discomfort as I shifted my bottom. "What's going on?"

"You remember me?"

"Mary Fran. Yes, I remember you," I informed her without smiling. My childhood nemesis. Maybe it was her strong hands that triggered the memory, those strong wiry fingers.

"Like I remember my worst nightmares," I went on. "When we were kids, you had about twenty pounds and three inches on me. You were a fighter who meted out punishment for real or imagined reasons with no mercy. I used to run the other way when I saw you coming."

"Sorry about that. Now let's move on. I–"

"I always wore my running shoes," I cut in, not ready to move on. "Come summer, no cute little open-toed sandals for me. No. I had to wear canvas Keds."

"What's wrong with Keds?"

Mary Fran was rail thin, with makeup that could have doubled for wall spackle.

"You used to bend my fingers back," I announced in a no-nonsense voice.

"Nora, I have no time to rehash old times. Here's what I need."

Rehash old times?

"I need a private investigator. I heard all about you this morning, being as how I own and operate the beauty salon on Main Street. Hot Heads Heaven. Maybe you noticed my new magenta marquee? Silver stars around silver heads on a magenta background? Kendall: Proprietor written on the door?"

"No, I didn't notice."

I seldom lie. But this was Mary Fran. Besides, that sign was appalling, a blight on an otherwise quaint and attractive main street.

She gave my hair a professional glance and declared, "You could use a touch up. But I digress. I heard you're a hotshot detective from New York City. I'm willing to pay. Do you know much about computers?"

"I do not need a touch up."

She let out a heavy sigh. "Computers? How good are you?"

I debated whether to tell her I was better than good. I was a computer analyst, and one of the best at my job until I got laid off when the company downsized last week. However, I was not, and never had been, a detective on the New York City Police Department. That story had been fabricated by Great-Aunt Ida to get the sheriff's attention when she had tried to convince him that she'd overhead two people in the library plotting a murder. Aunt Ida reads a lot of mysteries and watches every crime show on television. The woman has a vivid imagination.

I said simply, "I know a thing or two about computers."

"Perfect. I gotta find out who my husband—that would be smooth-talker and all-around ass Percy Kendall," she paused and nodded toward the SUV, "has connected with over the Internet. Some little whore. I know he's screwing around, but I need ironclad evidence. Emails. Some videos or photos, too. He's very clever. It will take someone clever to catch him. That would be you. I always thought you were clever, you know."

I wouldn't let praise go to my head. I was firm. "I don't think so, Mary Fran." I went to stand up, but she pressed her hand on my shoulder. She was very strong. Must work out.

"We were talking about you in the salon today. So when you stopped in front, I decided to follow you."

"I was at that stop sign for a few seconds. You hadn't seen me in twenty years," I scoffed. "So don't tell me you recognized me."

She waved her hand, dismissing this as trivial. "So I hopped in my car and followed you. I must say, and this is not a criticism, mind you, but you were playing your stereo way too loud. I could have followed the noise alone. It sounded like someone screeching off-key. Why would you buy a CD with such a weird sound? But, I digress again. There's no accounting for taste in music and that's that. You also have a loud rattle. Maybe you should have JT look at it. He's pretty good."

"That's why I'm here. The rattle's in—"

"Don't sidetrack me with your car trouble. I have enough trouble of my own. I need a detective, fast."

I shook my head. No, I was not going to do this. Even if I

were a detective, I would not want to help this woman. Didn't like her as a kid. Didn't like her now. End of conversation. Time to tell her the truth about Aunt Ida's fabrication. "Mary Fran, the reason I can't possibly do this—"

She grabbed my hand. I winced although she didn't hurt me. Sometimes anticipation is everything.

"It won't be hard," she said. "Just listen before you say no, and keep in mind I'll pay your fee, whatever you ask, plus a bonus."

Fee? Bonus? I was out of a job and my American Express bill was a whopper this month. Never should have gone on that shopping spree after I was laid off. I suppose it was only polite to listen.

"Okay, Mary Fran." I gently extricated my hand and peeked through the bush to see if the men had left.

"Your husband's one of the guys talking to JT?"

"Yes. I hid my car around back. I don't want him to see me talking to you. He'd know I'd hired a PI. It would ruin everything."

She opened her wallet, yanked out a fistful of bills, grabbed my hand and began counting out twenties. All the while her gaze never stopped shifting between the bills and me. "A retainer," she explained. "To show I'm serious."

Taken aback, I glanced at the pile of bills in my hand. "But Mary Fran you don't understand."

She handed me four more twenties, to shut me up, I suppose. The ploy worked.

"Let me explain what happened just before Percy and me got married. My mother, who was married to the town Casanova, insisted I get Percy to sign a prenup. Do you believe that? Nobody, and I mean nobody, around here signs a prenup. That's for folks like Donald Trump and Julia Roberts. The night I mentioned it to Percy I acted as if it was some big joke. I told him it was to please my mother. He was a little drunk at the time. I had waited for that. He may not even remember because I never mentioned it again. Stupid I am not. Anyway, the prenup said that if he fooled around and I could prove it, and we got a divorce, there'd be no fifty-fifty split of assets. It would be eighty-twenty, my favor. That paper is in my mother's safe deposit box even as we speak."

I folded the money in my hand. "How devious. But it might not stand up in court."

"It will. I checked with a lawyer."

Mary Fran stood, parted the branches, and peeked out.

"Percy's the guy in the red tie, the pompous ass standing next to JT. Looks like a slick infomercial salesman. Thinks he's king of everything. The other guy's his partner, the jerk with the stupid patches on his elbows and the big can, which you'll notice when he turns around. Lard Ass Collins. Percy and him. Perfect team."

"Lard Ass? I hadn't noticed."

As if on cue, Collins turned his back to us. Since I am totally lacking in self-control at times, I laughed out loud. My God. Perfect nickname. How could I not have noticed that shelf?

"Shhh." Mary Fran elbowed me. It had been a long time since anyone elbowed me. Startled, I stared at her. I was not going to work for this woman. And that was that.

Out front, JT waved both hands and smacked the fender. Even from here, I could see the color rising in his cheeks.

"Why are they here?" I asked. "What's going on?"

"Don't know. Don't care." She shrugged. "I guess your curiosity is the sign of a good detective."

"What does your husband do?" I asked instead of telling her the truth.

"Sells cars. Him and Lard Ass have a place on the edge of town. Biggest Little Auto Mart in Maine. They sell used cars and trucks. Maybe you remember it? It was here when you lived here. Percy's father owned it. He was murdered years ago."

Mouth agape, I stared at her. "Murdered. Who did it? Why?"

"Don't know the answer to that one. It was never solved. If his father was anything like him, he probably fooled around and got caught with his pants down. Some jealous husband probably coshed him a good one and it was lights out."

Mary Fran shrugged as if it wasn't important and continued,

"JT does repairs on used cars for the Auto Mart."

I was barely listening. Silver Stream is a small, isolated town. Good people live here. First Aunt Ida mentions a possible coming murder, and now I hear about this happening years ago. Omigod.

I focused on the three men. Lots of agitation. I wished I could hear.

I wished I were a hotshot New York detective who could get the goods on her husband. I thought about it. Maybe I could. Ability with computers seemed to be key. I knew I could find out who Percy was emailing. I could be a first-class hacker if I wanted to, a small detail few people knew. I was friends with a bunch of computer nerds and we still got together from time to time.

All I had to do to catch Percy was find out when he was meeting the woman, follow him and snap a few shots of them coming and going. Piece of cake. I was good with cameras, a hobby I'd played around with since I was a teenager. Intending to take pictures of the family, I'd packed my Canon XTi. I even packed the high powered telephoto lens that cost more than the camera, both bought back in the days when I was flush.

I fingered the wad of bills in my hand that I'd almost decided to give back.

"Yes. I'll take the case," I told Mary Fran, my heart thrumming up a storm.

If it became necessary, I'd spend a few more days here. It's not as if I had a job to go home to. Or a fiancé. Both were part of the recent past that I'd come up here to put behind me.

"Come by my salon Monday morning, first thing," Mary Fran said.

When JT returned, the glowing cigar clamped tightly in his mouth, he launched right into a discussion about my car problem, as if nothing unusual had happened. So much for our happy reunion. He set to work, and cleared up the rattle in the front wheel well of my rented PT Cruiser in no time.

There were so many things I wanted to ask to him, mostly about the family, especially my father. I wanted to find out why Dad had left Silver Stream so suddenly. At the time, he told me he didn't get along with Grandpa who wanted him to go into the lumber business. They had fought. As I got older I suspected there was more to it because Dad didn't want us to even mention his family.

JT was on edge after the visit from Lard Ass and Big-shot Percy so I decided not to launch into any discussion about family. But I did have to ask one thing.

"Did Aunt Ida tell you what she overheard in the library?" I said as I got back into the car.

He shook his head and laughed. "She told all of us. She thinks someone's going to be murdered. Crazy old broad. She's a joke. Overheard someone whispering in the library about getting rid of someone. They were probably talking about a mystery book."

My hands clutched the wheel. Only the fact that I intended to leave in four days kept me from firing back at him, from alienating my deceased father's only brother. Then I noticed the twitch in his left eye. A family trait? That used to happen to Dad. I figured out at an early age that it had to do with tension, and I remembered clearly the first time I realized that. It was right before we moved to the New York City all those years ago.

TWO

Aunt Ida and I had stayed in contact mainly though letters. My father tolerated this. I suppose he felt he had little choice. In the beginning, I'd given him Aunt Ida's letters to read, but he handed them back immediately. Not interested, he'd say. Eventually I stopped offering. He must have been curious though. He had such a large family in Silver Stream—parents, grandparents, aunts, uncles, cousins, his brother.

But only Ida wrote to me.

Ida loved to write. I tolerated it, especially as I got older. I tried to talk her into email a few years back, but she considered that in the same league with intergalactic travel, so at some point we'd switched to monthly phone calls. I decided not to mention texting.

Ida lived in my great-grandmother's house, an old Victorian set back in the woods, with original gingerbread trim, and a wide front porch with a hanging swing. The whole thing looked like it wouldn't be out of place on a birthday cake. I loved it. The rooms were large, with overstuffed furniture, dark wood tables freshly lemon-oiled, lace on every available surface, and a definite hint of lavender in the air.

Ida had put me in Great-grandma Evie's old room. Said she'd cleaned it especially for me. Evie, my father's grandmother, had married the oldest Lassiter brother. Her room was frilly, a girly room from long ago with lace curtains, knick-knacks, and a ruffled, flower-patterned bedspread on the double bed. Great-grandma Evie had crocheted the lace canopy that draped over the top of the dark mahogany frame, and it had been carefully mended over the years.

It was Friday, my second day in Silver Stream. I planned to leave Monday after the reading of the will, or maybe early Tuesday morning. In the short time I had, I wanted to see the house I used to live in, the one Uncle JT now owned, visit as many relatives as I could, see if I could find out why Dad left, and get a few shots of Mary Fran's husband and his lady friend. Feeling better than I had in weeks, I hopped into the shower. It was a short shower. The water went from lukewarm to cold after a minute or two. I toweled off quickly, shivering the whole time. September was chilly in Silver Stream.

I put on my only pair of Laurel Canyon jeans, an extravagance I will never allow myself again, and a blue ribbed turtleneck that matched my eyes, then hurried downstairs, following the scent of something wonderful baking in the oven. One of the *CSI* shows that Ida'd recorded was playing on the small kitchen television. I had a feeling Ida wouldn't approve of the job I'd taken for Mary Fran, but I'd have to tell her anyway.

"Ida. Blueberry muffins."

I threw my arms around her as she set the last muffin in a Tupperware container. "You treat me like this, I may never leave."

"Wicked good muffins, just for you." She smiled and hugged me back, then put her show on Pause. At eighty-four, Ida was still going strong, a little overweight with grey hair secured in a bun at the nape of her neck, wearing coral polyester slacks and a flowered blouse in the same color family.

"Maybe you shouldn't leave. You could live here with me. This is a big house for one woman. What's holding you in the city?"

"My life is there, Aunt Ida. Everything I know."

"But you have no job. You were fired, something I don't understand at all."

"I wasn't fired. I told you I was excessed. It's called downsizing. Big difference."

She looked doubtful and I didn't blame her. I was a little doubtful, too.

"You were their best computer analyst, weren't you? Didn't you get that Employee of the Month plaque a while back? I seem to remember you telling me."

"Yes. All past history." Unfortunately.

"Like your fiancé? Or do you think you'll get back with him?" Her brows shot up in question. "Reconcile, maybe?"

"That's not happening." I shook my head, more to dislodge the last awful scene with him and his bimbo in my shower, than to deny the likelihood of a reunion. "He's history. Let's not spoil this beautiful day by talking about any of this. I want to walk through the woods and see my old house this morning, then go with you to see Aunt Hannah and Aunt Agnes."

I sat down at the table. "Have you seen any moose in the woods around here lately?" I asked casually.

"There was one around back about a week ago. Haven't seen him since. Nothing to worry about. Mating season doesn't start for another few weeks."

I was about to ask what mating season had to do with anything but decided to let that go.

Over breakfast, Ida said, "The old logging trail you kids used as a shortcut is still there. JT plows it from time to time to keep it open. Not sure why. He hardly ever comes here to visit anymore. Anyway, you won't get lost. Just take the bridge over the stream. You'll remember the way."

She glanced at my feet. "Wicked smart boots you got on. Chic, I guess you'd call 'em. Maybe you'd better change into something a little more substantial for trekking through the woods. Help yourself to anything in the closet upstairs.

I thought my knee-high Bally boots were sturdy, but perhaps she was right. Didn't want to scrape these.

I went back upstairs, pulled on a pair of heavy socks and found ankle-high walking boots that probably belonged to some long-dead uncle, dusted them off and yanked them on. Unattractive, and definitely too large, but necessary.

Woods are dangerous. You need heavy boots.

I was careful on the trail. I walked head down, conscious of each step, knowing there were things here to be avoided at all costs, things like moose droppings and deer stuff. Scat, they called it.

There were even animal potholes. Of course, I knew they were not called potholes. I scared myself with the thought of animals waiting to pop up and get me, so I walked cautiously. Ever alert. It goes without saying that I was continually on the lookout for moose. Didn't want to run into any of those. How scared I was as a little kid when my brother Howie told me he'd seen a moose lurking around our driveway, and if I wasn't careful, I'd end up as moose meat. Of course, I later found out they were plant eaters, but still. . . .

Unbidden, came mental images of skunks and weasels and porcupines. Getting shot with a quill could probably kill a person. At the very least, it would hurt like hell.

Snakes? Could there be snakes? More vigilant, I stepped over broken branches and around small trees, on guard for any threat. I took my mace canister out of my bag and shoved it into my pocket for easy access. Like a gunslinger, I was ready.

The sun was visible through the burnished leaves fluttering above my head. Birches. I knew birches, the ones with the white bark. The morning frost had long since vanished, but bad weather was on the way. Red sky at morning, sailor take warning.

I wasn't sure where the property lines were, probably the stream off to my left. I could cross it ahead. Some of this land belonged to JT, some to Great-grandma Evie or Great-aunt Ida. What a feeling. Family woods. Once, Indians roamed here, hunting, making camp. As I stepped around a fallen branch, I pictured an Indian gathering firewood. My mind leaped from the Indians to my ancestors and I pictured Lassiters walking these same woods, maybe even this same trail, over a century ago. The sudden feeling of connection I experienced was so unexpected, I stopped dead in my tracks. But only for a second or two. Maine was not for me. I belonged in the city.

I followed the trail to where it forked. On the right, it sloped slightly toward a deadfall, and on the left it evened off and ran closer to the stream. Except for the softly rippling water, it was quiet here. No bird chatter, no small critters scurrying through the underbrush. I imagined I could hear my heartbeat. Strange, this stillness.

A ways down the path I spotted what looked like a brown alligator boot sticking out from behind a boulder.

"Hello?"

I stopped and waited.

No reply.

"Hello. You behind the rock." I took a deep breath, grabbed the mace in my bag and stepped closer, my heart picking up speed like a semi on a downhill run. I was hoping, hoping, hoping that someone was just sitting here, leaning against the boulder, enjoying the stream. But somehow, I didn't think so.

I should check. Take another step.

Or, I could run the other way.

I finally looked behind the rock. Even prepared as I was to find something awful, like a dead body, I gasped when I saw him. I knew he was dead. I knew *him*. Omigod. There was blood, so much of it. He'd been shot in the head, and I think an animal had nibbled on his fingers. Several of them were chewed to mere stubs. I hoped he was dead when that happened. I began to shake.

Suddenly, I couldn't look another second. I scrambled backwards, stuffed the mace in my pocket, and ran like all the animals in creation were on my heels. Breathing hard the whole way, feeling a wild hysteria that about choked me, I finally stopped and yanked out my cell phone. I dropped it twice. Butterfingers. When I had a firm grip, I hit 9-1-1, gave the operator a brief rundown and continued to Ida's at a fast clip.

Minutes later, the *Toreador March* played on my cell, and I answered.

"Nora Lassiter?" a man's voice said.

"Yes, it's me. Is this the police?"

"Yes. I'm Sheriff—"

"Help!" I yelled before he finished. "There's been a murder. I'll meet you at my aunt Ida's. That's Ida Lassiter in Silver Stream." I gave him Ida's address.

"Where are you now?"

"In the woods."

"Can you be more specific?"

Specific? What was wrong with this man? "Not even if I had a GPS," I replied, making no attempt to keep the sarcasm from my shaky voice.

"Are you near Ida's?"

"Not too far. Going back the way I came." My voice cracked as I skirted a snake and yelped.

"What happened?"

"I almost got attacked by a snake." I looked back at the snake to make sure it wasn't preparing to strike. "Cancel that. Just a dead branch." I took a deep breath, and continued running. "An animal chewed on his fingers."

Which reminded me of the mace. Better to be safe than sorry. I yanked the canister from my pocket.

"Do you know the victim?"

"Yes. It was. . ."

I stepped in a pothole and twisted my ankle. Yelped again. The phone went flying as I struggled to keep my balance.

"What happened? Nora. Nora Lassiter? Are you all right?"

Biting my bottom lip, I dropped to my knees, reached into the underbrush, retrieved the phone, and tossed it in my bag. I was not going to carry on a conversation with anyone while I negotiated this minefield.

Back at the house, I picked out a crummy-looking, old-lady sweater I found in Great-grandma Evie's closet and slipped it on. I was too distressed to care about my appearance, or the fact that I now smelled of moth balls. I was still shaking. I can't recall this ever happening before—not caring about my appearance, or how I smelled, or shaking like this.

Her hand on her chest, Ida listened to me, nodding the whole time, her face a mask of distress. Tears in her eyes, she said, "I hate to be one of those people who says 'I told you so,' but Nora, I did tell them. I warned them. Tried to tell that Renzo kid. He's a nitwit."

"The Renzo kid? Who's he?"

"Sheriff Nick Renzo."

"The sheriff's a kid?" He hadn't sounded like a kid. "And a nitwit?"

"Anyone under fifty is a kid." She sniffed into her lace-tatted handkerchief. "The worst was the family. That hurt. Only Hannah and Agnes believed me. At least I think they did."

"Your pals."

She nodded.

I hugged her.

"And now someone's dead because they wouldn't listen to you, wouldn't investigate what you overheard in the library."

"Just because I didn't hear anyone say outright that they were going to kill someone they figured I was reading into it." Ida sniffled again. "Phsew. Reading into it, my foot. They could all stand to do a bit of that. Too bad you don't know who it was, but we'll find out soon enough."

"Actually, I know who it is. I saw him when I went to see Uncle JT. His last name was Collins."

What I didn't say was that I'd seen him yelling at JT and I knew JT was afraid of him or maybe afraid of his partner. I wasn't sure.

"Oh, my. Collins works with Percy Kendall at the Auto Mall. I think he owns half of it. Bought into it years back when there were some financial troubles."

A short time later the sheriff drove up in an SUV, hopped out and raced onto the porch. I opened the screen door and stepped out to meet him. My heart gave a little jolt, just a small tremor, but completely out of character for me and my heart. This man was *not* a kid, and intuition signaled he was probably not a nitwit either.

"By the boulder next to the stream, just before you come to the bridge," I told him before he had a chance to ask. "Right along the path to JT's house. You can't miss him."

"Who is—"

"It's the guy who works at the Auto Mart. Al Collins, I think his name is."

"You all right?"

"Fine," I replied, still shaking like I was standing naked in a high wind at the North Pole.

He reached out his hand and I took it. "I'm Nick Renzo, sheriff of Silver Stream," he said.

The strangest thing happened. The shaking stopped. Suddenly. It's not that I was attracted to him, or anything crazy like that. I am a sensible woman, after all. He was a good looking man, no question about it. Not movie-star handsome, but there was a certain quality I couldn't put a name to. Well, maybe I could. I think the word was masculine with a capital M.

I didn't say anything as he held my hand. Couldn't think of a thing, not even my name, which would have been appropriate. It must have been the shock of seeing a murder victim that made my vocabulary dry up.

"You must be Nora Lassiter, the detective your aunt Ida told me about. The one who came up from New York to look into the murder she predicted?"

He let go of my hand. With the connection broken, I finally thought of something to say. "Yes, I'm Nora."

I didn't add the rest, the lie about being a detective. In fact, I should have taken this opportunity to straighten that out. My conscience danced around a bit. I thought of Mary Fran and the money she was paying me to get the skinny on her husband. If she knew the truth, I'd lose her business, and I needed the money.

I was a dishonest person.

"I need to talk to you. Get a statement. From Ida, too. Can

you both meet me at the station house in a couple of hours? I'll let you know when. Or would you prefer I come here?"

"Here," I said. "My aunt wouldn't want to go to the sheriff's office."

"Nonsense," Ida said as she came up in back of me. "I want to do my duty and go. The sheriff has to debrief us."

Debrief?

Nick nodded to me. "I'll call you. I have your cell phone number."

He took off. Minutes later Ida was on the phone to Great-aunt Hannah with the news of Collins' murder. I wasn't ready to call anyone, not even my brother Howie who's an officer on the Miami-Dade Police Department.

Shortly after noon, Sheriff Nick called from the murder site and said he'd be wrapping up soon. The forensics team was almost finished. He'd meet us at the station house.

THREE

There were so many vehicles parked in front of the sheriff's office that I had to park across the street by the Country Store. A big-breasted woman in a lime-colored sweater stood on the steps puffing a cigarette. I guessed she was in her mid-thirties. As I helped Aunt Ida out of the car, the woman said, "You hear what happened? The Collins' murder?"

"Yes. I'm the one who found him in the woods up by JT Lassiter's place. Shot to death."

"I heard." She took another puff of her cigarette and came down the steps. "I'm Amy. I waitress at the counter here. News travels fast in this town. How awful for you."

"Yes. Big shock."

"Certainly was," Ida put in as she smoothed the fresh orange flowered polyester blouse she'd changed into for this occasion.

"Maybe he committed suicide. No one gets murdered in Silver Stream. This here's always been a safe place to live," Amy said.

I knew that wasn't exactly true. Mary Fran's father-in-law had been murdered, but Amy obviously didn't remember that.

"Didn't someone get murdered around here about twenty years ago?"

Ida seemed to freeze. It was obvious that she remembered and was upset by it.

Amy wrinkled her brow. "Oh, yeah. Where's my head. I was in high school at the time. Had other things on my mind, I guess." She shrugged. "Someone out at the Auto Mart, I think it was."

"Did you know him?"

"Everybody around here knew Al."

I meant old Percy, but I let it go.

"Did people like Al?"

"The guy wouldn't have won no popularity contest, but he wasn't a bad sort. If he was murdered, maybe it had something to do with a car he sold that turned out to be a lemon." She dropped her cigarette and ground it out with the toe of her navy Nike sneaker. "What's the sheriff saying? He got any clues?"

"I don't know."

"Got to get back to work." Amy nodded and went back inside. I took a few steps after her, wanting to ask more questions. Such an odd thing for her to say, that someone would murder a man because he sold him a lemon. I hesitated. She must have been joking. I guess I didn't get Maine humor. When the screen door clapped shut, Ida and I headed to the sheriff's office.

"Did you know that old guy who got murdered about twenty years ago?"

Ida shook her head. "Not really. I guess I met him once or twice, this being a small town and all. Don't remember much about what happened though."

"And you a crime show enthusiast? Must have been a big thing in this town. A murder. I'm surprised you didn't go out and investigate yourself," I joked.

Aunt Ida didn't smile.

"Ay-uh, a big thing. The town was buzzing for weeks."

"They find out who killed him?"

Ida opened her purse, fiddled around, and closed it again before replying. "Not that I ever heard."

"You looking for something?"

"Just checking to see if I brought my glasses. I did. I'll need them in case I have to read something. I'll probably have to sign something, don't you think? And I have my camera, of course."

"I didn't bring mine," I said. "What was I thinking?"

Nick Renzo wasn't back from the murder site when we arrived at the station. The officer on duty behind the big desk was a skinny, nervous-looking guy with a pointy nose and small eyes.

"Howdy, Mrs. Lassiter." He nodded at Aunt Ida, then turned to me. "You must be Nora Lassiter. Sheriff said you'd be coming in. I'm Deputy Jay Trimble. You can both sit over there." He indicated the bench on the opposite wall.

The station house was a surprise. It was not the backwoods headquarters I'd expected. Someone had gone all out to make it imposing. The main desk looked like real mahogany. It was mammoth, twelve, maybe fifteen feet long, set on a foot-high platform that ran the length of the back wall. I pictured the sheriff sitting up there, looking authoritative, gazing down at some pathetic lawbreaker.

"This is my first time in this building," Ida said, her voice filled with the awe and reverence you might expect in an exquisite cathedral. "Imagine all these years and I've never been inside."

"I can imagine."

It took about four minutes for the awe to wear off. Suddenly, without so much as a word to me, and with more gusto than an average woman in her eighties should possess, Ida stood, marched to the desk and rapped with her purse. "Young man. What are you doing up there? Are you really busy?"

Startled, Officer Trimble blinked a few times. "Not too busy. Is there something I can do for you, Ma'am?"

In seconds I was at her side. "Aunt Ida, is there a problem?"

The *Toreador March* sounded and I foraged for the cell phone in the tote bag, swearing under my breath, shoving mace and mints and makeup out of the way. "Let me answer this first," I said, seeing the identity of the caller. I walked back to the bench.

"Howie. I was going to call you today. Did the list come out yet? Can I tell the world my brother is going to make sergeant on the Miami-Dade PD?"

"I'd like a tour of the station house," I heard Ida announce behind me.

A tour? I spun around.

"Not yet," Howie said. "I called to find out how your visit's going and tell you that–"

"Visits going fine, Howie," I spoke rapidly, my concentration on Aunt Ida. "Driving up here was the worst part."

"I wanted to give you a heads-up. There's been a murder in Silver Stream. It just came up on the computer in the station house. Hard to believe. Murder in Silver Stream."

"I already know about the murder. Hold on a sec."

I went over to Ida and touched her arm. "Aunt Ida, we don't really need a tour, do we?" I refrained from mentioning the obvious, that this was not a social occasion.

Officer Trimble stepped down from his perch, glanced at Ida, then back to me. "No problem, Ma'am, I'd be glad to show you both around. Follow me."

"Howie? I gotta go. I'll—"

"What do you mean you know about the murder? How could you know?" Howie cut in. "According to what I'm reading here, the coroner just picked up the body. Was it someone we knew? A relative?"

"Howie, I'm at the sheriff's office," I explained in a harsh whisper as I followed Ida down the hall. "I'll call you back."

"God almighty, Nora. What have you done now?"

"Nothing."

"What the hell're you doing there? Have you been arrested or something? You crash that rental car? I knew you shouldn't have driven up on your own. You're not a good driver. You know that."

My first impulse was to reassure him. But he was my brother, after all, the guy who had lied to me about moose when I was a kid, so I went with my second impulse. "Howie, I'll call you back." I paused dramatically. Sometimes I can't help myself. Howie is such a worrywart. "They're waiting for me," I said, an ominous tone in my voice. Smiling, I clicked off, and stood watching Ida check out the cells.

"Oh, my. Empty. No prisoners today. Soon though. When they catch the killer. Just look at these cells," Ida said as she touched the bars.

There was that reverence and awe again.

"Nora, we should take a picture. I have my digital that the nephews and nieces gave me for Christmas last year." She dug in her purse. "I haven't even filled the disk yet, but I've studied how it works."

No. "I don't think—"

"Oh, this nice Officer Trimble wouldn't mind."

"That's right, Ma'am. Snap away. I'll even open the door so you can go inside the cell. If you want to. Get some wicked good pictures."

Ida handed me the camera. "Here, I'll go in and you take my picture."

"Hello? Yoo-hoo. Anyone here?"

"Hannah. Agnes. We're back here," Ida called. "Come see this place and meet our Nora."

I rolled my eyes. My first meeting with the aunts I hadn't seen since I was a child was going to be by a jail cell. Wonderful.

The *Toreador March* sounded again. My friend Lori calling from New York.

"Lori?"

"Hi, Nora. How's it going?"

"Oh, just fine. I can't talk now. I'll call you back later."

"I'll send the résumé to your phone so you can check it before I print it."

"Okay," I said automatically.

"See ya."

"No, wait. Too many dead spots up here. You'd better fax it. I'll have to get back to you with a number. I'm pretty busy at the moment."

"Ida. Where are you?" one of the aunts called.

"Too busy? You are coming back, aren't you?" Lori asked.

"I-da." the other aunt called. "I-da."

I closed my eyes. "Absolutely." Why had I ever left?

FOUR

Hannah and Agnes, the great-aunts I hadn't seen since I was a child, were in their mid-eighties, like Ida. Hannah, a diminutive five-three with the whitest hair I'd ever seen, wore a purple blouse with a red ruffled scarf. As soon as she walked in, she grabbed me in a bear hug and got weepy.

"I'm so happy to see you," she said, making little sobbing noises that touched my heart. "At last. I just wish you hadn't found a body on your second day up here. How horrible for you. Are you all right?"

"It was a bit scary, but I'm all right now."

"Good. My poor little Nora." She touched my face and stood back, then sniffled again as she studied me. "Lots of Lassiter around the eyes. Same shade of blue as Viola's. Don't you think, Agnes?"

"Same trade as Viola?" Agnes repeated, cupping her ear.

"Geez," Ida mumbled impatiently, holding the jail cell open.

Trimble looked on with interest.

Hannah clarified, "Same *shade* eyes as Viola."

"Oh. Yes, yes. Beautiful eyes," Agnes agreed.

"Aunt Agnes," I said, moving from Hannah to hug her. My arms did not quite fit around Agnes, who was planetary in size.

"I remember you when you were a little girl. Such a darling girl."

"Who's Viola?" I asked.

"The vamp in the family tree," Hannah supplied immediately. "We'll not talk about that one. We don't speak unkindly about the deceased."

Hannah looked me over again, this time more slowly, from head to toe to left hand to fourth finger.

"You're not married yet, Nora. How is that?"

"I was engaged once," I blurted, defending my status, aware of Trimble hanging on every word. Then another cop appeared in the doorway behind him and Trimble acknowledged him.

"Chief."

Sheriff Nick Renzo's brows rose a notch when he looked at me. This was the first time I'd seen him without his uniform hat. I liked his hair. It was a touch longer than most cops wear it, dark, with a bit of a wave. I forced my recently un-engaged self to look away.

Hannah's hand went up, palm out like a traffic cop. "No explanations necessary. You're pretty enough to grace a magazine cover. What with your floppy, striped hair and your Viola-blue eyes you should meet a nice man and get married."

Floppy hair? Stripes? I'd paid a bundle for those highlights, and I'd used the hair dryer to style the floppy do this morning. I thought it looked fine.

The sheriff and his deputy seemed to be studying my hair, too.

"We'll see what we can do to move things along." Hannah looked from Agnes to Ida. "We'll have a party. That's the proper way of it. Shouldn't be a problem."

A party to meet a man? No. Please no. "Not necessary. I don't want to meet a man right now," I said, and that was the truth.

"But why?" Great-aunt Agnes asked.

The sheriff leaned against the door frame, arms folded, his expression hard to read as he took it all in, and waited for my answer like the rest of them. Well, he wasn't going to hear it.

I used his arrival to shift the aunts' focus. "I see the sheriff is here."

Despite his casual pose, he looked tense, stressed. This had to be the first murder case he'd handled. He was a novice.

Hannah nodded at Sheriff Nick Renzo in acknowledgment, but continued, "We'll have the party tomorrow night. Saturday.

Agnes," she shouted, "you make your famous strawberry short cake. You can use those berries we put up in June. We said they'd be for a special occasion and so they will. Ida, how about your famous banana nut bread? Maybe some zucchini bread, too? I'll make my prizewinning New England clam chowder. The young folks can do the main dishes. I'm thinking lobster salad, for one."

"Oh, yes." Ida smiled. "I just made banana bread this morning."

"We'll go straight to my place and make our plans," Hannah said. "When Nora is finished here with this nasty business, she can join us."

"Don't you want to stand in the jail cell first? Have your picture taken?" Ida asked the aunts as she handed me her camera.

"Absolutely," Hannah said looking around. "Not every day we get behind bars."

All three aunts chuckled. Next thing, they were in the closed cell, their hands on the bars, looking out. I took their picture while the sheriff, his deputy and one or two others came in to watch.

"How about you?" Nick asked me, holding out his hand for the camera. "Want to get in the picture?"

"No, sheriff." I gave the camera to Ida, and the aunt-trio emerged from incarceration.

Hannah headed down the hall, Agnes and Ida close on her heels. I followed behind the slow procession, shaking my head. I had to get out of here.

"Aunt Hannah, it's thoughtful of you to want to give me a party, but I'll be leaving Monday after the reading of the will, so maybe we'd better skip it."

The convoy stopped short in the hall. Had we been moving at anything approaching a normal clip, we would have piled up. As it was, some teetering took place.

"I was afraid she was going to say that," Ida said. "She did mention it when she first arrived. We'll have to lobby for her to change her mind."

Agnes bellowed, "Find? What did she find? Another body?

Oh, dear heaven. How does she keep finding bodies?"

"*Mind,* not find. Change her mind." Shaking her head, Ida repeated the rest of what she'd said.

Agnes frowned.

Hannah took the news in stride. "You'll meet the relatives, won't you?" She paused dramatically, adjusting her lacy red cuffs with the fussiness of an actress going onstage to accept an Oscar. "Unless you don't care about your relatives?"

Renzo and Trimble, along with the aunts, waited for any feeble reply I might come up with.

What could I say other than, "Relatives would be fine."

Everyone nodded and smiled, and the procession continued.

"Good. Before you return to the big city," Hannah said, "it's only proper you meet the family you haven't seen in so long. The Lassiters' heritage is here, Nora. That's not something to lose sight of in this fast-paced world. Family. Jeb Lassiter settled here in 1842 and founded this town. You were born here, your father was born here and his father before him, and so on back to Jed. Your father, God rest his soul, felt as if he had to leave all those years ago, and we lost you and Howie in the process."

Agnes said. "Nora, we're all so glad you're back."

"Ladies, I hate to hurry you along, but there's important business to take care of," Nick said when we reached the main room. "You go work on the party plans. I'll talk to Nora first, then you, Ida. Nora, if you'll come into my office. . . ."

As soon as he closed the door to his office, I asked, "Have you found out anything about the murder?"

"Like who did it?" he asked as he sat behind the gray metal desk, gesturing for me to take the chair in front.

I sat on the edge of the seat. "I don't suppose you're up to that part yet."

"Not likely. We know a shotgun was used. And where the shooter stood. Maybe fifty yards away. That's about it at the moment."

"How do you know that?"

"Good detective work."

"You have footprint evidence? Did you make a plaster cast? Did you bag any other trace evidence?"

He stared at me without replying, his forearms resting on the desk.

"What?" I demanded.

"I'm the cop. This is my investigation. I ask the questions."

"What's to ask? I don't know anything. I found him. I skipped the mouth-to-mouth because I knew he was dead. I called you. End of my report. Or *debriefing,* as Aunt Ida would say."

"Suppose you tell me again why you were in the woods this morning and how you found the body."

"Why? You think I shot the guy?"

He smiled. "If it eases your mind, you're not on my suspect list."

"You have a list already?"

He shook his head. "I wish."

"Okay. Like I told you. I was on my way to Uncle JT's house. I figured he was probably at work so I'd see his wife, my Aunt Ellie. Mainly, I just wanted to see the house because I used to live there. I'd decided to cut through the woods. It's miles shorter than going around by car. Besides, it was a beautiful day and I wanted to walk. And the trail? I used to take it as a kid, and miracle of miracles, it was still there. JT keeps it cleared. I was enjoying the walk, sort of, except for possible animal danger."

His eyes narrowed. "Animal danger?"

"Moose. Deer. Porcupines. Especially porcupines. No, especially moose." I shivered just thinking of such an awful encounter.

He nodded. "Okay." Then, "How well did you know Al Collins?"

"I didn't know him."

"You sure? You gave me his name easily enough."

"Oh, right. I had a thing going with Collins. That's why I came to Maine. Did I forget to mention that?"

Nick smirked at me. He had a cute smirk. "Just answer the question."

"I saw him for the first time yesterday at my Uncle JT's auto repair place. Period. Never spoke to the guy."

"What did he talk to your uncle about?"

"I don't know. They were outside, I was inside and couldn't hear them."

"Yoo-hoo. Nick. I'm up here," Ida called, looking down from the big desk as we came out of his office. "I don't want to be debriefed here, though."

All three aunts were seated up behind the big desk with the two deputies, Trimble and Miller. Miller was a hunk. This guy could be a whole calendar all by himself. No woman would mind looking at him twenty-four-seven. I thought Miller was winking at me, until I realized he had a twitch in his left eyelid.

"Where do you want to be . . . debriefed?" Nick asked.

"That room where they question the suspects. You know, the one with the two-way mirror."

"Sh-ur. We can do that."

Ida made her way down. "You going to videotape me?"

"Wasn't planning to."

"I think it would be best. That way you'll be able to refer back to it. Hear my testimony any time you need to."

"Good idea. We'll roll the camera, Ida."

I stood with the aunts on the other side of the two-way mirror, watching Ida recount her story, wondering what on earth I was doing in Maine. I didn't belong here, didn't fit in.

My sweet Aunt Ida was going on about overhearing two people in the library.

"So you have no idea who was speaking?" Nick asked Ida. "Don't recall anything special about their voices? An accent maybe?"

"No accent. They were from this area, I think. The only thing I can tell you definitely is that they weren't kids, but they weren't old either. I'm guessing middle-aged. Both of them moved fast. I heard their footsteps."

"Could you have heard the librarian?"

"Oh, no. This woman had a harsh voice. Not soft like Margaret's."

"Tell me again what was said. Exactly."

"Well, the woman said, 'You get rid of him. Soon. Scared people do stupid things and we can't afford that.' And then the man said, 'I can't.' The woman got angry and said, 'You wanted in big-time, didn't you? This has to be done. There's no other way.'"

"Anything else?" Nick asked.

"They mumbled the next part. Something about a meeting. I heard the words woods and stream."

Suddenly, she gasped. "I should have kept Nora from going along that trail, shouldn't I? I never thought of the stream. She could have been killed."

"Don't go there, Ida. Nora is fine."

"That's all I remember, Nick."

"I'm sorry I didn't listen to you, Ida. Real sorry. My mistake." He ran his hand through his hair. "From where you were standing could you guess their heights?"

Ida pursed her lips. "I was sitting on one of the step stools looking for a Sue Gafton mystery. Don't know why they put the good authors down so low. Anyway, I think he was tall, just above the second shelf down from the top. His voice came through the Ken Follet section."

Trimble, standing off to the side in the small room, smirked. But what Ida said had merit, and Nick seemed to realize it, too. He looked at Trimble and said, "Check it out. Take a tape measure with you."

"What's a Ken Follet section?" skinny Trimble asked.

"He's an author. Ask Margaret," Nick said bruskly. "Wait and take Ida to see exactly where she was sitting."

The disgruntled deputy nodded. "Ay-uh."

Ida announced, "Hannah and Agnes can come with me, then we'll all go to Hannah's. Nora can follow. We'll plan the party."

Nick thanked Ida for her information.

I kissed them all good-bye. Hannah whispered, "I'm so proud of our Ida. Hasn't she been wonderful?"

"Yes. Wonderful," I said. And I meant it.

"We all should have paid more attention to her. Like the sheriff, I'm sorry we didn't."

It was pouring by the time we got into the car for the drive home.

Hannah's house was the largest Lassiter home in Silver Stream, a sprawling colonial that started life as a cabin and grew over the years as the family grew. The child in me remembered the bigness. The adult saw beyond that. Here was something passed down through generations by folks who had broken away from the modern world and ventured far from the ease of the towns. Into the woods. Into the unknown.

I came from hardy stock.

The outrageous aroma of apple pies and blueberry turnovers warming in the oven wafted through the house. The dining room table was laden with all good things—shrimp with cocktail sauce, Swedish meatballs, chicken Marsala, lobster salad, a cauldron of beef barley soup and one of lobster bisque, both homemade. There were homemade breads, wheat and zucchini, crusty French and banana nut.

Hannah, Agnes and Ida had invited every Lassiter in Silver Stream and the surrounding towns, several friends and neighbors and, I suspected, a few single men. My three great-aunts wanted everyone to meet me. I was touched, not only by the gesture, but by the reception from the family. It was as warm and friendly as the big house felt.

I met cousins, aunts, uncles and longtime family friends. Since I was here for such a short time, I didn't bother trying to remember names, which I'm terrible at anyway. Most of the talk centered around the murder and I had to recount my discovery-of-the-body story several times.

Uncle JT waltzed in three hours late, removed his shoes, like everyone else in Hannah's house, and put on slippers. I was the only person in the house not wearing slippers, a tradition I'd forgotten about.

As I headed toward JT, his wife Ellie stepped into the entranceway, glared up at him and hissed, "You ass. Better watch your step. I have a key to that rifle cabinet."

Startled, I stepped behind a leafy ficus bush, not the greatest hiding place, but still . . . .

In the next instant I decided her words were just an exaggeration. Had to be. You know, like when someone says, 'I could kill you.' Not a nice thing to say, but not to be taken literally either. My mother used to say that to me all the time when I was a kid.

"Goes both ways," I heard him fire back. With that, Ellie spun on her heel and left. I tried to look casual, as if I wasn't eavesdropping, as I edged around the ficus. I examined a leaf with feigned interest, amazed to find it real. I once bought a real ficus and it lost all its leaves within a month. These Maine people knew a lot about plants. They could grow anything. I was a plastic plant person myself.

JT came over the minute he spotted me. "How's the car holding up? When you're ready to buy instead of rent, you should go over to the Auto Mart. They'll give you a good deal."

"I'll stick with the rental for now. I have to call them about the insurance. They should cover the money I paid out to have repairs made."

Wearing jeans and a green plaid shirt, he smelled like cigar smoke and beer.

"Still, buyin's your best option."

"I won't be here that long. Leaving Monday." I paused. "JT, can you tell me the real reason Dad left Silver Stream?" I asked, getting right to the point, not interested in his chit-chat."

He hesitated, "Come by Monday after the will's read. We'll talk."

I didn't like being put off. I watched him as he made he way to the buffet table, and couldn't help wondering why he was stalling and what it was that he didn't want me to know.

Nick Renzo arrived. My stomach did a little fluttery rotation. I was glad I looked better than the last time I'd seen him. My streaky blond hair, as Hannah calls it, which falls to my shoulders, looked like a shampoo commercial tonight. I know this because I was swinging it back and forth pretending I was in one of those commercials as I looked in the mirror. Shallow, shallow, shallow my mother would have said, and she'd have been right.

I had chosen my outfit with great care, a sky blue, soft-as-velvet lambskin jacket with an asymmetrical zipper up the front, and matching slim leather skirt. Men had told me I had a sexy caboose, and I knew this skirt accented it, which is why I bought it. Worse than shallow, Nora.

I watched Nick remove his shoes and slip into orange, day-glo scuffs? Good grief. Subtract a couple of points.

"Hello," I said. "Didn't know you were a Lassiter. Or a close family friend?"

"I'm a Renzo. Nobody was checking ancestry at the door so I slipped in."

"Security's loose here."

Fortunately, I had no intention of falling for this guy so I was relatively safe. Not only was I leaving soon, but I know a thing or two about cops. My father was a cop, and though I loved him, the hours he worked were horrible and the danger was worse, so I put cops on my negative-guy list.

"Love your slippers," I remarked.

"A gift. My mother picked them up at some big sale."

"Oh." It's not good to criticize a person's mother, so I

clamped my mouth shut.

"I don't like them," Nick said, "but it would be a waste not to use them, don't you think?"

"Absolutely. Thrifty you."

"Umm."

"Instead of wearing them you could stand on your roof and direct airplane traffic, I suppose."

The man actually smiled. Then he told me he'd talked to Mary Fran.

He waited for me to say something.

"The aunts thought my old 'friend' should be here. She's coming tonight," I said, wondering whether she'd told him about our agreement, hoping she hadn't. It would be better if no one knew that I was playing detective. As it was, I felt a little guilty taking money under false pretenses. I would give it all back if I couldn't do the job.

His stare made me uncomfortable. "You can't be serious about working for her."

My heart sunk a little, but I tried not to show it. "She told you?"

"Yes."

"I'm taking the case," I told him, watching his expression, wondering if he knew the truth about my detective status, and wondering whether he was going to call me a fraud.

He took a Bud Light instead.

"If Percy suspects for a second you're tailing him, he might get rough. He's different from most folks around here. He's . . . tougher. Can be ruthless."

I'd never considered that. "Has he ever been abusive to Mary Fran?" Hard to picture, recalling her finger-bending ability.

"Not that she'd ever acknowledge, but I've suspected it on more than one occasion."

I nodded. That gave a new dimension to the case, another reason to catch him.

Case. I had a case? I couldn't believe I'd committed myself.

"You shouldn't do this."

"I want to."

"Yes, I see. I just wonder why. You're putting yourself in jeopardy." He paused and took another sip. "You really should know what you're doing first."

Oh, crap. He had checked me out.

"You know, don't you?"

"I'm the sheriff. I know everything."

"You plan to expose me?" As soon as the words were out, I rephrased, "Tell Mary Fran?"

"Expose you?" He grinned down at me. "It's crossed my mind."

Ignoring the double entendre, I twirled a lock of hair around my index finger, giving my best dumb blonde imitation, and said, "I know what I'm doing. I'm a detective-show fanatic, you know. *Murder, She Wrote. CSI. Law and Order.* All the reruns. I've seen them all lots of times so I know lots of investigative things."

The corner of his mouth tipped and he nodded, then he pulled out a scrap of paper and wrote a number on it. "Keep this handy. Call if you run into trouble. Any trouble. Anywhere. Anytime."

Even though I was warmed by his gesture, I made no move to accept the paper. "I don't think I'll need your private number."

"Who said it was my private number?"

He looked at me with his dark bedroom eyes. I read the subtle challenge there, and took the damn paper.

"I cannot imagine ever having to call you. What trouble could I possibly get into, Nick Renzo?" I smiled sweetly.

When Mary Fran arrived, she introduced me to her husband Percy immediately. He was a big man, overweight by about fifty pounds, with slicked back hair, a red vest, and a salesman's phony smile.

"Shame about Al," he said to the sheriff and me. "Ay-uh. We'll all miss him." He shook his head, his mouth dipping down in sorrow. "Can't imagine who would want to kill such a great guy. If

I can be of any more help, Nick, you just let me know. Don't want any killers running loose in Silver Stream."

Phony, phony, phony.

The word swirled in my head like an F-5 tornado. That said, he invited me to view some used trucks. "I just picked up some kick-ass trucks at the auction," the man bragged, clearly not interested in the murder of his partner. "You might be in the market. I heard you're renting a car. Not economical. Renting and leasing? For suckers."

"Auction?" I said, not really interested, as Nick drifted away.

"Car auction. In Framingham, Massachusetts. My job takes me to the auto auctions." He smiled. "Pick up lots of good stuff there." He glanced at Mary Fran who seemed to be deliberately ignoring him. And me.

"JT already tried to get me to buy," I said, looking around for Ida, Hannah or Agnes. Anyone.

Like the angel she was, Hannah came over and told me she wanted me to meet another cousin.

Mary Fran managed to leave Percy's side for a few minutes and whispered, "See you in the morning."

When Nick was putting on his shoes to leave, he motioned me over. Once more, he repeated his warning. "Stay away from Percy."

FIVE

The interior of Hot Heads Heaven was everything I'd expected, and then some. The ceiling and walls were silver. Someone had run amuck with a magenta paint brush and done some freeform design damage.

It was exactly nine-thirty Monday morning. This would have been my last day in Maine, but I had to get the evidence—the emails and the photos—so I'd probably be here until Tuesday.

"Hi, Nora. Come on back and have a cup of coffee with me," Mary Fran called from a small alcove where she stood next to a steaming coffeepot.

Dressed in a magenta smock with silver trim, she blended into the decor.

"I make wicked good coffee, for sh-ur. Here's the key to the back door of my house, and the directions," she continued with barely a breath, skipping the small talk, her hand shaking like a woman with a major case of caffeine overdose as she gave me a key and a crumbled piece of paper. "I've never done anything like this. I couldn't sleep all night. This will not be my first cup of coffee today. I'm a wreck." Rat-ta-ta-ta-tat. She sent the words out machine-gun fire.

She'd be more of a wreck if she knew she'd hired a total novice, so in kindness, I decided to keep that to myself. I slipped the key into my purse where it clanked against the mace canister, then glanced at the hand-drawn map. Looked like some kid had scribbled it.

"Give me some details," I said, folding the map and stuffing it in my purse. I'd scrutinize it later.

She poured coffee for both of us, splashing it far enough to make me step back.

"Are you sure you want me to do this, Mary Fran?"

"I was in love with him, you know. Really. Maybe I still am. I can't believe he would jeopardize everything for some cheap fling." She took a sip of coffee. "For some tramp."

"Maybe he didn't," I offered, not believing it for a nanosecond. I could tell her about my ex-fiancé, Whatshisname, and the bimbo in the shower, but that wouldn't help either of us.

Her head snapped up. "Oh, he did, all right. Just get me the evidence I need. I'm feeling soft. I can't afford to. I couldn't sleep last night just thinking about this."

I added milk to my coffee as she explained what I needed to know.

"Percy's left already." She glanced at the clock. "He leaves at eight-fifty, on the dot. He takes Wendy, our seven-year-old, to school, then goes to the Auto Mart. He'll be gone all day, at least until five tonight. Unless, of course, he has to work late. Ho-ho-ho.

"Anyway, no need to worry you'll be discovered. As for my daughter, she'll be dropped off here at three-thirty. You should have no problems. You'll probably be done before then, right?"

"Absolutely," I said, projecting confidence I didn't feel. "I have the reading of the will at four."

"Good."

"I didn't know you had a daughter."

She smiled. "She's a great kid. Better than I ever was. Smarter, too."

"Well, that's nice." I smiled. "How about your neighbors?"

"Neighbors? No neighbors will drop by. They know I'm working. Oh, you mean will they think you don't belong there if they spot you going in?"

"Or be suspicious if they see my car parked out front?"

"Not to worry. Park in back. Best spot is behind the garage. No one will see the car there, not even someone pulling into the driveway. You'll be totally hidden. There's a cement slab, an unfinished basketball court that Percy began when I was pregnant. When our daughter was born he decided not to bother finishing it. He wanted a boy. The ass."

"Okay," I said calmly, keeping my unease in check. I had never done anything this furtive before. This was the kind of thing you saw in the movies that made you want to shout, "Hurry up, hurry up. Get out before someone discovers you."

There was still time to tell Mary Fran the truth. I considered it as she walked me out to the car. With trembling fingers she touched my arm. "How long did you say this would take?"

"I didn't. It depends on how quickly I can get into his email account. Then there's the amount of mail I have to go through before I find what you want. Some people delete stuff right away. Some save a ton of it. I'll run off whatever's pertinent."

Even as I said this, it occurred to me that I should have paper. He might notice if I used too much of his. Or he might be out of paper. Why hadn't I thought of this? Where was my head? I'd stop at the Country Store. I wanted to go in there anyway and see what it looked like. I had plenty of time.

"The computer's upstairs in the room between our room and the bathroom. You can't miss it," she told me as I got into the car. Reaching through the window, she grabbed my hand and held it to her chest. I held my breath.

"Good luck. Thanks for doing this for me."

I gently extricated my hand. "I'll call as soon as I find anything," I said, passing up the last opportunity to be an honest woman and change my mind.

The Country Store was down the road from Mary Fran's hair salon. There was no need to drive, but I did. The place was hopping with the breakfast crowd. Well, not exactly a crowd as I knew a crowd. Nine people sat at the counter. The waitress I'd met before, Amy, had a chest like Pam Anderson, which might explain why seven in the crowd were men. So transparent. So single-minded, the lot of them.

The place reminded me of one of those old-time general stores you see in Westerns. It smelled of bacon and hot coffee, toast and pancakes. If I were hungry, I'd be tempted. I walked through slowly, taking it all in as I looked for the stationery section. This was a multifunction establishment: a variety store, a post office, a luncheonette, a grocery store, a wine store, a video rental store. I loved it. Nothing had been overlooked.

When I found the computer paper, I noticed the room in the back with the potbelly stove and several men sitting around. That places like this still existed warmed my heart. I peeked in. Two of my uncles were in the group. Seeing them made me feel a part of something in a way I'd never been before. I was related to the in-crowd who sat around a potbelly stove. Just jawing. Old-fashioned. Nice. Ida had mentioned that the men came here to chat about important things, like world events and deer season.

From the doorway I gave the uncles a big hello.

"Morning," they said politely.

One of my uncles introduced me, and everyone nodded and wished me a good day. That was it. For a few awkward moments I stood there, unsure of what to do while they all stared silently at me. It was clear I was an intruder in the men's circle.

"Well, see ya," I finally said, and walked off, wondering what century I'd dropped into. Old-fashioned jerks.

I glanced at the waitress, who was watching me. Double-D for sure. When she turned away I inhaled, held my breath for a few seconds. Single-B, at the most. I was a foolish woman.

Amy was at the cash register when I paid for the paper.

"Don't pay attention to them, honey," she said, tipping her head in the direction of the back room. "They've got their ways. Change is slow in this part of the world. They're not a bad lot." She chuckled.

I nodded, but I wasn't sure we were on the same page. I was annoyed because my uncles had snubbed me. I didn't care about the rest of them and *their ways.*

"That's like a sacred spot," she explained. "No women allowed. Just the men, talking politics and such. Bunch of old farts. At least they're not as bad as my deceased husband used to be. Now there was a real jackass." She laughed, then yelled to a customer asking for coffee, "Keep your shorts on, Lenny, I'll be right with you."

Laughter greeted her reply.

I liked Amy. "I'm sorry your husband died."

"Don't be. I'm not. He left me a little something, more than I had when we was together. Where ya from, honey? I know you're not from these woods." She looked meaningfully at my violet cashmere sweater and black linen DKNY slacks. "You look so city-like."

"New York City. But my family's originally from Silver Stream."

"Oh, yeah," she said slowly, as if just remembering me, which I didn't believe for a minute. "Ida Lassiter was with you the day good old Al got himself shot. Someone told me you haven't been here in years. Smart lady." She checked out my apparel again, craning to look over the counter to see my shoes, which didn't match the outfit, since I was in stealth mode and wearing sneakers. She frowned. "Nice outfit," she commented insincerely. "I heard about you. A detective. You're up here on some case, right?"

I opened my mouth to reply as she handed me my change, then changed my mind. Instead of answering, I smiled, going for an enigmatic look. I don't know whether I was successful or not. I'd have to check it in the mirror later.

"Sort of," I said.

"Must be interesting work. Following clues, catching the bad guys."

What would Jessica Fletcher say, I wondered?

"A lot of it is routine. Even boring." Liar, liar, liar.

"I hear you're really good."

I smiled modestly. Who had she been talking to? Mary Fran?

"Are you?" she asked when I didn't comment.

What was I supposed to say? "I've had my moments."

She nodded. "Well, gotta run, honey. The natives are restless. Have to finish up the breakfast crowd."

Using the smudged, squiggly map from Mary Fran, I got lost and didn't arrive for over an hour. The house was a large red brick cape cod with two dormers, on a quiet street in a small cleared area surrounded by woods. It had a detached garage. I pulled behind the garage, nervous as a burglar on a virgin run, which, in a way, I was. Hands shaking, a little like Mary Fran's had been, I unlocked the back door, opened it slowly and went into the kitchen. It smelled of burnt toast and peanut butter. Breakfast dishes littered the table, a nice sight for Mary Fran to come home to.

I stood for a few seconds listening to house sounds–a grandfather clock ticking somewhere, a faucet dripping in the kitchen, the refrigerator humming.

Finally, I headed upstairs, stopping on the third step when it creaked.

Ba-boom, ba-boom. Who knew a heart could pound so loudly without bursting through the chest?

I wondered what I'd say if I were discovered. Foolish thought. I was here alone and would remain alone. I continued up, found the computer and turned it on, remembering when the desktop screen flashed on that I'd left the computer paper in the car. Where was my head today?

While the computer was warming up, I ran out to get the paper. More time lost. It was almost eleven already. When I returned, I tried the easy way first. Searched the desk drawers for evidence of passwords. Nothing. I checked under the keyboard, around the monitor, on the tower, beneath the lamp, the telephone, the pen holder.

Under the desk. Randy215. That had a certain ring to it.

My guess was that randy Percy had met his lady love last February fifteenth. I would soon see. I opened his email program, typed in the password, hit Enter, and waited. Like magic, I was in.

This was easier than I thought. If Mary Fran knew anything about computers and was able to find the password, she could have done this herself. I checked the folders, opened one named Marla, the only one with a woman's name on it.

Good guess.

My God. He had eighty-three messages stored here, the first one dated July twenty-eighth, about seven weeks ago. Chuck the theory about them meeting in February.

I began reading her mail to him and some of his to her that was on the same page. My face grew hot, and I do not consider myself a prude. Randy was a fitting password for both of them.

Wow.

Penned porn. No detail too small, too insignificant, too disgusting, to be mentioned. Why not just send the *Karma Sutra* back and forth, for God sakes? They included clothes, no, more like costumes, to be worn at the onset, descriptions of equipment to be utilized and a step by step on what the utilization entailed. I barely noticed the poor spelling and creative punctuation.

Dates were mentioned. No times or places though. Perhaps they always met at the same time, same place. I was looking for an email that mentioned a motel or some other destination.

Fifty-two emails later I decided to stop looking, and begin printing. I should have done that immediately. Not thinking. Too nervous. I pulled the dust cover off the printer. Omigod. An antique. One of the slowest printers HP ever made.

I pressed the On button and froze.

I heard a noise. In the next room. I stopped breathing and listened. A shuffling sound. Panicky feelings worked their way into my throat and I had trouble swallowing.

Like a big sissy, I grabbed my purse, bolted into the closet and yanked on the bifold doors, no easy task since I was off balance and immediately got entangled in long plastic dry cleaner bags and dropped my purse. A plastic bag caught my nose as I tried to turn. Dear God. I couldn't breathe. More panic as I tried to remove it, and, at the same time, keep myself from falling through the louvered bifolds.

Get a grip, Nora.

The noise came again. I pressed an ear to the closet wall, this time circumventing the bags.

A scraping sound. No, not quite scraping. It was like someone digging. They had sand in the bathroom?

Peeking through the slots, I could see the computer screen and the last email I'd read. I had to get out of this damn closet, turn it off, and quit this stupid stuff. Nick Renzo was right. I was no detective.

Just then, the *Toreador March* blasted from my purse. Oh, my God. I groped around the floor, hit my head on the partially opened door, but managed to snag the damn purse. I grabbed the damn phone and shut it off. I figured the jig was up now for sure. I was as good as dead. If anyone had not heard that damn music or the thump on the door, they were deaf.

Resigned to discovery, I stepped out, rubbing my head. That's when it suddenly hit me. The scraping sound. A cat in a litter box? Did Mary Fran have a cat? The thought was sunshine, even though I am severely allergic. Sneezing beats death by a Maine mile.

I tiptoed to the bathroom and glanced in just in time to see a fluffy white feline stepping primly from a litter box. I laughed with delight. Well, it was more like giddy relief, I suppose.

The snooty little cat spared me a brief glance as it strolled past with a get-out-of-my-way attitude that had me stepping aside.

For the next two hours I ran off emails on the slowest printer this side of the Rockies. I probably didn't have to run them all off, but I wanted to be efficient. Earn my fee.

I checked my watch. It was already two-ten. I was in that movie again saying hurry up, hurry up to the heroine.

Restless, waiting for the pages to print, I prowled the small office, then stopped to look out the back window. They had a lot of property. A tire swing hung from a tree and I imagined a child playing on it. I imagined swinging on it myself.

I heard the car before I saw it. Mary Fran? No, not in that big SUV. Possibly a neighbor. But why?

My throat went dry, my heart began a wild ba-boom, ba-boom, and I had to pee.

SIX

With unsteady hands, I cancelled the print and shut down the computer.

Outside, a car door slammed.

I grabbed the papers I'd run off, stuffed them into my tote, and, knowing it was too late to exit the house, desperately looked for a place to hide. The closet? Been there, done that. Where would he not notice me? Hall closet? Daughter's room? Under a bed? A bed.

It was almost two-fifteen. In a flash of insight that came too late, like a lot of my brilliant flashes, I understood the password. Not a date, not February fifteenth, but a time. His dates with Marla were at two-fifteen. Here. The nerve.

Hide, hide, hide.

I quelled the urge to head for the stairs. Instead, I ran to his daughter's room across the hall from the master bedroom, a pink frilly place with an unmade bed and toys and clothing scattered from here to kingdom come and back again. The daughter was a messy kid. I shoved my tote under her bed and scrambled after it. The only plus was the dust ruffle that touched the floor. I was hidden. The mattress was low, making it a tight fit. If I'd had breakfast or lunch I might not have made it. For a panicky moment I pictured getting stuck under the bed, having to call 911 and explain the situation. Calling Nick. No, I'd stay here before I'd call him.

The place was dust-bunny heaven. I wondered whether the cat spent any time under here. I couldn't see too well. Could there be dangerous cat hairs lurking?

Something smelled sour.

When my eyes adjusted to the darkness, I made out a bowl in front of me. Something awful was in that bowl, something worse than dust bunnies or menacing cat hairs, something that might have been milk a long time ago. I slid the bowl to the side, out of nose range.

I heard footsteps on the oak stairs, heard Percy whistling a song I couldn't identify, not some mushy love song, but something hot and heavy, almost menacing.

I lifted the bed skirt a tiny bit and peeked out. I watched his black leather shoes march into the master bedroom. I dropped the bed skirt quickly. I felt nauseous. My head started to ache. And, of course, I still had to pee. I hadn't gone to the bathroom since before I had that cup of coffee at Hot Heads Heaven hours ago. Dear God, how long would he take? Did he and Marla do 'quickies?'

More shoe noises. I chanced a peek. A pair of black patent leather stilettos with ankle straps clicked on by. Queen Marla had arrived.

The session from hell began.

I wished I were in a position to take photos, but I couldn't chance it. I had the camera in my tote.

"You're very naughty," Percy said in an unctuous voice that sent a chill through me. "Coming this late? When I hired you as my maid I warned you not to be late, didn't I?" His accent had morphed from Maine-ish to German-ish, or I was hearing things? It was hard to tell under this bed.

"Yes, sir," came a high-pitched, meek voice.

He was walking around, each step smacking the floor loud enough to make me think Gestapo boots. Had he changed his shoes? I wished I could see. I risked another peek, lifting the bed skirt higher this time. He was walking around her. Inspecting her? He had a riding crop in his hand. I saw the bottom of it rap his boots. When his toes turned my way, I dropped the bed shirt. I heard sharp raps against leather. I think it was leather. I couldn't tell for sure. I could only imagine. And under this dark bed, my imagination took wing.

"At least your uniform is properly ironed."

I didn't have to see her to know she was in costume. I wished I could get my hands up to cover my ears, but the space was too confining to cover them comfortably for any length of time. Lifting the bed skirt was challenge enough.

I also wished I could get to a bathroom. If I could just cross my legs . . .

Time moved at a snail's pace. So much for the wish for a quickie. Marla was laughing one minute, bouncing on the bed the next, oofing and aahing and such. What was he doing to her? The pictures running through my head rivaled things I'd seen on the Playboy Channel. Not that I'm a big fan, but every now and again . . .

Then it began, the familiar symptoms that I had come to dread, the ones that signaled the presence of cat. My eyes began to tear. And itch. I had to rub them. I just had to. Despite the cramped position, I managed to get my hands near my face. Good thing, because I felt a sneeze coming, trying to work its way up and out.

While my hands were nearby, I held one over my mouth and nose and gave forth with an almost silent, but spitty, a-choo. In reflex my forehead struck the floor, and my arm upended the sour milk bowl.

"Ow."

No time to wallow in self-pity. Another sneeze was waiting in the wings, a slow moving one, the absolute worst kind. Think pressure on magma, building, building. Think volcano. I wished I could force it and get it over with, but no.

Ah . . . . aah . . . .aaah . . .

It wouldn't come. The blockbuster sneeze was gathering force for eruption.

What came was the damn cat, in person, nosing around, rubbing up against my leg. I tried to push him away. No such luck.

He thought I was playing with him. I now had both hands guarding my nose. No way was I going to pull them away from nose detail and risk the escape of a loud sneeze. Some of my sneezes are sound-barrier-breakers, not cute, not genteel. I used to wish I had a cute and delicate girlie sneeze. I still wished that.

Body sounds from the other room got more interesting, but I was too busy trying to control my own body to imagine what Percy and Marla were doing.

The sneeze finally broke loose, a rip-snorter, and I pressed both hands tighter to cover the noise. I almost blew up. My head smacked the floor again, a real hard wallop this time. I'd have a bump for sure. The cat approached to investigate. Damn cat.

I had to get out of this hellhole. I really had to get to a bathroom fast. This detective business was getting old. I decided to risk sneaking out before the happy couple was finished. I prayed they would be too busy to notice someone scuttling along on the floor. From the sounds they were making, I figured they were very busy. My one regret was that I couldn't peek in. Not that I'm a voyeur or anything, but God, they were going at it.

Percy's different from most folks around here. He's . . . tougher. Can be ruthless.

Nick's warning ran through my head as I squirmed to the side of the bed. The need to sneeze was working its way up again, and each sneeze increased my chances of discovery, along with the lumps on my forehead. I had to stop moving.

When the sneeze arrived, it was a winner, the champion of all sneezes, a hall of famer.

Aaa-choo!

Aaa-choo!

Thwack. Bang. Two more lumps for a grand total of four. Wonderful. How attractive, Nora.

Marla moaned in ecstasy. "Oh, Percy." Her voice still had that phony, high-pitched quality. "There's no one like you. No one, my love."

"Marla, Marla, I can't get enough of you."

Well, I'd had enough of both of them. I rubbed my eyes again and shifted my leg in an attempt to get the cat to move. He did. Right next to my face. Soon I'd be a candidate for the Emergency Room.

I pushed my tote, then myself, out from under the bed, not an easy task with the cat positioned where he was.

I squeaked as the cat's claw snagged my sweater, caught, penetrated, and scratched my shoulder. I went into a holding pattern until I was sure no one had heard. It gave me time to be thankful I had chosen to wear sneakers instead of leather-bottomed shoes or boots. True, they didn't go with the outfit, but Mary Fran equals sneakers. Hadn't I learned that years ago?

With great care, I inched toward the door on my belly, sweeping the floor with my cashmere sweater and good slacks. I wanted to go to the bathroom. No chance. I crossed my legs for a second, took a deep breath, then uncrossed them and slithered into the hall like a recruit in basic training crawling under barbed wire. The damn cat followed. Cats love me. Once, a long time ago before I found out I was allergic to cats, I loved them, too. Maybe they sensed that. It's like I'm the Pied Piper of felines.

After I successfully passed the bedroom door, I stood, and tiptoed to the stairs.

I remembered to skip the creaky third step on the way down.

When I finally reached the car, I was a wreck. Gasping for breath, heart slamming like a jackhammer, I started the engine and took off like I was shot from a cannon. I almost clipped a pickup truck stopped at the end of the driveway, a newspaper guy delivering papers.

Title me Desperate Detective. I was lost. I recognized this little bridge ahead since I'd been over it three times already. I looked around. Woods, woods and more woods, and a little stream. Where was I? I wondered, wriggling in my seat, seriously in need of a bathroom, considering getting out and peeing by the side of the road. The way things were going today, I'd probably squat in a patch of poison ivy.

Groping for Mary Fran's map on the passenger seat, I drove over the bridge and pulled to the side of the road. I hoped no one I knew would drive by and see me. I was a mess. My hair. My clothes. I smelled of dust and sour milk, and if I didn't find a toilet soon . . .

It was five minutes to four. I had to be at the lawyer's for the reading of the will in five minutes. That wasn't going to happen. I hated being late.

From the X that was Mary Fran's house, I ran my pinky along the chicken-scrawl route that led to Main Street in town. It veered to the right after the bridge. Well, I'd done that. Then a quick left. Yes, I'd gone left. Or was that left made by the smudge on the paper? Which way had I gone when I was coming? Right. No, left. No, maybe right was right.

I needed a GPS.

An SUV with a red blinking light on top pulled along side of me. The flutter of my foolish heart was matched only by my rising panic. I needed a hat, or even better, a paper bag to cover my head. No, I needed not to be here. Instead of wildly trying to adjust my appearance, I took the high road and acted as if nothing was amiss.

"Parked to enjoy the wicked good view of Hunter's Creek?" Nick asked.

I looked at him and smiled as if my hair stuck up this way every day. His expression was hard to read. And that was because he had no expression. He just stared. God, he was cute. Too bad I'd sworn off men for the rest of my natural life.

"I'm temporarily lost," I said.

"As long as it's only temporary."

"Could you point me toward town?"

"You in trench-coat mode?"

"Have trench coat, will travel. I've just completed today's mission."

"One would think most detectives would have checked

directions before going on assignment."

"I got there."

"I can see that." His gaze traveled to my hair. "Rough time?"

"Not at all," I said with a straight face.

"Did someone whack you in the forehead?"

I considered lying.

"No. I hit my head on the floor when I sneezed."

He nodded as if he understood, but I recognized confusion when I saw it.

Just then the *Toreador March* sounded, I saw that my friend Lori in New York was calling, and I answered.

"Hi. I've been meaning to get back to you, but I've been busy. Sorry. Can't talk now either."

"You coming home today?" Lori asked.

I glanced at Nick who made no pretense of not listening. "Maybe tonight, Lori. Maybe not until tomorrow. Depends. But I have to—"

"On what's in the will?"

"I'm . . . involved here."

"Uh-oh. Dare I ask in what?" Then she gasped. "Or is that the wrong question? Nora, have you met someone? This soon? I wouldn't put it passed you. Guys are drawn to you. You have all the luck. I think—"

"No. Of course not." I hesitated, unwilling to give Nick a clue about this conversation.

"Is someone else there?" she said finally.

"Yes."

"Is he cute?"

I didn't reply.

"I'm guessing it's a he. Am I correct?"

I had to get off the phone. "You are."

"About the cute part? Is that an affirmative?"

"Yes. Now, I gotta hang—"

"Damn. I knew it when I didn't hear from you."

"You are dead wrong, Lori. I've just been busy."

"Doing?"

"Can I call you back?"

"You'd damn well better. I want to hear everything you've been up to in the hinterlands. But before you hang, you'd better give me a fax number or a computer address, somewhere I can send this résumé. Pronto."

"Hold on." I lowered the phone. "Do you have a fax at your office?"

"Ay-uh. Fax machines, computers, indoor plumbing. All the latest. We're very modern."

I grinned at him. "Could I have someone fax me something there?"

He didn't answer, just reached for something below window level, then leaned over and passed me a card. "Number's on here. Can't guarantee it'll be kept private."

"Doesn't have to be. It's only my résumé. Thanks for this." I gave Lori the number.

I could see from Nick's expression that he had a lot of questions, none of which I wanted to answer, so before he could ask, I said, "Can you point me in the right direction?"

I needed to cross my legs. Hard to do behind the wheel.

"You spied on Percy?" he asked.

It was now four o'clock. I was late for the reading of the will, the official reason I'd given everyone for coming to Silver Stream in the first place. I'd never told them it had to do with losing my job and my fiancé in the same week.

"I had a key so I wasn't breaking and entering, if that's what you're thinking."

"You refuse to take my advice on this."

"I'm doing a favor for Mary Fran."

He grunted.

"Directions?" I asked, pressing my legs together. God, I had to find a bathroom, fast.

SEVEN

As soon as I reached Hot Heads Heaven, I raced for the ladies' room like a wild woman, not bothering to acknowledge Mary Fran or any of the other women, some of whom might have been frightened by my appearance.

"Nora? You all right?" Mary Fran called as she ran after me.

"Yes. Be out in a minute."

"You look awful," she informed me from the other side of the door. "Are you sure you're all right?"

I sneezed and let her stand there and wonder as she listened to Niagara Falls. Who knew a bladder could hold so much without bursting.

One glance in the mirror and I went white with shock. It was worse than I thought. Omigod. Nick had seen me like this. My hair wasn't just sticking up. It looked like some school science experiment gone awry. The designer clothes I'd bought on sale when I was a working woman were a mosaic of cat hair and dust balls. Worse, now that I didn't have the car window open, that under-the-bed-aroma was stronger. Which way had the wind been blowing? Had Nick smelled this?

Mary Fran pounded on the door. "Nora. Come out and tell me what you found. You never called like you promised."

Where, exactly, was that odor coming from? I sniffed here and there.

"Nora Lassiter. Answer me."

I checked back and front, up and under, and finally spotted the telltale white chunks on the back of my sleeve.

"Did you fall in? What's happening in there?"

It was quarter after four. The family was gathered in the lawyer's office wondering where I was. I'd come four days early for this event.

"Noorrrraah!"

I yanked open the door. "I have to get cleaned up and out of here. I'm late."

"First, tell me–"

"Yes, he's cheating. Yes, I got the emails to back it up, and when I return from the lawyer's I'll give them to you and tell you all about it. Not another word on the subject until then. Help me look presentable."

"He's cheating. I knew it," she said with a grimace. "No surprise there." She grabbed a towel and brushed me down, then nudged me into a magenta chair and worked on my hair.

"Where the hell were you? How'd this happen? Look at the bumps on your forehead. My God. Were you attacked? Did you fall? Have a car accident?"

"I'm fine. I bumped my head."

"Maybe you should see a doctor."

"My hair, Mary Fran. Just do my hair. Fast. I hate to be late for anything." I did not want to tell her right now that Percy had been at the house today.

In the shop, all pretense of not listening ceased. I became the cynosure of all eyes.

"You look like you've been crawling around in a cellar. You're usually such a prissy little neat-freak."

Prissy? Me? "I prefer to think of myself as being well-groomed."

"I'll do what I can," Mary Fran said, but her tone implied I was a hopeless case and she wouldn't take total responsibility for the end result.

By the time I headed for the lawyer's office in his home just outside of town, a straight run, thank heavens, it was four-forty. Every eye focused on me as I walked into the main room. Today seemed to be my day to be onstage.

And the Oscar goes to. . . .

Hannah motioned me to the chair next to her.

"Finally," Agnes commented. "My knee's been bothering me, sittin' on these metal chairs so long. He should get better chairs."

"I'm sorry, Aunt Agnes," I said. "I was . . . busy."

"She's dizzy." Agnes called out. "Someone help. Quick. Before she faints."

"*Busy.* She said she was busy," Ida clarified with a smirk that resembled a twisted pretzel."

"Doing what?" Agnes asked.

"You need that knee surgery," Hannah told Agnes. "I've been telling you for about a year now. You've got to make the decision. Just do it, for heaven sakes. We're sick of hearing about your gosh darn knee.

Ida suggested, "You should talk to Helen in Senior Citizens. She had her knee done last year. She's up and running around like nobody's business."

"Oh, that one," Hannah said. "Ever since her operation, she thinks she's a regular Marilyn Monroe. Dyed her hair brassy blond. Wears those tight clothes."

The uncles exchanged approving glances. They gave me a big hello, big smile, nothing like the reserved reception at the Country Store earlier today. I played the game, and gave them an equally big hello. Strange people, these Mainers.

Exhausted, I slumped in the chair. My detective career had about done me in.

"Where's Uncle JT?" I whispered to Hannah.

She nodded toward Ellie. "Don't know. Ellie said he was off somewhere on business." Her tone implied this was strange, and she wasn't sure Ellie had told her the truth.

The lawyer, a man I thought looked a little like George Washington on the dollar bill, without the wig, of course, sat at a huge oak desk angled in front of a bay window. My eyes were drawn to a view of towering pines, a pond, a small dock. In summer it would be the perfect place to sit and listen to the loons.

That made me smile. Today I'd listened to human loons.

Looking at me, the lawyer cleared his throat. "I think we should get started. This won't take long."

Hannah waved her hand. "Everyone's here. Read away." She smiled at the uncles, and finally me, the smile losing a shade of brightness the longer she looked at me. "Are you all right, Nora? You look different. Your hair is so high."

I tried to press it down, not an easy task. Damn Mary Fran and her teasing comb. And her trigger-finger on that hair spray can. I had Brillo hair.

"And your forehead . . . did you get stung by wasps? Do you need treatment?"

"I'm fine. I just need to sit here."

Hannah leaned over to give me a kiss and I leaned toward her. My hair touched her face, and she flinched. I quickly checked her for cheek abrasions. She seemed all right. However, when she sat back, she wrinkled her nose, looked around and sniffed the air as if she'd smelled something unpleasant. I casually lifted my arm and sure enough, that sour milk was more than a memory. I thought I'd cleaned it. Instead of enlightening Hannah, I feigned ignorance.

The lawyer had several pages in front of him. I didn't understand why he couldn't have given them to someone in the family instead of having this formal reading, or even mailed them out. He'd explained in his letter that Great-grandma Evie had requested a reading with the family assembled, and everyone had agreed to respect her wishes. I suppose when you reach ninety-five and make requests, people try to oblige. Evie was a strong woman, leader of the Lassiter clan for many years.

The lawyer read off a list of items—nothing of consequence—that Grandma wanted family members to have. I was bequeathed a hankie with lavender lace tatting. I was a little hurt, but bobbed my head graciously to hide my feelings. I'd driven hundreds of miles for a hankie? Well, what did I expect? I was out of the loop, an estranged family member, and I should be grateful, I suppose, that I'd even been invited to this reading.

I tried not to smirk.

Or cry.

So far, this had not been a banner day. Crappy. It had been crappy. I tried to tuck a strand of hair behind my ear and almost cut my finger. I smelled my sleeve again while it was up there. Not too bad. Hannah's nose must be ultra sensitive. Or maybe I was getting used to the smell?

I closed my eyes. I was so tired. If I were lying down I'd be asleep in minutes. The lawyer was reading about some land. I drifted mentally. Who cared? Everyone knew Ida got everything, house and land. She deserved it, earned it. For years Ida had taken care of Great-grandma Evie. She had cooked and cleaned, taken her to doctors' offices and on visits to relatives and friends. Ida was a good woman and deserved the security of the house and property, even if she was getting on in years and would probably not be here much longer.

"Nora Lassiter," the lawyer said aloud. All heads swiveled in my direction.

What?

I knew I should have been paying attention. This used to happen in school. All of a sudden the teacher would call on me, and I had no idea of what the question was.

"Nora," Hannah said gleefully. "I'm so happy for you."

Before I could respond to Hannah, the lawyer said, "You can remain and we'll go over the paperwork. I wish your brother Howard had been able to make it today, Nora."

What had we inherited?

"You can do so much with the property," Ida said, smiling. "Build a house, tap the maples and make syrup."

"You could tap the maple trees and make syrup," Agnes said.

"I just said that," Ida told her. "Plug in your hearing aid."

Ignoring the comment, Agnes said, "Many years back Grandma Evie was famous, at least in the family, for her maple syrup. No one's bothered since she stopped. More's the pity. But someone could show you how it's done. You can even make maple candy. That's one of my favorites. Maple candy."

Holy crap! Land. Howie and I had inherited some land, a section of Ida's property? Me, Nora Lassiter, a landowner. A maker of maple syrup? Hard to picture.

I looked at Ida and she didn't seem upset. Surprisingly, neither did any other members of the family. Had they known? And approved? Strange. With all the nodding and smiling, they seemed to. I wondered how much the property was worth. I'd be able to pay the American Express bill, for sure.

"Why me?" I asked the lawyer after everyone left.

"Evelyn 'Evie' Lassiter and her husband Charles, who died five years ago, decided they wanted you and your family back in Silver Stream, Nora. Even your mother, if she would come. They felt this would be a draw."

The lawyer held out an envelope. "I was to give you this. Evie said it explained what she wanted to explain."

I took the envelope with my name and Howie's written in flowing, old-fashioned script across the front. More than anything I wanted to rip it open and read it immediately, but caution, which I believe runs only surface-deep in me most of the time, urged me to hold off until I was alone.

"Thank you," I said to the lawyer as I slipped the envelope into my purse. "Can I sell this land, or hand it over to Ida?"

"Both, I suppose. Ask the family if any of them want to buy it. Or you could live there, as your great-grandmother wanted. Perhaps a trailer to start out. Later, a house. I did not read the letter she wrote to you. It was sealed by her, kept private, the way she wanted it. She considered it extremely important. She did tell me there was something she wanted you to do."

He seemed to leave the last sentence hanging, implying I should do what Grandma Evie wanted before I returned to New York.

"One more thing."

He hesitated, and I realized he was going to say something he felt uneasy about, which, of course, made me uneasy, too.

"Several years back, when your great-grandmother was ninety-one, but in full control of her faculties, she was very troubled about something. Maybe she tells you about it in the letter. I hope so. Ninety-one should be a time of peace. Clearly it wasn't peaceful for her, at least where you and your brother and your parents were concerned."

Okay, now I was definitely uneasy. I figured it had something to do with Dad and the move to New York. Perhaps I would finally find out what had happened all those years ago.

As I signed more papers, he promised to help with any details he could.

I drove back to Ida's place, thinking about how much my life had changed in four days. Not only had I taken on a "job" for Mary Fran, but I'd inherited a large tract of land, fifty acres. With the loss of my city job, my life had been in the toilet financially. Now, I had land I could sell.

Unbidden, Whatshisname flashed through my thoughts, and I felt a sharp stab of grief. As much as I wanted to be rid of him, he still invaded my head. I wished I could press a mental eject button, especially of that last crushing scene when he had been naked in my shower with that woman.

Ida was watching *Crime Stoppers* when I arrived back at the house, so I gave her a quick kiss and went up to my room. With great care, I opened the letter. It was written in the same flowing script as the names on the envelope: Howard and Nora.

I quickly read to the end, then sat there with my mouth open. Stunned, I read it again, more slowly this time.

EIGHT

Dear Nora and Howie,

I've seen lots in my time. Some good, some bad. One of the bad was your father leaving Silver Stream. It was my fault.

Maybe we should have come together more as a family and backed him. The offender should have been brought to justice like he wanted originally. I begged him not to pursue the matter. I had visions of the family name being dragged through the mud. I shouldn't have meddled. I should have let him handle it any way he chose, being that his wife was the affronted party.

Although your dad did what I wanted, he thought we were choosing to sweep it all under the rug. That wasn't so. Sexual harassment is wrong. Plain and simple.

Back then, we thought since your mother was okay, the matter should be put behind us. After much ado, your father finally agreed and I thought that was the end of it. But of course, it wasn't.

I won't go into the details. By now, you know them. The matter is long over and should remain so. I just want you to know that I'm sorry I meddled. I, for one, didn't think he was guilty of anything, although some did, but I may have been the cause of the tragic consequences. I'm sorry I didn't understand how upset your father was before it was too late.

Afterwards, he was in such a hurry to get away that he sold his house and property to JT for much less than it was worth.

I've been saving to pay back some of what he lost. Since he died before me, I can't do that. I want to give you what I did manage to put away. I know your mother won't take it, or anything else from me. She'll never speak to me again. Can't say as I blame her.

You'll notice I included a map. Follow it to the box that I buried out back beyond the creek.

I wish it could be more. No one in the family knows about this. I'd prefer you keep it quiet, but the decision about telling is yours. My meddling days are over.

No logging's been done on the property for years, so if you stay maybe you could look into it. That will help you keep the place going. If you let it, the land will draw you and you will grow to love it.

I love you, sweet Nora and Howie.

  Your Grandma Evie

Sexual harassment.

My jaw had dropped at the mention of my mother, and it was still open when I finished reading. What did Grandma Evie mean that she didn't think dad was guilty? Of what? What had happened? Who was involved? Why hadn't Dad ever told me about this? Told me the truth when I asked? Or Mom? Neither had said a word.

I closed my mouth. My parents had never discussed sex with me, ever, so I guessed it wasn't surprising that neither of them mentioned this.

Sexual harassment.

I wanted to run downstairs and demand Ida tell me everything. I wasn't sure what stopped me. I told myself it was my concern for her.

Troubled, I read the letter a third time. I wondered what Mom would say now if I called and asked her outright. Howie would have a better chance of finding out. Mom was more open with him than she was with me.

On Tuesday morning I got up early. I had a plan for the day, formulated as I took the fastest shower of my life in water way below lukewarm. Damn water heater. Good for nothing.

Shivering as I toweled dry, I glanced out the window. Frost. In September? I'd forgotten about Maine mornings in late summer. I opened the window. Frost laced the bushes and lawn, the trees and old flower stalks. Despite the white puffs of steam coming from my mouth, I remained staring. How could I have forgotten how beautiful this place could look?

The land will draw you and you will grow to love it.

No. And no.

I stood back and closed the window on that thought.

I honed my day's plan.

I decided to leave the mystery box buried for another day. It wasn't going anywhere.

Seeing Ellie was a priority. And not just because I wanted to see my old house, which I still hadn't managed to see. I'd been too busy visiting relatives, and hiding under beds.

Ellie had been a friend of my mother's. She'd tell me what had happened all those years ago, what they all thought Dad might be guilty of, and who was involved in the sexual harassment incident. She'd know more than Aunt Ida, I figured.

I tried to call Ellie, but kept getting a busy signal. She didn't have Call Waiting? Well, I'd pack so I was ready to leave tonight or tomorrow. After packing, I'd drive into town to Mary Fran's and give her the emails. I hadn't done that yesterday as I'd promised. Emails should be enough. I'd offer to write out what I'd heard and seen. Maybe that would take the place of photos. While I was in town I'd stop and pick up my résumé at the sheriff's office, go over it carefully and call Lori with any changes I wanted. That way it would be ready tomorrow when I arrived back in New York. Then I'd go see Ellie whether she answered the phone or not.

Last on the list, I'd gather the old aunts and figure out what to do about the land. Even though part of me wanted to stay, I couldn't. The Big Apple was home.

This all sounded good. Positive. I wrote it down. A certain satisfaction comes when you have a plan, especially when you commit it to paper in list form. You can cross things off a list and see that you've accomplished something. Nothing tops a visual.

Once in a while if I do something that is not on my list, I cheat, and add it, just so I can cross it off. It's the crossing off that's satisfying. I didn't see that happening today, of course, because I'd written down everything. Everything. Today was going to be a perfect day. No bodies, no rain, no snooping in someone's computer, no hiding under beds. No lawyers.

With this in mind, I slipped into my black knit vee-neck dress, grabbed my camera and went downstairs. I'd take some scenery shots today, some by the stream.

Ida was at the stove making pancakes, watching a rerun of *Murder, She Wrote* when I came down.

She pressed Pause and said, "Hannah just called. Wants me to move in with her now that it's official and you own so much land around here. Says I should let you have the house, too. Ever since she became president of the Senior Citizens she thinks she's Queen of the World and can order everyone about."

I wanted to ask about the sexual harassment. Instead, I said, "I don't want the house, Ida. I'm not sure about the land either. Maybe I'll just deed it to you."

I wanted to tell her about the letter, question her about what had happened back then, but I decided to hold off until I'd spoken to Ellie.

"I'm not interested in ownership any more. House or land. I'm too old. A body only needs so much," Ida said, flipping three pancakes onto my plate. "Where you off to this morning?"

"To town, then to JT's. Want to come?"

Looking unsettled, she put the pan down. "I don't particularly want to see Ellie. Something's not right over there and I'd rather not know about it. I sensed friction at the party."

Ida, like Hannah, wanted nothing to do with any unpleasantness. Did this come with age? I wondered, or was it something peculiar to Mainers?

"Well, while I'm there I'll take some pictures. I'm sure the place has changed a lot since I lived there."

The tote with the emails felt heavy. I wondered if I should

deliver only a few to Mary Fran instead of this massive pack. I'd feel awful if I got all this stuff about a man I had loved. On the other hand, she already knew he was cheating.

By the time I reached the beauty parlor, I realized that kindness was not what she wanted. She wanted the truth, the cold, hard, devil-in-the-details truth.

When I entered, all spraying ceased in mid-spritz along with the conversation. Likewise, the hair dryers. I don't usually have this effect on people so it wasn't much of a mental leap to conclude they either knew what I'd been up to for Mary Fran, and I hoped that wasn't it, or else they knew I'd found the body and were staring for ghoulish reasons, which I figured was more likely. All eyes followed Mary Fran as she left her customer. Before she spoke, I handed her the stack of papers.

"Thanks," she said, clasping them to the chest, her eyes watering. "Let's go to the back."

Once out of earshot, I knew the time had come. I had to tell her. "Mary Fran, Percy was at the house yesterday." I swallowed hard. "With . . . the woman."

She staggered backwards and gasped as if she'd been punched. "In my home? The bastard. How low can he get?"

I hated to tell her the next part. "Yes. They . . . were in your bedroom. I didn't have a chance to leave. I hid under your daughter's bed. They didn't see me."

The color drained from her face. "He took that slut to my bed?"

I nodded.

"I'm thinking really bad thoughts, Nora," she whispered, leaning toward me. "I want to kill him. Slowly." She paused. "No. I just changed my mind. Not kill. I want to cut it off. Maybe throw it in the blender, make some chunky soup, so when he got out of the hospital I could serve it to him in a nice bowl. Maybe with a few crackers on the side. He likes crackers."

She slumped into a chair next to the coffee machine, and I put my hand on her shoulder.

"How could he do this to me? How could he? I've been a good wife."

"I'm sure you have. I know how you feel. Something similar happened to me a short time ago. Of course, I wasn't married to the jerk, but it was close. You don't want to do anything foolish, Mary Fran. It wouldn't be worth it. You know that, don't you?"

"Don't worry. Getting his money will hurt him. I know him well enough to know that. I was feeling a bit guilty about using the prenup. Not any more."

She swiped at the tears. "But it still hurts."

Relieved that she wasn't going to hack off Percy's body parts, I said, "You'll get through this, Mary Fran. You will. And the pain will go away." I wasn't sure about that last part, but it sounded good.

She straightened her shoulders. I could almost see the steel stiffening her spine.

"He just called, you know. About Collins."

I followed her back into the shop. "What did he say?"

"Who could have murdered him?" Mary Fran said, ignoring my question. "And why? I know the guy was a first class ass but murdering him. That's a little extreme, don't ya think?"

I nodded. "I do think that. Absolutely."

Her customers stared at me as if they were waiting for me to say more. What? I had no idea. Mary Fran continued to the front desk and I followed. All eyes tracked our progress. She picked up a huge, multi-colored bundle of beads and I figured she was going to hang these around her neck, but they turned out to be her purse. She stuffed the papers inside.

"This probably means nothing," she whispered quickly, "but Percy left early the last few mornings. Very early. He returned before my alarm went off. I was awake, of course, but I never spoke to him. I figured he'd been out owlin' around with his 'ho, but maybe not."

Was she implying that Percy might have killed his partner? I wondered whether she was in danger.

"Did he know you heard him, Mary Fran?" I whispered.

"No. I never moved and I was breathing like I was asleep. I've had practice."

I whispered, "Do you think he had anything to do with his partner's death? Is that what you're implying?"

She didn't say anything immediately. Then she put her hand up to cup her mouth and whispered, "I don't know. I don't think so, but I'm not sure. Lately there was friction between them. Don't know what it was all about. I was too pissed at him to show much interest and he keeps things close to the vest."

I nodded, then changed the subject as I walked toward the door. "I planned to leave today or tomorrow, probably tomorrow."

"No!" She grabbed my hand and I froze and tried to wriggle free.

"You can't leave, Nora. You haven't taken the photos yet. The prenup states that I have to have irrefutable proof. That would be photos. You promised me photos."

She dragged me back to the magenta-laminated counter, released my hand, thank God, and opened the cash register. She counted out a small pile of twenties. "Here, I didn't pay you yet. It's not that I forgot. I didn't. Believe me. I just don't know the protocol here. Hiring a private investigator is not something I've done before."

"But you already gave me money."

I refused to put my hand out. I do have some scruples.

"Yes. But even I know that was just a retainer. Now, I insist you take the rest for doing what you've done so far." She forced the money into my hand.

I tried to return it. No luck.

"No. Keep it," she insisted. "People should get paid for their services."

Well, I had gotten the emails she wanted. I'd also suffered an allergy attack, ruined my clothes, endangered my body. I looked at the money, thinking a person could make a living this way.

"What's the matter? Did I do a *faux pas*? I'm supposed to pay it all together? Come-on, tell me. I'm no good at this stuff."

Standing there like a goof, I made a decision.

"You did it perfectly, Mary Fran. I'll get those photos as soon as he sets up another meeting with her. I thought the emails would be enough, but I'll get photos. As insurance. You'll get your eighty percent. I'll have to get into the computer again in a day or so. There was nothing there about the next meeting."

Already I was thinking, next time I went to her house I'd bring a mask, wear old clothes, maybe bring some cat repellent spray, if there was such a thing.

Mary Fran looked relieved. I was scared. The limb I'd climbed out on was dipping dangerously.

"Wonderful. Super-dupe. The sooner the better . . . you know, just in case."

Second thoughts hit me immediately. What had I done? Then the "in case" registered.

"In case what?" I asked.

"Well, if Percy's arrested for murder he'll need a lawyer and that'll take a bundle. Can you imagine how it'll eat into my part of the settlement?"

I smiled. "You're always thinking, Mary Fran. On top of things."

I was out the door when a woman wearing one of those plastic caps with the holes in it, came charging out.

"Stop!"

NINE

"I need your services," the chubby woman with the holey cap said, panting as if she'd just finished the Boston Marathon. "Mary Fran told me how good you are at what you do, and that's all the recommendation I need."

Hair stuck through the holes on the right side of her cap giving her a lopsided appearance. I tried to concentrate on her less distracting left side, but the breeze swayed her bleached strands with a rhythm that was almost hypnotic.

"I'm Vivian. I need a detective," she said. "I never thought I'd say this. But I do. The sheriff isn't helping one bit."

I really had to tell people I was not a detective. Now was my chance. I started with a shake of the head. Nothing too vigorous, just a small negative shake. Then the protest. "I really—"

She raised her hand. "Don't say a word. First let me tell you about Dora."

I suppose I could listen to the Dora story. It was only polite. But after that I had to say no. An honest woman would say no. And I pride myself on being an honest woman. Most of the time.

"She was poisoned."

My hand went to my heart. "Oh, my God."

Three murders in Silver Stream. Had I come to the murder capital of the world? What was that sheriff doing to earn his paycheck? He'd hear a thing or two from me when I saw him.

"I think I know who did it, but I can't prove a thing, which is where you come in."

So this wasn't recent. Thank God. I fingered the bills in my pocket. "And Dora is?"

"Was."

I nodded somberly. "Was a friend? A relative?"

"My Pomeranian.

What on earth was a Pomeranian?

A fruit? I thought about it. No, that was a pomegranate.

"Describe her to me," I said.

She gave me an odd look. "Dora had a long black coat that was especially full on the neck and chest. She was about six or seven inches high and weighed about five pounds."

So we were talking about a sack-of-potatoes-size dog. I nodded sagely, like I knew it was a dog all along.

"So it was black," I said, glancing down the street to see if the sheriff's SUV was parked in front of his office. I wanted to see if he'd interviewed Percy yet.

"I'll save you some trouble," she said as I fished in my tote for a scrap of paper. "My next door neighbor is the perp. You can start there."

Perp? Hunh.

I handed her an appointment card from my dentist in New York. "Write down your name and phone number," I said, passing her a pen.

As long as I had to stay and do photos for Mary Fran, I might as well check out this dog poisoning business. Keep myself busy. Make a few bucks. Maybe I could buy Aunt Ida a new hot water heater before I even sold the land. A person could make a business out of this detecting work.

I took the card and dropped it into my almost empty tote. "I'll be in touch, Vivian," I promised as I headed for the sheriff's office to pick up the résumé that Lori had faxed.

Seated at the big desk, Trimble peered down his pointy nose at me when I entered the station house. He had a strange look on his face. At least I thought it was stranger than usual. It was hard to tell, but he looked like he was leering. I usually smile when I speak to people, but I made an exception and just asked him if knew anything about my résumé.

"Everyone knows," skinny Trimble said, smiling his little smirky smile. "Your résumé came in late yesterday, Ma'am." He moved to another section of the big desk, and with a flourish, scooped up some papers, and instead of reaching over the desk, came down to stand in front of me. "Here it is," he said, handing the pages to me.

Dumbfounded, embarrassed, I stared at the photo Lori had scanned onto the draft copy. She had a great sense of humor, I had to give her that, and I would have laughed if I'd received this in private. We had both thought a photo would be good and I trusted her to pick a nice head shot from my disks. Hell. I should have told her this would be coming into the sheriff's office. I wondered if every Silver Stream deputy had seen this picture of me. No use wondering. I knew.

I looked at Trimble standing there, arms folded, grinning like a loon, waiting for me to say something.

In the photo, posing a Playboy-type pose, I stood on the sand at Coney Island in the world's sexiest bikini, a black number with a few strings and wisps of cloth covering vital spots. I had worn this creation only once, for about six seconds, and then covered up. I must have been possessed to buy it in the first place. It was one of my few purchasing mistakes. I admit to making them. I'm human.

Knowing that Trimble had seen this, probably stared at it, maybe even drooled over it, made me cringe inside. He'd probably made copies of it. Enlarged it. I wanted to slink into a corner and hide. Or stammer that it really wasn't me. Or explain about Lori's humor. Of course, I knew all of these things would be wrong.

"Whadda you looking at?" I fired at him, my voice harsh, as close to a bark as I could get it.

Trimble actually took a step back. Good. I remembered how to do this. When he didn't say anything, I pummeled him again. "You got a problem with this? A problem with me, maybe? Or maybe you're never seen a woman in a bikini?"

I was back in high school where you never backed down, where toughness counted, where it equated with survival. Trimble was at a definite disadvantage here. He had never gone to a high school that bordered the Bronx.

"Got a problem with me? With my résumé? My picture, maybe?" The last words were pure challenge. I took a step toward him and he took another step back, this guy who wore a badge and carried a gun.

"No . . . no problem," he stammered as he hurried back to the safety of the desk.

I knocked on Nick's open office door, poked my head in and asked, "You talk to Percy yet?"

"I see you got your résumé," he said, sidestepping my question.

My first thought was: What do you think of me in a bikini? How shallow am I? My next thought was that Mister Big Ears Trimble was nearby, pretending to be busy.

"Yes, I got it. Thanks for letting my friend fax it here."

Nodding, as if to say touché, he got up and came over. "Trimble, I'm going to the Country Store for lunch. Don't bother me unless aliens land or the President calls."

"Ay-uh, Sheriff."

"You eat yet?" he asked me, grabbing his brown campaign-style hat.

"No."

"Come on."

I was going to have lunch with the boss. I should be thinking about Percy who might have murdered his partner instead of picturing myself sitting across from this romantic devil. Good thing I planned to leave Maine shortly. Without another word, I walked beside him, hurrying a bit to keep pace with his long strides.

As soon as we stepped outside, the wind twirled my hair up and around. It still had to look better than it did yesterday.

"I have to ask a few more questions," Nick began, eyeing my forehead.

Reflexively, I touched my lumps. "The result of an allergy." At the lift of his brows, I clarified, "I sneezed and bumped my head."

"So you said on your way back from Kendall's. On the floor, wasn't it? And it happened four times?"

"You're half right."

"Half right? Two sneezes, four lumps? Okay. Just seems a sensible woman would have moved back before the fourth hit. That's just my uninformed male opinion, of course," Nick said.

"Uninformed is your key word."

"Suppose you explain."

"Do you think this has anything to do with the murder?" I asked.

The *Toreador March* sounded in my pocket. I glanced at the caller's name. My brother again. I didn't want to talk to him in front of Nick, but I knew he was worried since I'd never called him back. I figured I owed him a short conversation.

"Hi, Howie. Everything's okay," I assured him immediately. I explained about finding the body. He told me to be careful. It's like a mantra with him: Be careful, Nora. Be careful, Nora. Be careful, Nora.

Howie thought I was a calamity magnet, which was absolutely not true. But I loved my brother Howie, so I accepted.

"Don't you want to know about the will?" I asked Howie, conscious of Nick beside me.

"Sure."

"We have inherited about fifty acres of woods around Aunt Ida's place. She'll keep a few acres."

No reaction.

"Howie? You still there?"

"What's wrong with the land? Is it under water?"

"Don't be ridiculous. This is not Florida."

"Has a huge lien against it, doesn't it?"

"That depends on how you define huge," I lied, unable to help myself. Teasing Howie was one of the small pleasures in my life. It takes so little to get him going and it's such fun to watch.

"I knew it. I'll sign it over to you. It's yours, Nora."

I laughed. "Howie, we have to talk." I thought of Mom and the sexual harassment business, but I didn't want to talk about that now.

"Sure, but not about the land. Just mail me the papers. Are you planning to move to Maine?"

"Absolutely not."

Nick and I reached the steps of the Country Store. "Howie, I can't talk any more now. I'm going to lunch with the sheriff."

"The sheriff. Are you sure you weren't arrested, Nora?"

Smiling, I said, "I won't even dignify that with an answer. I'll call you tonight."

I returned the phone to my purse. "That was my brother. He heard about the murder."

When Nick's brows shot up, I explained that Howie was a Miami-Dade cop.

As we climbed the steps, I asked, "Have you got any leads in the murder?"

He held the door. "Nothing much."

We took a small booth in the back and before I was settled in my seat, he asked, "What did you find at Percy's house?"

The question caught me off guard, which was a good thing because it kept me from answering immediately, which allowed me to consider the consequences. Could Mary Fran be affected? Could I? Was it illegal to snoop in Percy's computer even though Mary Fran had given me access to the house? Maybe I should find out first.

"That's private," I answered.

Waitress Amy arrived and handed us menus. "Hi Nick." She nodded at me. "The back room's been all abuzz. Folks can't seem to talk about anything else but the Collins murder. You got any leads?"

"None."

"Such a shame. What's this world coming to?"

"Amy, this is Nora Lassiter."

"We've met. How you doing, honey? You recovered from your shock?"

Before I could answer, Nick cut in, "Amy, you knew Al for a long time, didn't you?"

"Years. We were in high school together. He was a year ahead of me. 'Course we weren't great friends, but still . . ."

"He come in here much?"

"Few times a week."

"When was the last time?"

Amy rested her order pad against her Pam Anderson double-Ds, maybe triple-Ds—I wondered whether there was an E, an F?—and considered the question. "Several days ago he came in with another guy. Don't think the he was from around here."

I could see Nick's cop antenna stand at attention.

"What day was that?"

"Hmm. Let's see. Maybe last Monday or Tuesday."

"Have you seen this guy since?"

"Nope. Just that one time. I figured him to be a customer at the car place. Ay-uh. Maybe picking up a car?"

"What'd he look like?"

"Short guy, maybe five-seven or so, dark hair, wore a baseball cap. His hair stuck out. Slim, wore jeans."

"Anything else? A name maybe?"

"Nothing. Sorry, Nick. Lunchtime we get pretty busy. Don't leave much time for gettin' acquainted." She adjusted her AMY badge as she spoke. What a figure the woman had. I'd have to get triple implants to rival those melons. I tried not to stare.

"Thanks, Amy. It's a place to start." He handed her back his menu. "I'll have coffee and ham on rye, extra pickles, Muenster cheese."

"A lobster roll for me," I said.

"Coming up."

"Since I've been in Maine I've eaten about seven lobster rolls. I started when I crossed the New Hampshire border. They're my absolute favorite, after homemade chocolate chip cookies, that is."

"Interesting," Nick said, tilting his head slightly as he stared at me. "Easy woman to please."

A man wearing a suit walked into the place and made a beeline for our table like a hound dog who's spotted the fox.

"You Sheriff Renzo?" the guy asked.

Nick said, "Ay-uh," his look, implying he didn't appreciate being disturbed.

With that, the guy signaled a pony-tailed man with a professional camcorder on his shoulder. Oh, hell. We were about to make the six o'clock news. Furiously, I patted my hair. I grabbed my purse and touched up my lipstick as the guy asked Nick about the murder. Glancing into my compact mirror, I realized I needed a complete overhaul. My national debut was minutes away.

"Can you tell us about the man who was murdered, Sheriff Renzo?

"No."

The reporter looked stunned. "The camera's rolling, Sheriff. The world is watching."

"The world'll have to wait until I finish my lunch. You going to film me eating?"

Not completely discouraged, the reporter turned to me. I was tempted to smile when the camera was aimed at me. I always wanted to be a performer, a singer maybe, or a dancer. I took tap as a kid. I still remember a few steps.

"And you are?" The reporter asked me.

I wished my hair looked better. That wind. . . .

"Nora Lassiter," I replied with a smoothness that surprised me. The show must go on.

"Did you know the murdered man?"

I wanted to tell him I'd found the body. Nick stepped on my toe under the table. When I looked at him, he stared back and tapped my foot a few more times. I wondered whether it was Morse code. I sighed and said, "We'll eat lunch first."

"Are you two an item?" the reporter asked, taking a new tack.

I laughed. The sheriff rolled his eyes.

"An item of what?" I asked before Nick found my foot again and tapped furiously. Lucky for him I didn't have my Bruno Maglis on, or he would have felt more than tapping on his own damn foot, scuffing up my shoe like that.

"Are you a couple?" the reporter asked, his annoyance evident.

"We're a couple of people who want to eat lunch at the moment," I said. I watched the camera zoom in on me for a close-up. I think it was aimed at my forehead. My lumps would make the news.

"I'll have a brief statement later," Nick cut in, the authority in his voice ending further discussion. He checked his watch. "Be in front of the station house around four."

It was almost three now.

"Sure thing," the guy said. He made a move to leave, then stopped short as if a light bulb had gone on in his head. It was creepy.

"Nick and Nora?" he questioned. "Like Nick and Nora Charles, the famous detective duo in those old movies? What a coincidence. That's cool. Do you two crack cases together?" He chuckled. "Do you have a dog named . . . I forget what their dog was called. My grandfather used to watch those old movies."

He chuckled again and left, muttering about the dog.

"When I'm in my crossword puzzle mode, I do a puzzle every night. On Sundays I do the *New York Times* crossword. So I know the name of the dog."

Nick tapped a rhythmic tattoo on the table. "Should I care about this?"

"Asta. The terrier in the *Thin Man* series. Nick and Nora Charles' dog was named Asta."

The lobster roll was delicious, better than any they served in New York. As we ate, Nick peppered me with questions, most of them routine. Then he asked about Percy again and I decided to tell him about the visit to the Kendall house, leaving out the sexual playacting parts, of course.

"You think he did it?" I asked when I finished. "Did you question him yet?"

Nick didn't answer immediately. "Right now I don't know what to think. I'll talk to him after I get rid of the press. Look into his business dealings with Collins."

"Get rid of the press? Gonna shoot them, are you?"

He shrugged, smiled. "We'll see."

I liked his smile. Broad. Warm. He had a dimple that showed up when he smiled. I felt the urge to kiss his dimple. *Geez.*

"I have to go to Percy's house again," I said. "Maybe I'll find out more this time. Do you want me to check a few programs on his computer? Like Quicken? Or Microsoft Money?"

"No. Stay out of it. Stay out of his house. I told you Percy's no one to mess around with. Besides, it's none of your business."

He was right. But it didn't change my mind. The determination must have shown on my face because he said, "I want to be very clear about this, Nora. I'm in charge of this investigation. I don't want you involved, especially where Percy Kendall is concerned."

"I promised Mary Fran I'd get photos."

His mouth thinned. "All right. Take your damn photos. Of him coming out of some motel, or out of his house with this woman, but that's it. That should be enough."

"Of course."

As we headed back to the station house, he said, "The first murder in Silver Stream was back in 1855. Some guy shot another guy for horse theft. Then about twenty years ago we had a real brutal murder."

"Percy, senior."

"So you heard. Guess it'll be talked about now. He was bashed with a baseball bat."

"What an awful way to die."

"Yes. A crime of passion, for sh-ur. It was the bat the Auto Mart guys used when they played on the local softball team. Very handy weapon."

He stopped and looked at me. "I only have book knowledge of this type of investigation. I wish you really were a hotshot New York Detective. I could use the expertise."

The admission surprised me. Not many men would admit they needed help. I was impressed. This was a notch above asking for directions.

"Sorry," I said grimly. "Maybe I could help anyway."

"No."

"How soon did you check me out?"

"I didn't have to."

"But you did?"

"Within a hour of meeting you."

"No grass growing under your feet."

We spotted the reporter and the video guy waiting on the station steps.

"I'll head home now," I told him. "Good luck with the sharks."

He reached for my hand and gave it a slight squeeze. "Thanks." Then he added, "I've had your statement about the murder typed up. You can read it over, make any corrections and sign it later."

"Okay. I know you think you don't want my help, but you saw my résumé, so you know . . . my areas of expertise." Nora, Nora, Nora.

He raised his brows, and grinned at me. "It caused quite a stir among the boys, you know. I don't think they bothered to read it. Never got past the picture."

"I'm guessing Trimble enjoyed it."

"Hell, I enjoyed it. If your "detective" career doesn't pan out, you could try modeling for *Sports Illustrated*."

I felt so pleased I wanted him to say more. "Yeah? You think so?"

"Oh, yes ma'am."

TEN

I couldn't get Percy out of my head. Mary Fran didn't think he was capable of killing his partner, but I thought she might be wrong. Had she ever heard his Gestapo boots stomping on the floor?

I stopped the car in front of the library, and called myself ten kinds of a fool for even letting my thoughts run in this direction. What dreamland had I mentally moved into? I was going home in a day or so, and I had no business even thinking about what Ida overheard here. That was the sheriff's business. I stared at the library building. I should not go in. Should not. There were three pickup trucks and a red Honda Civic parked out front. It wasn't crowded.

The Silver Stream Public Library did not look like most libraries I'd been in. It was a small, one-story wooden building with a steeply pitched metal roof, one of those special roofs you see in Maine that the snow can slide off of easily. I guessed the building would fit into a ladies' room of the New York Public Library with a few cubicles to spare. Since I was here, I might as well check it out, for nostalgia reasons, if nothing else. My lifelong love affair with books had begun here. I was at home here.

I should return the overdue library book I found when I unpacked my books in my new apartment about two years ago. I wondered what the fine was for twenty years. I had a book about Abraham Lincoln that I used for a fifth grade history report. We'd moved before I had a chance to return it.

Feeling a little guilty about the book, I walked up to the

librarian's desk, solid oak, from another century. The years vanished in an instant as I closed my eyes and breathed in the place. Even after all this time, I could identify *my* library by scent. Warmth and books and a hint of lemon oil polish.

A woman around forty years old, dressed in a green skirt, a severe gray blazer and cream-colored blouse, and looking tidier than any woman should ever look, unless she was in a convent, greeted me with a perfunctory—and a neat, I must say—smile, when I entered. Every hair on her head was in place. I immediately guessed she was a customer of that mad sprayer, Mary Fran.

"Good afternoon. May I help you?"

If I said I was just snooping, I suppose she would have asked me to leave, so I said, "I'd like a library card."

She handed me an application. "Just fill this out, in pen, and add a reference at the bottom. That's essential. Without a reference, you cannot take out books. When the application is complete, I'll approve it and give you a number."

Approve it? Was it possible that I wouldn't be approved? And I needed a reference?

They still used numbers here instead of computer-read cards. I already had a number. I figured after all this time it was not on record. Good thing. They could open up a new wing if I paid my fine. Ms. Efficiency would not like to hear about that book.

"I need a reference?" I asked, wondering if I'd misheard.

"Certainly."

"Sounds like an exclusive club. What people are you trying to keep out?"

"We like to know our patrons."

I reached across the desk to shake her hand. "My name is Nora Lassiter."

She took my hand hesitantly. "Related to the Lassiters in town?"

"Ida, Hannah, Agnes, Ellie, JT. Well, I could go on."

"No need. They're a wonderful family. One of their ancestors founded this town." She flashed a smile as big as Alabama. "But I suppose you know that. My name is Margaret. Happy to have you as a new library member."

There was a possibility that one of the people Ida overheard that day had returned a book. Not likely that they stopped to take one out, of course, but that could be checked, too. I wondered if the sheriff had looked into that.

For now, I filled out the application, turned it in and got a number.

"Each time you check out a book," she explained, "I'll stamp a date on the card and you'll write your number on the card and in the book."

Very high tech, I almost said, wondering where they kept the files that matched up the names with numbers. I asked about it and she indicated a drawer beneath the desk. "We keep all our lists on file here. When a book is overdue, we call the person. If that doesn't succeed, we mail out a card."

I thought about that, then asked, "Margaret, if a person returns a book, do you keep a record of the date it was returned?"

She nodded. "Naturally. But only for a week or less. No need to collect unnecessary paperwork. That's what garbage cans are for. Efficiency is my watchword. Every Monday, the previous week's returns' list is tossed. Anything still owed is noted."

Since today was Tuesday, last week's returns were already in the garbage. I was a little disappointed.

Could you have heard the librarian? Ida had been asked.

Oh, no. This woman had a harsh voice. Not soft like Margaret's.

Margaret, sweet though she appeared, and soft-spoken as she was, could not be eliminated as the woman Ida overheard. Almost any woman could make her voice harsh, I figured, if she were angry enough.

"Was there something else you wanted?"

"No. No, thank you." How foolish to be wandering off mentally. Margaret looked like a good and decent woman. What was I thinking!

I poked around for a while, checked out the Ken Follet

section where Ida had been, sat on the foot stool she had probably sat on, and decided she was right about the guy being tall. At least six feet, maybe more, I'd guess, if his voice came through that Follet shelf. I tried to think of all the men around here who were six feet or over. Uncle JT, Percy, Al Collins, Nick. Too many to mean anything.

There wasn't much to do here, so I picked up a Ken Follett book and brought it to the checkout desk. I tried to think of what else to ask the librarian.

"I know Ida Lassiter overhead people talking in here about a week ago. Do you know—"

"Deputy Trimble was here with your aunt," she interrupted, as she stamped my card with a thump. "I answered all his questions. I saw nothing."

She picked up some books, put them on a cart and headed away. I had been dismissed. Interesting. I thought she liked Lassiters.

I arrived back at Ida's to absolute chaos. The family had gathered in the kitchen. Everyone seemed to be talking at once. "What happened?" I asked. "This about Collins?"

"Worse," Hannah said with a heavy sigh.

"What could be worse? Collins was murdered."

"JT is missing," Ida said. "He never came home last night. Sheriff Nick was just up to the house looking to question him and Ellie, but Ellie hasn't seen him since yesterday noon."

Ellie, wearing a silver-gray warm-up suit, sat dabbing her eyes, sniffling, taking in great gulps of air.

"Nick called about twenty minutes ago asking again to speak to JT and I had to tell him the truth," she said between gasps.

The truth? I looked at everyone here—Hannah, Agnes, Ida, Hannah's son and daughter-in-law. Just to be clear, I asked, "Do you think he—" I stopped short, backtracked. "What truth? That he's missing?"

Everyone ignored the three children, ranging in age from four, or so, to about ten, as they raced through the kitchen, dragging what sounded like a load of tin cans.

Ellie sobbed into her tissue. "He'd been acting strange lately. Nervous. Drinking more. Something's going on, that's for damn sure. He wouldn't tell me what. We've been fighting for the past few months. More than usual, and that's saying something. That's why he left."

Her angry words the night of the party came back to me. *You ass. Better watch your step. I have a key to that rifle cabinet.*

"You can't think he murdered Collins." I said.

Ellie grabbed another tissue to sop up a new flood of tears. "I don't know."

That set me on my heels.

Aunt Agnes passed Ellie a handkerchief. "Use this. Much better than a tissue. I wouldn't give you two cents for those tissues. They fall apart."

"I agree. We should all go back to handkerchiefs," Hannah said.

"Here, here," put in Ida.

"Oh, but they get so dirty. Better to throw them away," Hannah's daughter-in-law chimed in.

"They're wasteful," Agnes said. "'Course, nobody cares about being wasteful any more. Throw this out. Throw that out. They don't care."

Handkerchiefs? Tissues? My uncle was missing. A man had been murdered on his property, or maybe my property, and they were talking about the best way to blow your nose.

Something crashed in a back room. Nobody even flinched. I felt a headache coming on.

"Does the sheriff think he killed Collins?" I asked Ellie, determined not to be sidetracked by the tissue debate, or distracted by the children who were now—judging from the noise—wrecking one of the back rooms.

No one answered. Ida finally nodded, and said softly, "He's a suspect."

ELEVEN

I called Howie and told him everything. The business about Mom and the sexual harassment at her job just about shocked him out of his shorts. Like me, he wondered why our parents never told us. He said he'd talk to Mom about it, in person, and let me know the results. I was glad about that. "Better you than me."

He laughed when I told him about the buried box.

"A buried treasure, Nora." He laughed some more, then said, "And you have to hunt in the woods for this?"

I smirked. "I'm glad you're enjoying this, Howie. This is exactly why I called, you know. To add a bit of amusement to your otherwise dull life."

Then I told him about JT.

"Oh, God. Taking off right after the murder? The guilty have a tendency to run, Nora. The law will be hot on that trail."

At two in the morning, my eyes popped open. Instantly awake, my thoughts flew to the library's returns' list, and I wondered where the library garbage went. Was there a dump around here somewhere? The more I thought about it, the more important the list seemed. The killer might be on the list. Any six-footer on the list should be checked out. How many men went to the library around here? Tall men. Without wasting another second, I grabbed my cell phone and hit Nick's private number, which I'd programmed in after all.

The rough sound of his voice told me he had been sleeping.

"I think the returns' list at the library is important. I can feel it in my bones," I said without bothering with niceties like "Sorry I woke you," or "This is Nora."

"Damnit, Nora. It's two in the morning. I didn't get to bed until after midnight and I have to be up by five."

I noticed he never asked who it was. Either he recognized my voice or looked at the caller ID.

"Sorry," I said to appease him. "Did you ever check that list?"

"No. It had already been tossed."

"Where does the library garbage go?"

I heard a groan. "What the hell're you talking about?"

I could tell he was having trouble focusing. Some folks, like me, wake and hit the ground running, others are sluggish, grumpy even. Plain to see which category Nick fell into.

"The library garbage?" I repeated. "Where does it go?"

"You're conducting an environmental survey? That's why you called at his hour?"

"Where?" I persisted, ignoring the escalating annoyance in his voice.

"I already thought about that angle and dismissed it. What would the list prove? Besides, you probably couldn't read it after it's been slopped over with garbage."

"Where?" I said again.

He made an odd sound, a cross between a groan and a roar, then used a few expletives that I didn't think were very nice at all. Finally, he said, "The garbage from the Main Street businesses and from the library go into the Dumpster behind the Country Store. They'll be picked up this morning, near five A.M."

"It's still there. Great. Don't you think we should go look for that list? It might be helpful."

"We? No. Not you, not me. Once and for all, no. No one should look. And in case you need to be reminded, again, you are not part of this investigation."

I held the phone away from my ear. Did the man think I was hard of hearing? He hung up without even saying goodbye.

Silver light from a fat moon lit up the far wall of my bedroom.

The rosebuds on the wallpaper seemed to shift back and forth as I stared at them. I should get up and close the shade.

Back and forth. Back and forth. Dancing rosebuds. I was being hypnotized.

Of course, that wasn't why I couldn't get back to sleep. My head was filled with thoughts of Uncle JT and Ellie, Collins and Percy. Mary Fran, too. And cranky Nick who had a sexy phone voice when he was half asleep.

I'm no expert, but it seemed to me that this whole murder business could be solved more easily if Nick had the library list. We needed it. The more I thought about it, the more convinced I became. If Ida's two plotters met in a library, they had to have a reason to choose that location. Otherwise, why not a store, or a side road, or a gas station? Millions of choices existed, so why the library? The answer? Obvious. It would appear natural for them to be there. They had been there before, both of them. At least one of them was a reader, or had a family member who was a reader. It annoyed me that Nick couldn't see this. He'd regret it in the morning when his mind was firing on all cylinders. Too bad the garbage would be gone by then.

I watched the rosebuds some more.

I had just found my family after years of separation. I liked them, all of them. If JT were arrested for this murder, I believed it would wound them as much as my father's leaving had wounded them and me. I had to help Nick find out who had murdered Collins. Had to help him prove it wasn't JT. No big deal time-wise since I had to hang around until I got those pictures for Mary Fran.

Suddenly, unable to remain passive another second, I hopped out of bed, rummaged through the closet and dug out some clothes of questionable origin, jeans that were way too big and a sweatshirt with paint stains. I found old clodhopper shoes. It was dark. Who would see me? While I laced up the shoes, I hummed a song I used to sing as a kid when I wore my Wonder Woman outfit. *Won-der Wom-an. Ta-da, Ta-da!* I finished tying the shoes and stood up. With a flick of my shoulders, I resettled my imaginary cape. Ta-da, Ta-da! I was ready to go.

Shortly after three in the morning, I drove into the lot behind the Country Store and pulled next to the Dumpster. The damn thing had to be about seven or eight feet high and maybe ten feet long, a behemoth. Who ever heard of such a big Dumpster! I stood on the bottom lip and grabbed hold of the rim. I could barely touch the plastic top that covered this section, so I hopped down. I beamed my flashlight around and found a pile of wooden crates. I was in luck.

This was going well.

I piled the crates up, climbed on top with great care, and lifted a section of the plastic top. "Oof!" The odor almost knocked me over. I should have brought a scarf for my nose. I wondered if there were rats or mice or worse inside.

I passed the light around the garbage. Over to one side I saw a bunch of papers. Could it be this easy? I moved the crates and aimed the flashlight at the papers. If I hadn't been gagging on the smell, I would have hooted when I saw the words Silver Stream Library on one large envelope.

Piece of cake! Oh, this was going so well.

To make matters easier, I spotted several wooden crates at the far end that I could use to get out. Perfect. I had all bases covered, all facets of the mission lined up. What surprised me was that the Dumpster wasn't totally full on pick-up day. What a waste of space.

I stepped down, flipped my imaginary cape and began to hum as I added another crate to my pile to make entry easier. Once up, I stood on tiptoes, swung my right leg over like I was mounting a horse, and rolled in, quite smoothly, I thought. The landing wasn't as smooth. I fell forward into what might have been rotten egg salad. I gagged, got up, and assured myself all was still going well. I groped around for my flashlight. I'd wash when I got home. Scrub myself. Throw these clothes out.

I fought my way to the library papers. They were soggy. With what, I didn't want to know. I picked up a pile, discarded the lettuce leaves and skimmed through the papers, the flashlight braced between my neck and shoulder. A few minutes later, gagging, close to puking, I found the returns' list. Hallelujah! The takeout list was here, too. A bonus. I could compare the two. The bad guys may have returned books that day, without taking anything out. Too busy plotting a murder.

I headed for the boxes in the corner, more than ready to leave, and grabbed the nearest box.

Not wood. Cardboard.

Omigod.

I grabbed the others. All cardboard. Someone had painted wood-like stripes on them. Who? What demented person painted wooden slats on a cardboard box? I flashed my light around, inspecting the rest of this section. I stared at what was probably scenery discards from a school play or something. Lots of painted stuff.

Frantic, I beamed the flashlight over every foul-smelling inch, looking for something solid to stand on. Two little beady eyes glowed back. I whimpered.

Determined to find a way out, I set my flashlight down and angled it so I could see what I was doing. Then I began to pile garbage next to the wall—cardboard boxes, milk cartons, potato peels, pizza crusts. I skipped the dirty diapers. Why hadn't I thought to wear gloves? When the heap was knee-high I picked up my flashlight and papers, and climbed on the pile.

I sank.

Knee deep in garbage, but refusing to admit defeat, I folded the paper, stuffed it in my pocket, then stepped out of the pile. I needed more solid garbage. I added more stuff, period. Then I climbed up, slid down, fell, gagged. Tried again.

Finally, I slogged to the opposite side and took a running leap, hands extended for a grab at the lip.

Shh-woosh.

I slid down the greasy wall and landed on my rear end in the dirty diaper section. Oh, shit. I even dropped my flashlight. I stood quickly and snatched up the flashlight. Breathing hard, thinking about how to get out, wondering where the beady eyes were, knowing they were monitoring my every move, made me feel like crying. I bit my bottom lip instead.

It was hard to tell how long I'd been at this, but I needed to stop before I contracted the E-bola virus, or was attacked by that rat and his relatives. I did the one thing I'd been resisting. I yanked out my cell phone. Hit a number.

"I'm stuck in the Dumpster behind the Country Store. I've tried, but I can't get out."

"Damnit all, Nora. I should leave you in there," Nick yelled from the bed of his pickup truck. "Where's your head? Didn't it occur to you that you'd want to get out at some point?"

"I found the papers," I announced as he lowered a ladder. I was too tired to argue with him, and besides, I was really glad to see him. Maybe I'd give him a kiss. And a hug. I smiled in the dark Dumpster as I kicked aside some garbage so I could settle the ladder firmly.

"This Dumpster stinks more than usual," he said. "You've stirred it up."

"Some of that smell is me."

"There are probably rats in there. Did you ever think of that?"

I peered up at him as I climbed the ladder slowly, my legs wobbly from all the jumping. I hadn't jumped in years. I was never good at jumping or hopping, especially hopping. In kindergarten pre-screening, I failed left-foot hopping. My mother used to tell everyone that. I never thought it meant much, but here I was stuck in a Dumpster, a hopping failure. A better hopper might have made it out. I should have taken remedial hopping. Maybe it wasn't too late. I could get one of those mini trampolines and practice.

"I saw rat eyes," I told him as I stepped on the top rung. "I was scared. I don't care much for certain animals. Mind you, I have nothing against them and I would never harm one, but I'm not a big animal person. Mainly, because of my allergies."

"Psheeew!"

Although it was dark, I could see him shake his head in disgust.

"Move it," he said. "I want to get out of here before someone comes along."

Minutes later, I was standing in his truck bed. Thank God. It felt wonderful. Sometimes happiness is as simple as a garbage-free spot to stand on.

"My hero," I said quietly, meaning it so much I decided not to hug him.

He ignored the praise, at least outwardly.

"I'll get you a blanket. If you sit on my seat, I'll never get the stench out." He jumped down. "That may happen anyway. God, you smell awful."

He passed me a small plastic bag with damp paper towels in it.

He'd thought to bring me something to clean myself with? He had dampened his paper towels for me.

Mute, I wiped my hands and face.

Clean again, the pleasure was intense. He opened the tailgate and tossed me a blanket. "Wrap up. I'll drive you to my place so you can shower before you go home. No need to let Ida in on your possible insanity. I have old sweats you can use. There's no way you can put those rags back on."

He paused, hands on hips. "You know what surprises me?"

I shook my head.

"That this doesn't surprise me. I've known you less than a week and I'm not surprised that you pulled this stunt. Not at all. I should have known. Really should have known. I'm slipping up."

Shaking his head, he walked to the driver's door. "Let's go, Sherlock. Move it. Dawn waits for no one."

I didn't say a word. I figured he was entitled to blow off a little steam. I hopped down and wrapped the blanket around me. Even though he was annoyed, I sensed the concern in him. He had gone out of his way, done more than just rescue me. Nick Renzo was a thoughtful man. Kindness is a rare thing in my life so when it happens I have the strangest reaction. I become a big baby. My eyes fill with tears and my throat closes. For the first time tonight, I felt both those things happening. I turned my head to keep him from seeing too much.

Being stuck in a Dumpster hadn't made me cry, neither had falling into the dirty diaper section, or spying a rat's eyes, or feeling desperate and desolate. In most ways I'm a strong woman. I can handle adversity. But kindness. . . .

As I sat in the front seat, I used the last of his damp paper towels to wipe away my tears. I was glad it was dark.

"Are you crying?"

"No."

"Good. I don't want to make you cry," he said softly.

Turning toward the window, I sniffled as quietly as I could. If he heard, he refrained from mentioning it.

TWELVE

Heaven is a warm shower when what you need most is a warm shower. I lathered up and rinsed, lathered up and rinsed again. The nicest part was the water stayed hot, unlike Ida's shower. Face to the spray, I let the water cascade over me, rinsing away every trace of garbage, wishing I could rinse away every trace of sadness as easily. Ever since my life in New York had fallen apart, first with the loss of my job, then the loss of my fiancé, the sadness lingered deep inside regardless of what I did to uproot it. I concentrated on positive thoughts, like what I'd accomplished tonight.

Nick had left a huge towel, a thick fluffy one that felt wonderful when I wrapped it around my clean body.

His house was different than I expected. Polished hardwood floors, taupe walls, white crown molding, a central kitchen open to the living room, dark shiny granite countertops. I pictured him eating soup there. Why soup, I have no idea, but soup popped into my head. Chicken noodle. That's the only kind of soup I like.

I toweled dry. I was in the guest bathroom that opened into a sparsely furnished, good-sized bedroom. I wondered who stayed here. Parents? Relatives? Other women? No, the women would stay in his room. Why that should bother me, I have no idea.

Naked, I went into the bedroom and slipped into the clean sweats he had tossed on the bed. The paper bag he had given me for my smelly clothes was gone. I couldn't help wondering whether he'd peeked in the bathroom when he was here. Probably not. I have a feeling he's very honorable. How rare.

The sweats were enormous on my five-foot, six-inch frame. I

tied the waist, rolled up the legs and sleeves, pulled on a pair of white socks, and headed to the kitchen. I passed a small laundry room and heard the washing machine cranking away. He was washing clothes?

I'm sure he had a dark side, like Whatshisname, and it would show at the worst possible moment. But for now, Nick Renzo was a good guy.

The moment I entered, his head shot up. I don't think he actually heard me, not with the washing machine running, not with me in these silent socks. I think he sensed my presence.

The intensity of his gaze shook me. Long seconds passed and neither of us spoke. This was one sexy man. He had changed clothes. He was dressed in his khaki uniform. I was aware that I had no underwear on. Of course, I had to think of that right now. My delicate petal pink bikinis, which were in a bag somewhere, had been a Victoria Secret special last month. How can you pass up those specials? Not possible. And the matching lace demi bra? Also on special. They made a great combo.

"Doing laundry?" I asked.

"Threw your clothes in."

He was doing *my* laundry? Geez. I thought guys like him were only part of female fantasies.

My underwear should be on the delicate cycle. Would a man consider a thing like that? I think not. I had to retrieve them before they were ruined. How to mention my unmentionables?

Nick glanced at the clock. "It's after five. Another hour or so and it'll be light, so we best head out now. You can get your clothes later today or tomorrow. Or whenever."

He grabbed a brown lightweight sheriff's jacket from the closet. He'd had little sleep last night because of me, but he didn't look tired.

I walked over to him. "I want to thank you for everything—rescuing me, letting me shower here, washing my clothes." I bit my bottom lip. "I'm sorry I got you up twice tonight."

He held my gaze. "If you ever wake me again in the wee hours of the morning it better be for something better than a trip to the Dumpster." He lifted my chin with his index finger. "Deal?"

He was standing so close I could smell his soap, his aftershave. He must have showered when I did. "Deal," I agreed, wondering whether I was agreeing to what I thought I was agreeing to and hoping I was. I wanted him to kiss me. So bad. I thought he was going to, but he let his finger trace down the side of my jaw. I wanted to do an awful thing. I wanted to bite his finger. Suck on it. The finger in question fell to the rim of my sweatshirt, then dropped to his side. I had missed my chance. I could feel my heart thrumming double-time. I wanted to grab him and kiss him senseless. Reserved, unaggressive, sweet little me. I stepped back and shelved my salacious thoughts.

In the quiet between us I heard the washing machine again. "Did you put those clothes on the delicate cycle?"

"I only use one cycle. I doubt there's anything delicate about it."

I hurried to the laundry room, fished around for my petal pinks, rinsed them by hand and hung them in the guest bathroom. In a discreet spot.

When I returned, he was buckling on his gun belt. He nodded toward the returns' list. "That library was a popular place last week. JT, Collins, Percy—all there. Along with a few dozen other people I'll check out. I hate to admit it, but it's good to have the list. I should have done it."

I was amazed he admitted this so freely. Most men weren't big on admitting mistakes.

"Great. I'm glad I could help," I said, feeling redeemed as we glanced over the list together. I recognized Vivian's name. She was the Pomeranian Lady. The only other person I recognized on the list was my Aunt Ellie. Ellen Lassiter.

I have a key to that rifle cabinet.

I deep-sixed the thought. Couldn't be. Just couldn't.

"Who's A.M. Yanetti?"

"A-M-Y. Amy, the waitress at the Country Store."

Nick glanced over my shoulder and said, "I considered Percy Kendall and JT suspects even before I saw this. Your uncle JT's repair shop works on the vehicles Percy sells. Collins often brought cars over there, and picked them up."

"Percy and Al came to talk to JT when I was getting my car fixed on Saturday. They all seemed angry."

Nick nodded. "Something's going on. But I don't want to talk about the investigation. Sheriff's business."

I studied him a moment, but he was too busy gathering his gear to look at me, probably on purpose. "Do you have other evidence linking JT with the murder?"

As he slipped a small mag light into his belt, he said simply, "Yes."

Oh, God.

"What? Tell me," I demanded.

"No."

"Why?"

"You know why," he said.

"But I'm the retriever of the library returns' list. And let's not forget the library takeout list. After all the time, energy and talent I expended to secure these vital papers, you should assuage my curiosity—"

"I'm not into assuaging. Besides, you have to watch your curiosity. It could have gotten you killed tonight. Do you realize that if you'd fallen on your head and passed out, no one would have known where you were. And—"

Hands up, palms out, I cut him off. "Okay, okay. You're right, Nick. But JT's in the family. Is telling me against some oath you took?"

He picked up his car keys. "No oath, just common sense."

"I have plenty of common sense. Tons of it, in fact."

He rolled his eyes, switched off a few lights and headed for the door. "Come on. I'll drive you to your car."

Exasperated, yet incapable of getting annoyed because I was too tired, not to mention super-grateful that he had come for me, I looked around for something to put on my feet. My shoes were garbage. I'd put them in the paper bag with my clothes. He probably threw them out. Nick nodded in the direction of his orange Day-Glo slippers, which sat side by side at the front door like two flattened road cones.

"You're kidding?" I said.

He shrugged. "Your choice."

"Are these battery operated?"

He smiled, but said nothing.

I had no choice. It was chilly and damp out. I slipped into the horrendous slippers. Come to Maine and look what happens. How low I had fallen.

As I was getting out of his truck in back of the Country Store, he said, "The patch from JT's work jacket, *JT Auto Repair*, was found not far from the body, caught on a tree branch. Threads still on it. Like he was running away and it snagged."

Before I could question him about it, he took off.

The sun was high in the September sky when I finally dragged myself out of bed, dumpster flashbacks racing through my head so vividly that I headed for the shower. The lukewarm shower. Before I could rinse the shampoo from my hair, the water turned icy cold. Damn, no-good water heater.

I was toweling dry, grumbling up a storm, when it occurred to me that someone should check Kendall's Auto Mart, see what wily Percy was up to, see if he'd heard from JT, or from Marla. Who could do that? I wasn't going to call Nick again with my suggestions. Although he'd said he wished I were a real hotshot detective and could help with the case, he'd made it super clear that he didn't want my amateur interference. Well, amateur me had helped professional him last night. True, there had been a snag or two, but still.

I was stepping into my lavender bikinis when I remembered the purple PT Cruiser was due back today. I could turn it in up here. I considered renewing my rental agreement versus blowing my rainy day money on a used car. What would I do with a used car when I left Maine? I wouldn't need a car in the city. On one hand, renting was expensive. Might as well open the window and tip your wallet into a high wind. On the other hand, buying was an investment.

I hooked the lavender lace bra. I'd buy a used car, sell it when I got back home, and make a few bucks. That was the act of a thrifty woman.

I yanked up my gray wool slacks as I mentally ticked off the other things I had to handle. There was the little matter of the land that Howie and I had inherited. I had to meet with the family soon about it. See if anybody wanted it. And the buried box. I'd do that today. By the end of the week I'd be on my way back home. I pulled the soft periwinkle sweater over my head. I'd picked it up at a Saks' sale for seventy-five percent off.

Downstairs, I found a note from Aunt Ida taped to the refrigerator. She'd gone to a senior citizens' meeting at the church with Hannah and Agnes to help plan Silver Stream Days, a celebration I had a vague childhood memory of. It was a good memory. A wicked good memory, as Mainers would say. Good food, music, games.

Besides the car situation, I had to go to my former house today and visit Aunt Ellie. I also had to check out Percy's computer and pick up batteries for my camera's flash attachment. Might need those for the coming photo shoot with Percy and his 'ho friend.

I had so much to do. Too much. I'd never get to everything. First things first. I called Hot Heads Heaven and Mary Fran answered.

"Can I get into the house today to check the computer again?" was all I said.

"Nora. Yes. He won't be home until four, the earliest."

I decided not to point out that she had told me once before that he wouldn't be home. "I'll see you shortly for the key."

Collins' wake and funeral would keep Percy and Marla from

meeting for the next few days, I figured, but they still might make future plans. I wanted to check out Percy's bookkeeping software, too. He did business with Uncle JT. I couldn't get JT out of my head. I hoped he hadn't killed Collins. I felt a shiver race up my spine. Aunt Ellie must be devastated by all this. I wondered if JT could be dead, too? Murdered like Collins? No one mentioned that. They must have considered it.

When I entered Mary Fran's house, I wasted no time. In a flash I was at the computer opening Quicken. I scanned the records, looking for . . . what, I didn't know. I found that Percy made more than a decent living selling cars, both new and used. So Mary Fran's eighty percent would be considerable. No wonder she wanted to hire a detective. According to these records Al Collins took home less than Percy. Unequal partners. I wondered why.

I checked out the records that involved JT and found nothing unusual. He made decent money, but it didn't seem to me that it was enough to buy all the land he had bought unless he had a lot of other business. A possibility. Maybe he and Ellie saved a lot. I wondered what his property was worth.

I finally checked Percy's email and found a small surprise.

THIRTEEN

By the time I got to Hot Heads Heaven to drop off Mary Fran's key, it was lunchtime.

"So what did you find out?" Mary Fran whispered, leaving a woman with a section of hair unbleached. She clasped my hand and dragged me back by the coffee pot. "Have they set another date?"

I yanked my hand back. "Yes. And I'll be nearby snapping pictures. Not to worry." I couldn't bring myself to tell her more. I hoped she wouldn't ask.

"The skunk. How could he? His partner's not even in the ground and already he's planning a romp in the hay. What makes her so special anyway? Is it lined with gold or something?"

I had no answer for that, so I bit my bottom lip and waited a full minute. "Is the Auto Mart open today?"

"Uh-huh. At noon. Two part-timers are working. Percy thought it wouldn't look right if he was there. 'Course he has to go to the sheriff's office, then over to the Collins' place to visit the widow again. What a wreck that poor woman is. We were over there last night. Percy's taking care of the funeral details for her." She paused. "Nora, when's he meeting the slut? You didn't say."

"Don't ask. Please. It's better if you don't think about it."

She grabbed my arm. "I want to know."

What the heck. "They plan to meet the day of the funeral. Friday."

"What!" She stared at me. "My God. The man has no sense of propriety. He can't even mourn his partner." She paused, then whispered, "He couldn't have killed him. Could he?"

I had no answer, just suspicion.

As I left Hot Heads Heaven, I saw Percy leaving the sheriff's office down the street. Instead of taking off, I sat in my car and watched him cross to the Country Store. Mary Fran stood at her window and gave me a what's-going-on shrug. I smiled, waved and took off, but only far enough to get out of her line of vision.

Percy came out minutes later with a newspaper tucked under his arm and got into a new-ish looking Toyota pickup. Did everyone drive pickups or SUVs around here? I followed at a discreet distance. It was a strange feeling, tailing someone. I'd never done it before.

I had the feeling I had missed something. Something I should zero in on. The more I thought about it, the more illusive it became.

Percy passed his Auto Mart, slowed, but didn't stop. Several miles farther along, he pulled into a driveway. I slowed, then cruised by. The Collins name was on the mailbox.

This was a waste of time. What was I doing? I was no detective. I probably couldn't find a murderer if he was right under my nose. I went a little farther, turned and drove back to the Auto Mart. I wanted Percy to be the murderer. That was my problem. He was such an underhanded cheater of a guy, just like Whatshisname had been. No sense of loyalty, a trait that may well have carried over to his regard for his partner.

Had Collins somehow gotten in Percy's way? Been such a threat that Percy had to kill him? Was something underhanded going on at the Auto Mart? Or had Collins simply demanded a bigger cut? Money was a powerful motivator.

A woman was involved. Ida had overheard a woman in the library. Marla? Was she behind this? Maybe Percy was doing something to please her.

On the way back, I pulled into the Auto Mart and got out of the car. A young guy with navy slacks and a burgundy sweater came out to help me.

"Looking for something new to drive?" he asked.

As I stood staring at rows and rows of autos, I was tempted to tell him, "No, I was looking for the Goodyear blimp and thought it might be parked here." But self-control prevailed and I said, "Yes. A car or maybe a truck."

"Nothing special in mind then."

"Something not too expensive. Something that runs."

We both smiled at that. It occurred to me that I should have a car-knowledgeable person with me. I understood a thing or two about interiors, like leather seats and eight-speaker Bose stereos, but what was under the hood was pure mystery. I know this tiger shark intended to take advantage of my lack of expertise, but I was sure I could handle it. I was a black belt shopper, after all.

He stuck out his hand. "Name's Pete."

"Nora."

"Well, Nora, let's find something you'd like. Maybe a pickup?"

"Okay. I think."

I told him how much I had to spend, thinking there goes the nest egg. Pete looked disappointed. I followed him down a row of neat pickups to the section where the less neat were kept.

I wondered whether Percy would stop here on his way back. I had no idea of what I'd say to him.

"I was surprised to see you open today, Pete. I hear one of the owners was killed a day or so ago."

Pete's grin dipped a few watts. "Yes. We're closing for his funeral."

How considerate. "You know him long?"

"Since I started here about a year and a half ago."

Pete stopped near a shiny, but very old-looking Dodge Ram with lots of chrome, and placed his hand on the fender. "You might like this baby. Plenty of power under the hood."

"Must be sad for you," I persisted.

He didn't speak right away, just stared off into the distance. I tried to read him, but wasn't getting anything. Stoic people, these Mainers. I was about to apologize for being so insensitive when he said, "We weren't close."

"Didn't get along, huh?"

"You a cop?"

I laughed. Did I look like a cop?

"Me? Absolutely not. I'm just visiting relatives around here. Naturally I'm curious."

Pete said nothing.

If I was going to learn anything I realized I had to take a chance, so I said, "I didn't particularly care for him. Met him a few days ago," I lied. "He seemed . . . pushy." Quickly, I backpedaled. "I shouldn't speak ill of the dead. I suppose it was just his way. He was a businessman who had a product to sell."

Pete gave a snort that bordered on a laugh. "Yep. Sure did."

"What do you mean?" I asked.

"Oh, nothing," he said in a way guaranteed to made me think there was something. I wondered what this guy had told the sheriff.

He launched into a sale's pitch about the Dodge, explaining all sorts of things I didn't understand. I tuned him out and let him practice his spiel.

Minutes later, Percy drove in. I watched him go inside, a newspaper tucked under his arm. Something about the paper niggled. Then it hit me. He had the paper home-delivered and he'd bought one at the Country Store? The only reason I knew this was that I'd almost smashed into the newspaper delivery truck when I blasted out of his driveway on Monday. It probably meant nothing. But I did pat myself on the back for noticing.

"I need a drink of water," I told Pete, holding my throat, going for a parched look. "I'll be right back."

Pete followed. I turned and suggested, "Find me something smaller. This Ram is way too big. You saw me drive up in a PT Cruiser. Diminutive, Pete, that's what I want. Skip the heavyweights and proceed to bantam."

When I reached the offices inside, I stuck my head in the one marked Percy Kendall. "Hello, Percy. You might not remember me. I met you at Hannah Lassiter's on Saturday night?"

He nodded in recognition. "Yes. Hannah's niece. You in the market for a vehicle?"

The newspaper was open in front of him on his desk.

"I'm sorry about your partner. Terrible thing, his murder."

Without being invited, I stepped inside, looked around. Nubby gray carpeting, scraped metal furniture, faded geraniums that screamed plastic. Awful room. They should hang the decorator.

I glanced down at his newspaper, then back at him quickly. A small square of paper had been attached to the top of one page. Even though I'm new to this detective business, it didn't take a bona fide Sherlock to know that was odd. Without missing a beat, he removed the square of paper and slipped it into his middle drawer.

I found myself staring at him, seeing him as the philanderer, hearing again the crack of the riding crop, the stomp of the boots, but most of all, wondering about the little piece of paper in his middle drawer. I sensed it was important and I wanted to see it.

"Yes, terrible. Thank you for the condolences. Now, can I help you?"

"I found the body."

"I heard. I'm sorry." No sorrow in his voice. No emotion. And I knew Percy was a man who could muster a lot of emotion.

Pete poked his head in the door. "I was showing Nora some pickups. I think I found one she'll really like."

Looking relieved, Percy came from behind the desk. "Take good care of Ms. Lassiter. I know her family."

"A nice Ford pickup, Nora."

"Yeah, sure," I said.

I had to back up and step outside the door to make room for Percy to pass. Neat maneuver on his part. Get the nosy lady out of his office.

"If you'll excuse me, I have a few things to take care of," he said.

I watched him head upstairs, probably to some other office, maybe just to the men's room. That paper was so close, just a few steps away. It could be from the woman he spoke to in the library.

Maybe she congratulated him on a job well done? I stopped myself in mid-thought. I didn't know for a fact that he was the guy in the library. It was a guess. I was jumping ahead.

"The pickup?" Pete prompted, his professional smile locked in place as he gestured toward the lot.

"Find me something else," I said. "I don't want a Ford. It's personal. My ex had a Ford."

My ex didn't own a car, and if I stood in front of a dozen cars, I couldn't tell the difference without checking the names on them.

"Sh-ur. I understand. I have an ex, too."

"I didn't get my drink yet, and I have to use the ladies' room. Be out in a sec." My smile was bright, my heart pounding, palms sweating.

I went to the water cooler and filled a cup. I sipped slowly as I watched the eager beaver grab several keys and hurry outside again. My gaze shot to the stairs Percy had taken. I could only see one other person in the building, a chunky guy—a salesman?—sitting by the side door reading a Batman comic and eating a Twinkie.

Knees knocking, I edged into Percy's office, set my water down and yanked open the drawer. I grabbed the paper he'd hidden from me. It was a list of names with a series of numbers next to them. I had no idea what it meant, but I knew, really knew, it was critical.

I wanted to stuff the paper in my purse. Study it later. In lieu of that stupidity, I glanced at the first name and number. I grabbed a pen from the desk and a piece of paper that said From the Desk of Percy Kendall, and began to copy the first name and the numbers that followed.

I heard footsteps. My heartbeat rocketed. Off the charts, thumping, thumping, so intense I thought my chest would burst. He couldn't be back this soon. My hand flew as I copied a second name and the set of numbers that followed it.

Percy's different from most folks around here. He's . . . tougher. Can be ruthless.

Panting with fear, I shoved the original paper back in the

drawer. Grabbed my cup, knocked it over. Water splashed on the desk, drenching the newspaper.

Gestapo bootsteps came closer. He was going to find me in his office at his wet desk. What could I say? Or do?

Think. Think.

I seemed to have shut down mentally. Brain freeze. I heard him pause outside the door and speak to the comic book kid, something about cleaning the cars.

Think. A plan. A plan.

FOURTEEN

Shaking, as I listened to Percy chat outside the door, I snatched up his phone and punched in my home number in New York.

"Well, I'm going to use the money whether you think it's a good deal or not." I shouted over the ringing at the other end of the line. "I need a truck. Something substantial. Winter's coming. You think I can manage up here without a truck?"

Percy stepped through the door, his eyes hard, assessing. I paused, held up my hand, giving him the universal wait-a-minute sign.

I hoped he couldn't hear the ringing. To cover the sound, I waved his wet newspaper as if I were trying to dry it. When my answering machine kicked in, I talked louder to cover the generic man's voice. "We're not available right now," it informed me in a deep sonorous tone. "At the sound of the beep. . . ."

"I'll have someone else check out the truck before I buy, but I do intend to buy," I shouted. That said, I hung up with a dramatic flourish.

"Sorry to use your phone without asking. My cell phone is dead. I forgot to charge it, and I just had to make a call. Right away. I'll pay you the charges." Opening my purse, I reached for my wallet.

I could see his suspicions ebb, not entirely, but enough. "You needn't bother," he assured me in a cool voice, eyeing his newspaper.

"I knocked my water over." I did a meek Marla impersonation. "I'm so clumsy sometimes. I'll get a paper towel and clean it up."

"Never mind."

Smiling Pete returned. "I think I found one with your name on it. Like to take her for a test drive? I have the key." He held it up in case I needed proof. "Just let me put these others back."

Her? Take *her* for a test drive? If I wasn't so glad to see him, I'd call him on that *her* business.

Relieved that I'd managed to escape detection—I thought it went well, considering—I followed Pete, happy to put distance between myself and Gestapo man, who stood by his door like a sentinel, arms folded, watching our exit. I'd bet a winning lottery ticket that once we were outside, he'd check to see what number I'd called.

Pete and I were close to the exit when the *Toreador March* blasted from my purse. Omigod. No and no. What timing. I didn't look directly at Percy. Didn't need to. My peripheral vision picked up his form. I saw his arms drop to his sides. Saw him take a step toward us. Then stop.

To answer the phone, or not to answer? That was the question. Decisions, decisions.

"Imagine that. It *is* charged," I said as I grabbed the phone, turned to Percy with a helpless Who knew? kind of look, accompanied by appropriate gestures like shrugging and such. I was in a high school play once and my friends told me I should be an actress.

I quickly answered, "Hello, Lori."

She started to discuss my résumé. I cut her off. "Can't talk now. My phone is almost dead. I'll call you back later."

I'm not sure Percy bought it. I wouldn't have. With a sinking feeling, I made a quick exit.

I drove a Chevy S-10 around and liked it. It was small and had a nice stereo with a CD player. Of course, the engine could be ready to drop and I wouldn't know it, but Pete looked trustworthy.

Had I once thought that about Whatshisname? I gave a mental shake and tossed my ex from my thoughts. The bottom line was that I needed something to drive. Should I bother to have anyone check it out, like I said on the phone? I didn't want to bother. I'd tell Percy that JT would check it over and charge him if anything needed fixing. I hoped he didn't know that JT was missing. "Petey, let's talk money. What are you asking?" I added quickly, "And don't quote me that ridiculous price on the windshield. I'm from New York."

Percy would be less suspicious when I bought a truck from him. I was almost sure of it. Almost. Worrying about my phone ringing was getting me no place. I decided since I could do nothing to change the situation, I wouldn't waste my time thinking about it.

By late afternoon I had turned in the rented PT Cruiser, and was driving the neat silver Chevy S-10 pickup with only a few dings and dents. The purchase had sent my bank account into double digit country.

I needed a real job. Pronto.

I had a feeling of accomplishment as I tooled along in my very own truck. I felt Maine-ish, too. I tooted and waved as I passed another truck, just for the heck of it. I decided to name this truck. Let's see. Chevy Charles? No. Chevy Bevy? Dumb. Chevy Charlene? That had a nice ring to it.

"I christen thee Chevy Charlene," I declared loudly. To make it official, I banged on the dashboard. The glove compartment popped open and the door fell on the floor.

It was late afternoon, but I figured I had time to go to Aunt Ellie's. See the house. Talk about Dad's missing brother. Maybe there'd be some news about JT.

When I pulled up to the front door, I sat for a moment, my thoughts heavy with memory. The house had changed, had been bricked and sided, an extension added. It looked good. Not just good. Spectacular. Maybe they'd won the lottery and no one had mentioned it to me.

I got out and stood on the bottom step. The last time my feet rested here they were pointed in the other direction. I had been leaving Maine. I remembered thinking, with the optimism of childhood, that I'd be back soon. Good thing I didn't know then that it would be twenty years before I returned.

The southwest sky, awash in shades of purple, pink and indigo, was dotted with those puffy backlit clouds edged in silver. Exquisite. I was a sky person. If I were a painter, most of my work would have sky. As an amateur photographer, I included it as often as I could. I picked up my camera and snapped a few pictures.

When I was a kid I used to stare at this same sky from my second-floor window. I looked up at my old room and saw white ruffled tie-backs and a shade pulled mid-way down. I wondered whose room it was now. And did she look out as I had? Strange, how this feeling of belonging and not belonging melded together.

I knocked.

Ellie answered the door. "Come in, come in, Nora."

She gave me a quick kiss on the cheek. Her eyes were red-rimmed. From crying or lack of sleep? Strain was evident. She wore a wrinkled blue warm-up suit and her makeup was spotty except for the blue eye shadow. Basically, she looked ten years older than she had Saturday night.

Standing in the foyer, we made small talk. I couldn't help noticing how different this house was from the other houses I'd visited up here. So different from the way it was when I was a child. Not Maine-like at all. More like designer showcase.

Ellie said, "I'm sure you'd love to see the house. Come on. Take the ten-cent tour."

I glanced around. If the outside looked spectacular, the inside dazzled by comparison. I considered myself a connoisseur of sorts when it came to designer clothes, but I also knew a thing or two about furnishings. Granted, not as much as about clothes, but still enough to recognize the hand of an interior designer when I saw it. Or was Aunt Ellie this good?

The living room's antique sofa, upholstered in white leather, anchored the space set off by a red Persian carpet. Solid oak flooring had replaced my mother's linoleum. Custom made cabinetry showcased what I thought might be a Dresden porcelain collection. I'd have to see it close up, of course, but my guess was Dresden. Expensive stuff.

Dragging my attention from the house, I said, "I wanted to see you, too. I'm so sorry about JT. I wish I could help."

This was true. Even though Ellie hadn't been that welcoming, I couldn't abandon her. She was family.

"Have you heard from him?" I asked.

"No." She hesitated and I thought it was anger I saw, not sadness behind the damp eyes. Then she said, "It's no surprise. The man's an ass."

Suddenly, she took a deep breath, looked so intense that I reached for her hand.

"Aunt Ellie?"

She pulled back before I could touch her and said, "Nick informed me that JT's a suspect. I guess you probably knew that."

I expected her to cry, or at least get choked up. She didn't. She told me about the patch the forensic team had found.

"That doesn't prove a thing," I said. "The patch was on his property and could have been lost there at any time."

"Maybe. But it was brand new, not weathered. I remember when he brought it home. It was one of the new patches they had made up."

Then it hit me like a punch to the midsection: she thought he was guilty. I wondered if any other family members felt the same. Great-grandma Evie's words about my father flashed through my mind.

Maybe we should have come together more as a family and backed him.

Was family history repeating itself? Was anyone backing JT, or did the family think he was guilty, too?

"Has the family been around?" I asked.

"I sent everyone home. Different ones have been here off and on since I told them he was missing. They're wonderful . . . keeping me company and all. I appreciated it, but I wanted to be alone for a few hours so I sent them home. Come suppertime, a few will be back, I suppose."

"And now I come barging in on your private time. I'm sorry."

"It's fine. I thought I could nap, but I can't. Sit, please. I'll make some tea. I need to be busy."

"I don't drink tea, but if you have coffee?"

"Done." She opened the refrigerator and took out a bag a coffee beans with a Starbuck's label. I actually got excited. I hadn't had Starbuck's in over a week. I mentioned it to her and we both smiled.

"That patch. It was my fault it came off at all. When he got the damn thing he asked me to sew it on, and I refused. I was too mad at him to do anything for him, so he sewed it himself. He did a lousy job."

"Don't you think it's strange that JT wouldn't have stopped and pulled it off the branch? He must have felt it tear. Why leave evidence like that?"

"I mentioned that to Nick, and he said when people panic they're not as aware as they would normally be. But JT never panicked easily. Believe me. My husband may be ten kinds of a fool, a drinker, he may have been unfaithful . . ." She paused. "But he's not a panicky person."

Unfaithful? This was the first I'd heard about him being with another woman. "Are you sure he's been unfaithful?" I blurted, my tact having been left at the door.

Holding the refrigerator open, Ellie stared at me as if I had just dropped in from Mars. "Yes," she said cooly.

"It's none of my business. Forget I asked."

My thoughts jumped to faithless Percy and I wondered if the same woman could be involved. How much bed-hopping took place in Silver Stream anyway? Or were most men bed-hoppers? Like Whatshisname.

She put the milk in a delicate china pitcher and set it on the table. "Would you like to see the rest of the house while the coffee's brewing?"

"Sure." Anything. Get me outta here.

The house was elegant, a show place. In the den I noticed the gun cabinet. Empty.

You ass. Better watch your step. I have a key to that rifle cabinet.

I wondered what had happened to those guns. With JT missing and Collins murdered, Ellie's angry threat to JT on Saturday night seemed ominous. Ellie could have murdered JT. Or Collins. The thought was barely formed when I sacked it. No. Not possible. She was my aunt, a Lassiter by marriage. We Lassiters didn't murder people. We were the good guys. JT was a good guy.

"Isn't that a gun cabinet?"

"Yes."

"No guns in the house?"

"I removed them. For safe keeping."

I followed her upstairs, wondering where she had stashed the ordnance.

She was talking to me. I hadn't processed a word she'd said. Something about her daughter.

"What?" I asked as I stepped into my old room.

"My daughter's an art teacher. She did that horse painting when she was twelve. Talented, isn't she?"

"Very."

I barely glanced at the painting, a white stallion poised on a ridge overlooking a lake. Woods all around. I had come home again. I went to the window, leaned my hands on the sill and gazed at the driveway, at the trees rising up on either side. I knew this sight. How many times had I closed my eyes and been right here? I opened the window and leaned as far as the screen would allow, and looked down at the front porch. I could see the steps and the last few feet of porch, could make out the edges of the green Adirondack chairs.

The sun tipped the treetops, casting a reddish-orange glow over everything. I felt my breath catch. The years fell away. I was a child again. I was safe. I was in my own room.

My eyes suddenly filled with tears. That mushy side that I usually manage to keep hidden leaked out. Aunt Ellie left me alone. Whether she'd noticed or not, I wasn't sure.

I snatched one of my cousin's tissues, dabbed my eyes and blew my nose. Then I took a good look around. My cousin had a flare for decorating. Lots of beige and white and muted shades of blue, a dresser full of pictures in assorted frames, mosaic-tiled tables, an old fashioned secretary with horse statues in ceramic and brass and copper. The room looked better than when I lived here. For just the briefest moment I wished I were a child again and life were simpler.

Back downstairs, composed, I had a cup of coffee and some lemon cake with Ellie.

"I'd like to talk to you about my mother. You were both around the same age, both friends. Can you tell me more about what happened back when they left? Any specifics?"

"I can tell you it shouldn't have happened," she said immediately. I had the feeling she was happy to talk about someone else's troubles, so I pressed on.

"What did the sexual harassment involve?"

"I don't know why your mother didn't tell you. What's the big deal with the way the world is going these days?"

She folded her arms and leaned forward. "Some of it was my fault. We were young. Free-spirited. Your Mom was having problems with your father."

Free-spirited? My mother? We were talking about the same woman?

"She told me your father didn't find her attractive any more. They hadn't had sex in months. It was my idea for her to make him jealous."

The impulse to cover my ears was strong. I didn't want to hear about my parents' sex life. At all.

"We went shopping. I helped her pick out a few outfits, all sexy things your father would disapprove of, but maybe be turned on by. The black leather pants and the really short skirt were the best."

"I can't picture my mother in black leather. No way."

"She looked spectacular. She had a great figure, like you. The kind guys love."

"Uh-huh."

"She wore the slacks to work one day. Just once. After that, there were remarks on a regular basis, more than remarks. The boss grabbed her several times. I guess he considered her fair game. Said she was advertising it."

"So why didn't she just tell this jerk off? Or claim sexual harassment and sue? Or leave? What was the big deal?"

"Back then, that would have been unusual, especially around here. For one thing, she wanted to keep her job, and opposing the boss was not the way to do that. The term political correctness hadn't been coined yet. Things are different today. Back then a man could get away with a lot more."

"My dad didn't do anything?"

"Oh, he did. He beat him up."

Omigod.

"Who was the man? I recall Mom working part-time at the library for a while. What man worked there? I don't remember any."

"I don't remember any man working there either. But what does it matter? The harassment business happened at Kendall's Auto Mart. Your mother had just gotten the job. The S-O-B involved was old man Kendall."

"Percy's father?" I asked on a wisp of breath.

"The one and only."

FIFTEEN

I needed to get back to New York City soon. I'd been without gainful employment for a month now, the last week of which had been spent dawdling around my old hometown, checking out a Dumpster, hiding under a bed, finding a dead body, buying a truck, and such. Not my bailiwick. Not the kind of activity I expected when I drove up here, that's for sure.

Of course, none of this compared to finding out that Mom had suffered sexual harassment at the hands of Percy's father, and then the guy had been murdered. No wonder the aunts didn't want to talk about it.

I had thought about it for a good part of the night. It had kept me awake. I wanted to call Mom and talk about it. Tell her she was not to blame, if that's what she thought. Tell her I understood why we had moved. But Mom was a hard person, at least when it came to me. She never let up on me, I guess because she thought I never measured up to her high standards. When Whatshisname moved in with me, she outright refused to talk to me. Howie could handle this better.

Before taking my shower—I wasn't in any hurry to subject my body parts to that icy water—I went over my résumé and made a few minor changes. I'd fax it back to Lori today. Then I'd call and tell her about my new truck and about how great her timing was yesterday.

I finally mustered the courage to jump in the shower. I soaped up like I was going for the gold in an Olympic lathering race, rinsed off, and hopped out just as the water was turning really, really cold. Shivering, I slipped on my sky blue bra and matching lace panties. I pulled on black Guess jeans, a blue, pointed-collar blouse that matched my eyes perfectly, and a pair of black leather ankle boots with a low heel.

I worked in a bit of gel, then used the blow dryer till my hair fell softly around my face. I added color and a bit more shape to my brows, and a touch of mascara to my lashes. They were too short and too light to leave as nature intended. Nature makes mistakes. I correct them. I finished up with my lipstick brush. Since I blended my own colors, this took a while. Some things are not meant to be rushed.

Before heading downstairs for breakfast I studied the paper I'd written yesterday in Percy's office. Michelle Gray. Her numbers were 8011a0920. The second name was Phil Clinton, 401p0925.

I had no idea what these numbers meant, or who these people were. I thought the number immediately before the a or p might refer to a time. A.M or P.M.? Was Percy supposed to know the times for something that was going to happen? I wondered, too, if this was connected to his partner's death. The more I thought about it, the more I realized I had to find out who gave him this paper. I also had to show Nick.

I headed downstairs, wondering whether the uncles had been in the back room when Percy arrived at the Country Store. Before I hit the bottom step, I inhaled the delicious aroma of apples cooking. Ida stood at the stove stirring a pot of oatmeal. Before coming here, I only used oatmeal that came in the paper envelope that you heated in the microwave with water. This was a new world up here.

"Aunt Ida, I want to take you home with me."

"Just about done, Nora," she said as she stirred some of her freshly made chunky apple sauce into the oatmeal.

Oh, God, how good was this. I'd sure miss it when I left. I'd miss her lots more. I kissed her lined cheek and set the table.

One of the *Law and Order* reruns was playing on the kitchen television.

After breakfast, I called the uncles and asked each of them if they'd been in the Country Store yesterday, hoping they may have seen who Percy met. They'd seen Percy say hello to Margaret and Vivian, who were chatting with the waitress. One other guy they didn't recognize also stopped by briefly. No one knew whether Percy spoke to the guy or not.

I drove Ida to the library in my new truck. She loved it.

"Isn't this something. You in a silver truck." She dabbed a tear from her eye. "This is the answer to my prayers. Now I know you're going to stay."

"Aunt Ida, I needed something to drive. That's why I got this. It doesn't mean I'm staying."

"Oh. Okay. Sh-ur."

I knew she didn't believe me.

She sniffed for what I hoped was the last time.

When I pulled up in front of the library, I said, "Ida, I haven't discussed selling the land with you and the relatives yet, but I want to. Maybe today. I'm thinking I'll either sign it over to one of you, or sell it and give you any profit after a few repairs are made on the house, like a new hot water heater."

Just saying that out loud made me feel a weight had been lifted from my shoulders. When she didn't respond, I went on, "I'll visit often, I promise. But my life is back in New York."

"I understand."

She did? How easy was that. Too easy. She still wasn't buying it. After we talked deeds and details, she'd believe. A part of me was sorry I couldn't stay. Maine wasn't so bad, not nearly as bad as I'd expected. I hadn't seen a moose at all.

The weight of Great-grandma Evie's request still pressed on my heart. Somehow, I'd try to fix what she asked me to fix. Grandma Evie, I said silently, I'll get Howie and Mom up here yet for a visit, I promise. Get them back in the fold.

"Aunt Ida, Ellie told me about the sexual harassment business with my mother. So I know." I pulled into the library lot and parked. Tapping my fingers on the steering wheel, I waited for her reaction.

"It was a long time ago," Ida said. "Does no good to rake up old dirt."

That said, she opened the door. "I best be getting these books back and pick out seven new mysteries. I do love my mysteries."

When she was out of the truck, she leaned in and said, "If I hear anything out of the ordinary today, I'll check out who's doing the talking."

"Good idea." I smiled at her, but my heart wasn't in it. She still didn't want to talk about my parents.

I had to pick up a new disk for the Canon Rebel. Tomorrow afternoon I planned to wind up the Mary Fran business, and I didn't want any other pictures on the card. I would use my new lens. I hadn't used it before, so I was looking forward to that.

The Country Store was close enough to the library that I could have walked, but I didn't, not with my new truck, and all. This was the first vehicle I'd ever owned and I wanted to drive it everywhere before it came time to sell.

Percy's days were numbered. Marla's, too. I'd love to get a shot of them doing the dirty, to really nail it for Mary Fran. I pictured sneaking into the house, catching them in bed. Too risky. I'd never do that.

As I opened the door to the Country Store, it occurred to me that it might be a good idea to take pictures at the funeral. I could use the small pocket-size digital. It would be unobtrusive. I'd seen movies where the murderer showed up for a burial. Even though I was ninety percent sure that Percy was the killer, there was still that ten percent chance that it was someone else.

The store was almost empty. Amy was taking a break, sitting at a back booth across from some guy. She got up when she saw me.

"Hi, Nora. Can I help you?"

How nice to walk into a store and be recognized. "I just need a memory card for my camera, a four-gig would be good.

Amy pointed me in the right direction. "Taking photos, are you? The leaves will be in full color in another few weeks. That's quite a sight."

"I'm going back to New York City. I probably won't be around for that," I said as I took what I needed and placed it on the counter. "I'll have to do my picture-taking before then."

My hand was on the door, when I turned and asked, "Amy, did you know the senior Percy, the one who was murdered?"

She gave me a strange look.

No one gets murdered in Silver Stream. This here's always been a safe place to live.

She had said that to me the day I found Al Collins, but when I reminded her about the other murder, she had remembered it.

"Not really. I knew who he was and all, like the other kids. I was in high school at the time. I remember we all thought Mister Kendall must have done something really bad to be murdered the way he was."

"With a bat?"

"Yup. His head was bashed in. So were his privates."

Margaret was checking out Ida's books as I walked up to the big oak desk. The librarian, dressed in a navy polyester suit and the neatest, crispest, most wrinkle-free white blouse on the planet, smiled perfunctorily at me. I don't think she liked me. Perhaps she suspected I had the Lincoln book.

I figured she was old enough to have known something about the first Auto Mart murder. The fact that both murders involved men who worked in the same place was a coincidence too huge to be ignored. People had to be talking about it.

"Margaret, what do you remember about the murder of the senior Percy Kendall at the Auto Mart?"

Margaret's pale cheeks colored. Her eyes flashed when she spoke. "I know nothing. Just because I dated someone who worked there at the time, people thought I knew something. I didn't. I don't. And I don't appreciate you interrogating me about the murder."

Interrogating?

I caught myself before I took a step back in reaction to her sharp retort. I forced myself to stay rooted, and not look at Ida who had taken a step back. Instead of leaving, or at least dropping the topic, I pushed. "You dated someone from there? Who?"

Her chest heaved and I thought she wasn't going to answer. "My husband, deceased now."

Surprised, I said, "I'm sorry." I waited a beat. "Your husband must have talked about the murder. What did he say?"

Margaret pressed her lips together, and I expected her to remain silent. She did the unexpected and said in a cool voice, "He told me what everyone knew, that Mister Kendall was a harsh man. He was the boss, after all, and he ran a tight ship. Few employees liked him, including his own son."

"The present Percy worked there then?"

"Yes. Part time."

"And they didn't get along?"

"No one got along with that old man," Margaret said. "That's what my husband told me. I believe he used words like louse and skirt-chaser to describe Mister Kendall. That's what everyone called him, even his son."

"Nora, we best be going," Ida said as she picked up her books, clearly uncomfortable.

Without prompting, Margaret added, "His murder was a hard thing for this good community, but the truth was that no one really mourned the man. Good riddance to bad rubbish."

As soon as we got in the car, Ida said, "You shouldn't be asking about this, Nora. Brings back a lot of bad memories for folks. Margaret was upset. She's a nice woman, a widow. She's had a rough time of it, what with her husband sick for so long before he died."

SIXTEEN

After dropping Ida off, I drove back to the sheriff's office to fax my résumé. Nick was behind the desk when I walked in. He leaned forward and peered down, his forearms resting on the desk. What a picture he made. Even though I barely knew him, I decided I would probably miss him. Correction. I knew I'd miss him. There are some men who attract with looks alone, and others whose magnetism extends beyond their good looks. Nick was one of the latter.

Good thing I wasn't in the market for a new relationship or I'd really regret leaving the Maine woods.

"Afternoon Ma'am. Can I help you?"

"Yes, officer," I replied, sweet as spun sugar. Well, I could still flirt at bit. I wasn't dead, just guy-shy. "I have a résumé that needs faxing and I heard there was a very cooperative and competent sheriff in this department who would love to be of assistance. Do you know how I could . . . contact him?"

Nick's brows shot up. "Why, I surely do, Ma'am. And you'll be happy to know the charge will be . . . minimal."

We stared at each other. Sexy devil. With his dark hair and dark eyes. Nice lips, too. They probably worked their magic on a few lucky women.

"Shall I come up there, or will you come down here?"

"I'll come down." A predatory smile.

It had been a long time since a man made me nervous. I was nervous now. No, maybe excited was more accurate. Then he put his hand on my neck. A gentle touch. Nothing more. I felt juices flowing that hadn't flowed in a while. Dear God. Talk about the magic touch. Did he know what he was doing to me? Probably. Right here in the damn sheriff's office station. I was ready to melt. Core meltdown.

He removed his hand, smiled. "Follow me."

Anywhere.

He led me to the back section, pointed to the fax machine. "Help yourself. I'll see you when you're finished."

"Thanks."

When I returned, he was talking to his two officers, skinny Trimble and hunky Miller, and he barely looked at me. They finally nodded and left.

Hot Nick had disappeared, and cop Nick had replaced him, all efficient and official, even when we were alone. I stood there waiting for him to speak as he read some report. It should come as no surprise that sheriff's work was more important than I was. I'd learned that as a kid, hadn't I?

So why did it hurt?

Unbidden, came a memory of my junior prom night. Dad was supposed to take pictures. I had saved my own money to buy the gown, and it was a beauty, beige satin and soft tulle. My mother said it was too extravagant. "Over the top, Nora. This is a disgrace, spending money so foolishly. You should have saved that money for college. Instead, you've wasted it on one dress. And shoes." She had badgered me off and on the whole time I was getting dressed. I held on, kept the tears at bay, because I knew that when I walked into the living room Dad would look at me with approval and best of all, with love.

Just as I opened my bedroom door to make my entrance, the phone rang and within seconds Dad called, "Nora, I have to leave. It's important. A case we've been working on." In a heartbeat, he was gone. The case was more important than my prom. More important than me.

If ever I felt myself falling for Nick, I'd make it a point to resurrect that moment. I quickly dismissed it from my thoughts, but it was harder to dismiss the feelings it left in its wake. In that moment I decided Nick Renzo would be a friend. Period. With that decision, my nerves quieted, the pounding pulse at my neck returned to something resembling normal, and my sweaty palms dried up. Well, almost.

Nick finished reading and turned to me.

"Sorry about this," he said, holding up the papers in his hand. "I didn't mean to be rude, but I've been waiting for this lab report on a fiber found at the murder site. Might belong to the killer."

"What does it say?"

"Nothing too helpful. At least not yet. Common fiber. Half the people of Silver Stream probably have something to match it, including me. Green cotton thread." He put his hand on my shoulder. "Tell me about your day. I wondered off and on what you were up to."

"You did?" Now why that made me feel warm inside, just when I'd decided to keep him as a friend, I do not know.

"My father was a cop," I blurted to protect myself. "Did I tell you that?"

"No, you only mentioned your brother." He narrowed his eyes. "You trying to tell me something?"

"Just that he did the same kind of work. His life revolved around the job."

He stared at me a moment. "Do you think I'm like your father or your brother?"

"I don't know."

He nodded, accepting that. "I don't know either. But being sheriff is what I do. I like my work. When I'm working, I'm fully involved, but I try to put it aside when I leave here for the day. I keep my sanity that way."

I wanted to tell him about my prom, but I told him about my new truck instead, and about Percy being at the lot.

"Percy again. You followed him, didn't you?"

"You are so suspicious."

"Just a guess."

When I said nothing, he asked, "Well, did you?"

"I was going the same direction he was. Besides, I may have found out something." I told him about the newspaper and the paper that was stapled inside. Naturally, I omitted my evasive tactics. No need to draw attention to the risk.

"Follow me," he said as he headed for his office.

"Do you want to see the names or not?" I asked, reaching into my purse.

"Yes." He stepped to the side and held the door for me. "Let's see."

I gave him the paper. "There were other names, maybe ten more, but I didn't get them."

"Too dangerous?" He shook his head and exhaled a puff of breath. "Don't answer that. How many times do I have to tell you the same thing about Percy? You won't listen, will you?"

He looked at what I'd written and his expression changed, became intent as he studied the paper.

When he looked back up, his expression revealed nothing. "This could be completely innocent. Could be related to his business."

"You don't really believe that. You know it's nefarious."

"Nefarious? Who uses words like nefarious?" he asked, studying the numbers.

"An educated detective," I said.

He sighed.

I took the paper from his hand and placed it on his desk so we could both look at it.

"8011a0920 and 401p0927. I think the a and the p refer to time.

"Good guess," he said. "Eleven in the morning. One in the afternoon."

We studied the numbers together. Went back and forth about their meaning.

Nick said, "These last numbers could be dates. September twentieth. September twenty-seventh."

"Yes. Dates a week apart. They jump off the page. How come

I didn't see that?"

He checked the calendar on his desk. "Both are Saturdays."

"If we knew what Percy was up to," I said, "I bet we could figure this all out easily."

Nick copied the information and tacked the paper to a bulletin board near his desk. "This doesn't have anything to do with Mary Fran and her case against Percy, does it?"

"I'm not sure." This was definitely true. "I think Percy is into something and I want to know what it is, not only for Mary Fran's sake, but for JT's. I have a strong feeling that Uncle JT's disappearance is connected. Percy could be at the heart of it." Puzzles on top of puzzles.

"You're probably right about Percy being involved in something he shouldn't be," Nick said. "That wouldn't be a surprise. It might, or might not, be connected to JT's disappearance. We'll see."

He tapped the paper on his desk. "I'll check out these names. I don't recognize either, and I know just about everyone around here. Trimble can run them through the database."

"Good. Now come out and see my new truck."

He smiled. "I've been waiting for an invitation."

When we were outside, I said, "JT didn't murder Collins, you know. You're on the wrong track if you think so."

He lifted the silver hood and looked at the engine and whatever else was in there.

"And you know this how?" he asked.

I laid my hand over my heart. "I feel it. I know this sounds silly, but I think JT ran for another reason. I just don't know what it was at the moment."

"Intuition, huh?"

I pretended to consider this. "Is that the same as gut feeling? You know, the feeling cops get when they suspect something without hard evidence to go on."

He closed the hood, without commenting, and walked around the truck, inspecting stuff like the tires and the truck-bed. He checked to make sure there was a jack. I was tempted to tell him I didn't know how to use a jack so it didn't matter whether it was there or not, but I refrained. Men are funny about things like that.

"I have your clothes at my place," he said. "Want me to drop them off?"

"Sure," I said casually.

"I'm not free till dinnertime. That okay?"

What was he asking? Probably nothing. I was reading into it. I wondered whether hot Nick was back. I tested.

"How will you eat dinner if you're out delivering clothes to women?"

"Maybe the woman, not women, could have dinner with me."

A date. Hot Nick returns.

"That's an idea," I said pleasantly, calmly, as if I were considering it. "I eat every night."

"Something we have in common then."

"I haven't noticed a plethora of restaurants around here."

"Plethora? Is that anything like nefarious?"

"Very much," I said.

"I know a place that's not bad. You like Italian?"

"Some of my best friends are Italian."

"Good."

"This is like a date?" I said.

"No. Just dinner. I don't date."

"Whew. Thank goodness. Me neither."

"You have a few problems with your new truck."

"Oh?"

"The back tires are bald and the radiator leaks. You'll probably have to replace the tires yourself, but the radiator might be Percy's responsibility. Granted, it's a slow leak, but it will get bigger. Don't let it go. Check out your warranty."

Had that salesman given me the warranty? Yes, he talked about it so I probably had it. I now had an excuse to go back there again, maybe discover something else. Perhaps get the rest of the names on the list. Or find the key to the list?

"Good," I said without thinking.

"Good that things are wrong with your truck?" Nick asked, narrowing his eyes.

"Good that there's nothing *else* wrong with it," I said, covering my mis-speak.

"Can't say that for certain. I just mentioned the obvious things that were wrong."

I hopped into the truck. "Maybe when we go on that non-date, you could do me the favor of driving Chevy Charlene and letting me know what else you think is wrong. That way I can have my list ready when I go in about the leak."

"Chevy Charlene?"

"Ce-ce for short, if that's easier. What have you named your truck?"

Resting both hands on the window frame, he stared at me without speaking. I felt a little shiver. I suppressed a giggle, which was odd because I never giggle. I either laugh out loud in a bodacious manner, or I smile. Howie used to say I had a horse laugh. But giggle?

Finally, he said, "I hope you're not planning to nose around when you take *Ce-ce*—"I think he shuddered when he used the name—"back to the Auto Mart."

Sometimes, I find it difficult to lie, like now, so I just rolled my eyes as if he were way off base. Even that made me feel guilty, but I think he bought it.

Then again. . . .

SEVENTEEN

I phoned Lori. She'd received my résumé and put the changes in. My cover letter was waiting to be signed. I was ready for the job hunt. As usual, she asked when I planned to return to the City.

"I still haven't set a date," I told her. "I'll do that tomorrow and let you know. Good enough?"

"You're not planning to stay there, are you?"

"Don't be ridiculous."

"I have a feeling you're getting involved."

"Just tying up a few loose ends."

I told her that she'd faxed the résumé to the sheriff's office, and she groaned and apologized for the photo. I told her it wasn't so bad.

Next, I checked in with Howie. Quickly told him what Aunt Ellie had said about the sexual harassment. He was astounded. He hadn't spoken to Mom yet and was very busy working on a case so we couldn't talk much. Before he hung up he asked what was in the mystery box that Great-grandma Evie buried, and I told him I hadn't gone on the hunt yet.

"I'm surprised you're not curious. It could contain thousands. Or the family jewels. Or Pepsi stock bought when the company first went public."

He was laughing so hard I just hung up.

But he was right. I had to locate the box. I was wasting precious time. What was I waiting for? A big thunderstorm? Snow? Today was a beautiful day for a treasure hunt. The box probably wasn't far from the house. The letter said it was beyond the stream. It would be nice to have someone with me, but I could manage alone. Not that I was afraid of moose or anything like that, but company would be nice. I was used to having a lot of people around.

I crawled around in the closet, pushing the dangling hair from my eyes, sighing, groaning. I needed some boots when I crossed the stream.

Bingo. Found them.

I sat on the floor and pulled on a pair of clunky boots at least two sizes too big. They probably belonged to the original Silver Stream Lassiter, Jeb. I hoped I didn't catch a foot disease. Probably not with the thick socks. I tied the boots tightly and tested them, hoping the old shoelaces would hold. I grabbed the envelope with the map inside and lurched out to the shed.

I selected a shovel from a buffet of five different shovels. Who needed so many different kinds of shovels? I probably wouldn't need the shovel today, but optimism runs rampart in me sometimes. I planned to get as far as I could, mark the way like Hansel and Gretel, but not with bread crumbs, and then . . . Who knew? I smiled inwardly and clomped onward.

When I arrived, I set the shovel down, whipped out the map and studied it. Confusing squiggly lines ran every which way. There were direction markings for north and south and such. I had no idea which direction was which. Go north at the red pine. Which way was north? Had the sun come through my window in the morning? That would be east. If I faced east, north would be . . . to my left. Piece of cake.

Trees were penciled in with names on them. Names? She thought I could identify trees by name? I could recognize a total of three trees--white birch, red Japanese maple, and blue spruce, the distinguishing element in all three being the obvious. None of Grandma Evie's tree labels met my criteria, except for the red pine.

Okay. A good place to start. Elementary, my dear Nora. Red pines must be red. I could find this one, but I figured all the rest were green. Most green trees were a mystery.

Discouraged, but not enough to deter, I glanced around. The

red must be up farther. I picked up my shovel and plodded along the stream, which was more like a little creek here, looking for a red tree, or even one close to red. Occasionally, I banged the shovel against a rock to let the animals know I was not unarmed and they'd better beware: moose and bears in particular, although I didn't think there would be any this close to the house. You never know though. So far, it was an effective tactic. No animals dared to appear. I think I went about half a mile. It's hard to gauge distance in the woods when you're used to city blocks. Twenty blocks, one mile. At least that was the rumor.

How many trees equal a mile? Had anyone figured that out yet? I think not.

Nothing down this way. Not so much as a smear of red. I decided to retrace my steps and check out the opposite direction. The shovel was getting heavy and the shoes were rubbing against my heels, even through the thick socks. Great. A blister for sure. Maybe two blisters.

I passed the spot where I'd started out, and continued for another ten minutes. Nothing. No red pine in this area. Nothing red.

This wasn't working. I needed a tree expert. I knew that the aunts and uncles were tree people but I couldn't see them tramping through these woods.

I'd prefer you keep it quiet, but the decision about telling is yours. My meddling days are over.

That made me wonder about the contents again. Something sinister? Another secret? I hadn't considered either before.

I needed someone I could trust, someone who knew tree stuff. Nick? Mary Fran? Or maybe a book? I headed back to the house.

An hour later I pulled into the library parking lot. Margaret looked nervous when I walked in. I made her nervous?

"You here for anything in particular?"

No friendly hello this time.

"Books on trees," I said. "I want to be able to identify trees."

She directed me, and then went back to the book she was reading, probably some dry classic. I almost asked, but she seemed so remote, that I kept my distance.

I looked up red spruce first. *Geez.* It was green. Whoever named this tree should be shot. No. Tortured, then shot. How dare they deceive an unsuspecting public. I studied the picture and it looked like several trees I'd seen. Big help. I tried another book and found the pictures more annoying, many with a tree trunk, pine cones and a few pine needles. From these pictures I'd never be able to identify a thing. Who wrote these crappy books anyway? Bunch of jerks.

Three women came in as I was putting the books back on the shelf. As I was heading out, Margaret got up and walked to the children's section with them. I glanced at the book she'd turned face down on the desk and covered with her napkin.

I flipped the napkin. *Lascivious Lucinda.* Erotica.

Staid Margaret in the navy blue polyester reading a bodice-ripper. My thoughts scattered every which way. Of course, it probably didn't mean anything.

Quickly, I flipped the napkin back in place and left, my take on prissy Margaret upended once more.

This was a disaster. One of my own making. Just when I thought my days of being foolish about men had been consigned to the past, wham-bang, I stepped into it again. A date, for-god-sakes. I had to be out of my mind.

I know a place that's not bad. You like Italian?

Some of my best friends are Italian.

How cute was that? Coy and cute and let's not forget stupid. Starting a relationship when you're leaving the state? And with a cop no less. Stupid. Stupid.

Wrapped in a towel, still shaking, fresh from that icy shower, I looked at the clothes spread out on my bed, my entire Maine wardrobe. Not much. A week's worth of clothes for a woman planning to stay four days. I was into week two and down to my last pair of black slacks and one white silk blouse. I was in trouble. But thinking about clothes didn't work right now. I was in deep doo-doo. I was not prepared for a date with Nick the cop and it had nothing to do with clothes. If I didn't like him so much, wasn't so attracted, this would be easier. I could have dinner, enjoy the conversation, the company, the food, say goodnight and leave without looking back. Simple.

As I towel-dried my hair, the weight of the coming evening bore down on me. Feeling desperate, I dropped the towel, grabbed my pocketbook and found my appointment book. I could set a date to leave is what I could do. I'd promised myself I'd do that, and I would. Right now.

Tomorrow was out. First the funeral, then the Percy-Marla photo shoot. Then I'd have to get the pictures run off and give them to Mary Fran. That would take me into Saturday. Hmm. On Saturday I could finish up everything, conference with the family about the land, finalize details, say my good-byes. I'd have to tell Vivian the Pomeranian lady to find someone else to investigate her dog poisoning. I hated to do that, go back on my word, but it couldn't be helped. Self-preservation came first.

By Sunday morning, the latest, I'd be ready to leave. I circled Sunday and wrote Back to NYC in block letters and added an exclamation point. I double underlined it and tossed the book on the table. I felt better already.

Then I remembered the buried box, picked the book up and changed the date to the Monday.

I slipped into my white underwear, extra lacy to make up for the fact that it was white. I'd have preferred the red bra and panties, but the bra would show through the blouse and I figured I had enough trouble ahead without that teaser. I pulled on the black slacks and white blouse. I'd wear the white blazer. Nights were chilly here.

Cover up. Cover up, Nora.

Too bad I hadn't asked Margaret the Librarian for one of her navy suits. Ms. Erotica in a straight-laced suit. Who would have guessed?

I smoothed down the collar of my blouse as I looked in the mirror. I wondered whether Nick would drive the sheriff's car or his own. His own, definitely his own. I'd asked him to test drive my truck, but he might not need to take that very far.

I was excited about seeing him. I couldn't help it. Even though I knew I was flirting with disaster. Sometimes it's fun to flirt with disaster.

He was supposed to arrive around seven and I hoped Ida would be dozing by then. Less fuss. She often fell asleep in her chair while watching the news. I'd told her that Nick and I were going out to eat. Her grin was the broadest I'd seen since I'd arrived. I set her straight though. Told her it was strictly a platonic dinner. She mumbled something about those Renzos not knowing the meaning of the word. I could take that two ways. Either they suffered from limited vocabularies, or they were passionate men. I didn't think I needed clarification.

At the appointed time, I heard the doorbell ring and headed downstairs, feeling every bit as nervous as a teenager on a first date. I am a foolish woman.

That's when I heard them.

"Oh, he's here. Come on in, Nick. We've been waiting for you."

It was Hannah's voice. I couldn't believe it. What was she doing here?

"My, don't you look swell. All dressed up," Agnes said, loud enough for me to hear on the top step.

"Out of the way now, let the man in," Ida ordered officiously.

Frozen midway down the staircase, eyes closed in mortification, I considered going back upstairs, maybe jumping out a window.

"What's in the bag?" Hannah quizzed in a whisper loud enough to alert the Pomeranians several miles from here. "A present? My Henry used to bring me little gifts when he came courting."

Courting. Oh, my God. These women. Had they no sense of the appropriate?

I heard the paper bag rustle. Was he opening the bag? Shifting it? I couldn't tell. Would my petal pink underwear make an appearance?

"That's right," Agnes affirmed. "I recall your Henry once brought you a zucchini. Never saw such a big zucchini in all my days." She paused. "I forget. Did you cook that one with cheese or did you bread it, Hannah?"

I grunted to myself. I had to stop this. I peeled my fingers from the cherry wood bannister, and continued down.

"Now don't you folks go spoiling the surprise," Ida cut in. "Let Nick here give our Nora her bag, and if she wants she can tell us what's in it. We're not nosy."

In a pig's eye, I almost shouted, wondering even as the words formed in my head where they had come from. Straight out of left field, that's where. I'd never used an expression like that in my entire life. Had I heard Ida say that?

"It's not a present," Nick explained. "Just a bag I found out by Nora's truck. She must have dropped it," he lied.

I expelled a grateful breath as I hit the bottom step. When I turned the corner and saw him in the foyer, I gave him a huge smile. He smiled back over the sea of white heads. "Nora, hello."

The aunts turned, expectant, heads swiveling from me to Nick and back again as if they were following a tennis match.

I wanted to scowl at them, but I couldn't. I loved these ladies, Agnes with her chubby cheeks, Hannah with her purple silk scarf, Ida with her apron. I took the bag, excused myself and hurried back upstairs.

"What was a flag doing by her truck?" I heard Agnes say.

"*Bag*, not flag," Hannah said.

When I returned to the parlor, Hannah was chatting with Nick about the restaurant we were going to. Ida mentioned that the last time she'd been there she'd had their special three cheese lasagna.

"Oh, that's wicked good food, but all that cheese will bind you up for sh-ur," Agnes said. "Believe me, I know from personal experience. But if that's the dish you want, why go right ahead. There's always Metamucil."

I rolled my eyes.

"Call me old fashioned," Hannah said, "but I still prefer Exlax."

"You like that chocolate flavor," Ida pointed out. "Me, I like my prunes. They do the trick."

Nick stood when I entered. I expected a desperate, get-me-out-of-here look, but his broad smile held despite the laxative discussion. He looked good in a light blue, button-down shirt and stone-colored slacks. This was the first time I'd seen him out of uniform since the Dumpster episode.

We all sat and chatted, a rare experience for me. No, not rare. That would imply it had happened before. It never had. My parents never chatted freely with any guy I dated. It was more along the lines of the Spanish Inquisition.

The tension ebbed as I listened to them all. The aunts wanted an update on Collins' murder.

"We're checking out the folks who visited the library the day Ida overheard the conversation," he told them.

This pleased Ida. Me too, since I'd done Dumpster duty to retrieve that list.

"We have several suspects but nothing definite on any of them. Can't tell you who they are, of course."

Everyone nodded in understanding, including me, although I decided to pump him later.

"The shell caliber used is a common one, a 30-caliber. Collins was shot from a distance of about two hundred feet, give or take a few feet. We figure the shooter was standing by a tree, and probably steadied the rifle on a branch. We found a fiber."

Agnes leaned forward in her chair. "Red? A hunter?"

"Not exactly."

"Blue?" Ida asked.

"I can't reveal that information."

I almost said green, but I realized he didn't want it to be common knowledge. He had favored me with the information though. I felt privileged.

"You think he saw his killer?" Hannah asked.

"We can't know that, Ma'am."

We all nodded, but at two hundred feet there was a good chance Al Collins had seen his killer. Someone had been nearby in the woods and that someone had shot him.

"You have any idea why he was there in the first place?" I asked.

"Probably to meet someone. He wasn't dressed for a hike in the woods."

A mental image of JT's empty rifle cabinet flashed through my head again.

"Think you'll find the man who killed him?" Ida asked. "So we can all sleep at night."

"We'll find the killer," Nick assured them.

Not find *him*, I noticed. He'd said 'find the killer.' Did he suspect a woman?

I wondered if Ellie had heard from JT yet.

During a brief lull in the conversation, I mentioned that I was starving, and the aunts took the hint and agreed we should be on our way.

EIGHTEEN

When we stepped out the front door, to my credit, I didn't sigh loud enough to be heard. Nick had come in his official sheriff's vehicle. Great. Red bubble lights, a siren, a scanner, a two-way radio. What more could a woman want?

"You don't mind, do you?" he asked as he opened the door. "My truck is in the shop."

"Are you going to test drive my truck?" Even that would be better than this.

"When we get back I'll take it for a quick spin. I'm hungry now and your truck shouldn't be driven much until you get that radiator leak fixed."

"Right." I slid into the front seat. "You're not planning on running to any calls, are you?"

"No. My men can handle whatever comes up. I'm off duty."

"I've heard that before," I mumbled as he walked around and got in.

When he turned the key, the sheriff's radio gave a blast of static that startled me. He grinned and turned it down. Not off, just down. God forbid the man should not be tethered to his job.

"You look nice, Nora."

"Thank you. So do you."

"Thanks."

He pulled onto the road and I decided to relax, give up being annoyed about riding in his sheriff's vehicle. Once I did that, an amazing thing happened. Suddenly, I was feeling very at home sitting next to him, an unusual feeling. I should analyze the phenomenon.

He pointed out his parent's house as we drove past. All I saw was a green mailbox at the end of the driveway with faded mums spilling around it.

We drove by the lake and he pointed out where he used to swim as a kid. Then past the high school and the football field where he played on the varsity.

"Quarterback?"

"Good guess."

He was a man who took charge. "You called the plays."

"Umm."

We traveled through a thickly wooded area where the trees canopied the road, darkening it, then up an incline and finally into the light where the fields were rimmed with the pinks and golds of the setting sun. Clouds, like gauze, drifted above us.

"Beautiful," I said.

We crossed a bridge and I saw a restaurant ahead.

"Do you know much about trees?" I asked.

"I'm from Maine."

Ignoring the conceit, I said, "I went looking for a red pine yesterday and couldn't find any red trees, so I went—"

He started to laugh. Looked at me, then laughed some more.

I interrupted with, "Get a grip, Renzo. It's not that funny. I went to the library and found out they're really green. It's a common mistake, I'm sure."

He had the audacity to laugh louder. "Not around here it isn't."

I caught myself before I smacked his arm. That would be too familiar. I had to be careful. "Now I'm not going to ask you what I wanted to ask."

He pulled into the parking lot of the Bella Napoli Restaurant. "Even if I promise not to laugh?"

"I think I don't like you."

He turned off the engine and touched my arm. "I like you."

Damn man.

"I have to find something in Ida's woods, down by the brook.

Different trees are markers on the map."

"And if I offer to help?"

"Would you?" It came out as a whisper, although that's not what I intended.

"Yes," he whispered back, leaning so far toward me that I thought he was going to kiss me. I held my breath, which I realized was ridiculous, but I was on the verge of panting so what else could I do? My heart had kicked into overdrive, and my palms began to sweat. Instant sweating. How embarrassing. Then he placed his hand over my hand and pulled back, his eyes holding mine. After a few second, or was it hours, he removed his hand and turned off the engine. Without delay, I opened my door. Get me outta here.

All I could think of was that I used to be cool. I held my head up, in an attempt to recapture that cool as we went into the restaurant.

Red-checked tablecloths, candles in amber glasses, plastic grapes, vines up one side of the room and across the ceiling—not New York chic, a snobby thought that made me wish it was possible to take thoughts back.

The rich aroma of tomato sauce, garlic and onions filled the air. The place wasn't crowded, but one group of about a dozen people, all men, one with a paper hat with the word retired printed on it, was making so much noise I could barely hear Dean Martin going on about the moon hitting his eye like a-big a-pizza pie.

"The food's good here," Nick assured me after we ordered wine, a merlot for him, a pinot grigio for me.

"Even my parents come here," he said, "which is saying something for my dad who swears only my mother knows how to cook a decent beef braciole."

"Your family's close?"

"Yes." He took a sip of wine. "Which is why I have my own place," he added with a smile.

Eh, Cumparì began and the noisy table sang along. I found myself tapping my foot. If I knew the words, I might have sung with them.

Nick asked what I was looking for in the woods. I hesitated. I hadn't even told the aunts yet.

"You don't have to tell me if you don't want to," he said quickly.

I realized I wanted to share this with him. I made a quick decision that I hoped wasn't the result of wine on an empty stomach.

"My great-grandmother buried a box for me," I began. I told him about my father taking the family to New York, and asked if he'd ever heard anything about sexual harassment at the Auto Mart years ago.

"No. But I can check it out for you. Look up old records."

Exactly what I needed to see. So why, all of a sudden, did a chill of dread sweep up my spine.

There was a loud crash in the vicinity of the *Eh, Cumpari* singers. Glass breaking. Laughter.

Nick's gaze darted to the group, but he quickly turned his attention back to me. The noise level rose a few decibels as the refrain kicked in, for what I hoped was the last time.

Nick's gaze shifted between them and me. I wondered whether he'd get involved. Half expected he would.

"Is that why you sat on that side of the table? So you could keep an eye on them?"

He gazed at me for several moments, silent, not feeling the need, I knew, to verbalize his answer.

"The waitress is young and keeps serving them alcohol," he said. "Several of them should have been cut off a while back. And a few of the guys keep going outside to smoke. I caught the sweet smell when we entered."

"I didn't smell anything. There was a breeze. How could you smell anything but fresh air?"

"Well . . ."

"Never mind." I waved my hand. "You don't have to explain. You're more tuned in than I am. Right? More observant?"

He nodded. "It's what I do. I'd better be good at it."

I turned to look. A young guy, probably the maître d', was conferring with someone at the table. "Looks like the situation is under control."

Nick nodded, and his focus turned back to me.

"This is a non-date, right?" I said.

"Yes," he answered.

"Tell me about the woman who made you swear off dating."

I expected him to hem and haw a bit, like most guys would, but he said, "She was my ex-fiancée. She moved to the big city. That would be Boston. She called from there to cancel our engagement."

"Ouch." I stared at him. "And I do mean that with a capital O. Some people have no class. Did you suspect anything before that happened?"

"As the local sheriff, I don't like to answer that. Tarnish my reputation for following clues."

"To say nothing of gut instinct?"

"Thanks."

"I don't mean to offend. You'll get your chance. I hear payback is a bitch. Here goes." I paused for effect. Sometimes I can be a drama queen. "I walked into my apartment early one afternoon, due to the fact that I was laid off from my job that very day, and I heard the shower running. What a nice surprise. My fiancé was home early. Let me go see.

"He was living in my apartment. We were saving money to get married. I paid the rent. His check, or most of it, went into his bank account, *our* little nest egg. We never got around to putting my name on it. I trusted him, so there was no rush and we were both so busy. Please don't tell me I was dumb," I said quickly. "I know that."

"Love and trust go together. You loved him. There's no need to explain further."

That was the perfect thing to say. I was liking this guy more and more.

"Anyway, you can probably guess the rest."

He nodded. "I think so."

"*Bimbo*-slash-*fiancé-interruptus,* I think it's called."

I shoved down the urge to cry. I laughed lightly instead. Nick didn't. He held my gaze.

"This was recent, wasn't it?"

I nodded. "Shortly before I came here. A few days before."

"You never had a clue?" he asked gently.

"Not a one, says the hotshot detective from New York."

"I'm sorry."

"Me, too." I paused, trying to decide how much to tell him. "I jammed a chair under the bathroom door so they were both locked in, and then I tossed his clothes, his CDs, his tennis racket and his vitamins, which were all lined up in alphabetical order, out the window. It was sort of like a sidewalk sale for the folks walking by. Actually, a little crowd gathered. I even sent his Big Berthas down. He'd just bought those golf clubs. He loved them more that anything. Even me, as it turned out."

"Good move."

I tasted the veal Marsala. Melt-in-your-mouth wonderful.

"He was a cop," I said when I finished chewing. "Like my Dad. But not quite like my Dad."

Nick nodded. "So you're cop-shy."

"And you're city-girl shy."

"Nora Lassiter, we should never talk to each other again."

"We absolutely should not, Nick Renzo."

"Good thing this isn't a date."

"Truer words were never spoken."

"We should toast to that."

We raised our glasses and toasted.

The noisy table broke up and most of them went home. Three remained. They argued with the waitress about the bill.

During dessert, a chocolate mousse that was better than anything I'd tasted in my whole life, there was a loud crash. Nick stood abruptly, jostling the table, which jostled my spoon, which sent chocolate mousse blobbing down the front of my blouse. He didn't notice.

"Stay," he called over his shoulder.

Stay? Is that anything like *sit? Stand? Heel?*

I think not, mister.

I got up and followed him, mumbling a few choice expletives about my blouse. Two of the former *Eh, Cumpari* singers were duking it out. Maybe someone should change the present tarantella and put *Eh, Cumpari* back on.

Nick was attempting to separate the brawlers. Some guy, I think he may have been the manager, came running, followed by the Pillsbury Dough Boy in one of those bouffant chef's hats.

"Call nine-one-one." the manager yelled to the entire room, which consisted of me, the chef, and an elderly couple who may have been hard of hearing since they didn't seem disturbed by the racket, or perhaps were pretending it wasn't happening. Who knew? I didn't count the drunk with the paper hat who was now clapping his hands and rolling his shoulders in rhythm to the tarantella.

I grabbed my cell. Before I could dial, Nick and the two men fell to the floor in a big heap with Nick in the middle, kind of like a sheriff sandwich. I dropped the phone. What to do, what to do. Stay calm.

"Nick." I yelled in my calmest voice. He turned to look at me, and a fist clipped his chin.

Okay, calm didn't work. I needed a weapon.

I scanned the room. Knives. Not a good choice. I hate knives. Desperate, I grabbed a bowl of spaghetti with clam sauce from the old folks table. Now they were paying attention. Aiming for the guy on top, I flung the contents. Hit him square in the face. Faster than you can say linguine pescatora the guy was off the floor, sputtering, spitting, wiping. I thought he was going to kick Nick, so I sent the chocolate mousse his way, too, a sad waste, but you do what you have to do.

Mouth pressed into a straight line, chocolate fists raised, spaghetti dangling every which way, the bull charged. I grabbed a chair, and shoved it. Drunk, wobbly on his feet, he fell into it head first.

Seconds later, Nick had the guy's arms behind his back, and was cuffing him.

The tarantella ended, and *O Sole Mio* drifted through the speakers. The music seemed to match the action.

Nick escorted the two prisoners to the SUV and secured them in back. Just before we drove off, he reached for my hand, leaned over and whispered, "Lady, you are something else. You can be my wingman any time."

Pleased, I smiled. "I used to play Wonder Woman," I whispered, lifting my wrists to ward off imaginary bullets.

He brushed my lips, a feather-light kiss that I felt all the way down to my toes.

"Ah, shit. We gotta watch this crap."

Nick spun around, yanked the prisoner forward by the collar, and said through clenched teeth, "Shut ya mouth. Hear me? You ruined my meal, plus, I gotta put up with your stink. You reek of weed."

"Marlboro Lights," he declared.

Nick released him and shoved him back. "The hell it is."

Hunky Miller with the twitch was on duty when we walked into the station house. He assisted with the prisoners, then gave us both the once over, his brows shooting up a notch.

"Spaghetti, I see," he said to Nick, nodding toward a stand dangling from his shirt pocket. "If you'd asked, I bet they would have given you one of those take-home bags."

NINETEEN

I half-expected the aunts to be peeking out a window when we drove up, but Hannah's car, a huge thing that was many years old, was gone and Ida never stayed up beyond ten, so I figured I was safe. To my chagrin, I was nervous when he stopped. Felt awkward. And I haven't felt nervous or awkward around guys since college. No, make that high school.

I expected to sit in the seat a while, perhaps say a few words, maybe fiddle with my purse.

No such thing. Nick leaned over, cupped my neck with his palm and pulled me to him. The man wasn't one for preliminaries, and that's a fact. He kissed me, right smack on the mouth, a no-nonsense kiss that set my senses spinning. Now, I'm not saying that rockets went off or anything like that—I'm a realist—but the man did know how to kiss. It was one of those wet, smoochy affairs that you want to go on and on until it leads to other things. That thought made the sensible me pull back, but not too far, not too fast. I may be sensible, but I'm not a masochist.

"This doesn't mean anything more than friendship," Nick murmured, his lips skimming down my neck.

"I agree. We toasted to that," I mumbled as I turned my head, giving him better access to my lips. "Platonic friends," I murmured into his mouth.

"Two buddies," he agreed. "Out for an evening on a non-date."

"Yes," I breathed.

After a few minutes of this, my sensible side kicked in and I reached back for the door handle.

"Good night, Pal," I muttered, as I got out and stood on jello legs.

It was a clear September day, a perfect day, warm, deep blue, the kind of day that makes a person feel blessed to be alive, the kind of day that makes you want to stop by the side of the road, hop out of the car, and run through a field, arms wide, face to the heavens.

It was not the kind of day a person wanted to go to a funeral.

Yet here I was, driving the three aunts in Hannah's 1965 dark teal Pontiac GTO with the black leather interior. She insisted I try it out. It was a boat of a car. But power. With a touch of the gas pedal I threw everyone back in their seats, rocket-takeoff style. G-forces at work. Not being the best driver on the road, I was super cautious.

"V-8 engine," Hannah explained before I asked. "They called it a muscle car. It was my husband's favorite."

I was shaky by the time I braked to a stop in front of the funeral home. I'd made it without incident, hadn't hit a tree, a person, or an animal.

The aunts were in black today, traditional mourning clothes. As I got out of the car, I saw the Collins family, also in black.

"I'm glad to see that," Agnes commented as she huffed and puffed her way out of the back seat. "It's only proper. In the old days, widow's weeds were common."

Ida must have seen my questioning look, so she explained, "That's what we used to call the mourning clothes that widows wore. Some widows would dress in black for years after their husbands died."

Agnes finally made it out. Straightening her dress, she commented, "I wore this dress when my husband passed away a few years back. I've had to let the seams out since. Dry cleaning shrinks things, you know."

"You should sue." Hannah advised, adjusting her black

knitted shawl.

"Blue?" Agnes questioned. "Why should I wear blue? Black is for mourning."

"Agnes, that hearing aid works best when you take it out of the drawer," Ida said, brushing a speck of lint off her black polyester dress.

I listened without comment, my thoughts on the people around us. It looked as if the whole town had turned out. Percy and Mary Fran stood with two salesmen from the Auto Mart, all dressed in their Sunday best. Percy checked his watch and looked around. I followed his gaze, wondering if he was looking for Marla. Maybe he'd give himself away and I'd be lucky enough to find out who she was.

Michelle Gray, 8011a0920. Phil Clinton, 401p0925.

The names and numbers were committed to memory. Percy was up to something bad, and I suspected it paled beside his unfaithfulness to his wife.

Mary Fran saw me and nodded. Percy looked right through me, pretending, I suppose, that I didn't exist. I'm sure he wished I didn't. It made me a little nervous to think he suspected I was up to something in his office. I'd put the paper back exactly where I found it. He probably didn't buy the idea that I hadn't realized my cell was charged. Or maybe he had. To reinforce the idea, I tossed my head, sending my streaky blond locks sailing around. I selected one lock, and twirled it, twit-like, of course, as I gazed around.

Aunt Ellie arrived alone and parked across the street. She wore a black warm-up suit. Amy from the luncheonette pulled up in back of her. She wore an ecru blouse that scooped low enough to show hills and valleys. Her skirt was black, in deference to the occasion, I figured.

I didn't want to feel excited about all this, but I couldn't help it. Such intrigue. And I was going to catch some of it on camera. I was certain all would go smoothly. I hadn't told Nick what I intended to do. No reason to alarm him.

As the aunts chatted with neighbors, I smiled and nodded at

the appropriate moments, while continuing to check   the new arrivals. I fingered the compact Canon PowerShot in my pocket, the one with the powerful zoom lens. The big Canon was too obtrusive to use.

"Ida, I'm going to the ladies' room,' I announced. "I'll meet you inside."

I strode purposely across the lawn, and into the funeral parlor. Once inside, head down, I dodged the mourners, and found the door that led to the back parking lot.

No one here. I skirted the hearse and checked out both sides of the building. On the left, I spotted a broad-trunked tree, one big enough to hide behind. If I could get there without being seen, I'd be okay. I waited until I thought no one was watching, then dashed to the tree. Puffing from nerves more than physical exertion, I pulled out the camera and started snapping. After a while I sprinted to another tree, another angle, and got more people. The whole town must be here.

I watched Nick watching people. He looked sharp in his uniform with the razor-creased khaki slacks, the dark brown jacket with the transmitter clipped on the shoulder, and the sun glinting off the six-pointed star on his chest. Naturally my thoughts flew to last night, but I quickly diverted them as more people arrived. I needed to concentrate.

The funeral parlor was crowded when I finally went inside, standing room only. I stood next to the door where I could see everyone. Since I was a visitor to Silver Stream, I figured this looked okay. Natural, in fact.

From his seat across the room, Percy gazed around, nodded ever so slightly at someone. I followed his line of vision. Four women sat together, their backs to me. I couldn't tell which one he'd made eye contact with. Librarian Margaret, Waitress Amy, Vivian the Pomeranian lady, and Aunt Ellie. Ellie? Good God. I think not. She was too old. But the others? What was going on? Was he having an affair with someone besides Marla?

"Snap one more picture and I'll confiscate that damn camera,"

Nick whispered. I'd never heard him come up behind me.

"It's a free country," I whispered back, feeling a chill of excitement race up my spine. "You can't take my camera."

"Want to bet?"

"Maybe I do."

"Try me."

"I was well hidden," I whispered. "How did you make me?"

"Make? That cop talk?"

I smiled, but still didn't turn around. "How?"

"You were going from tree to tree like the Roadrunner. I'm a trained observer. Do the math."

"You were looking for me," I said smugly.

"Could be." He poked me in the back.

The minister began to speak and the room quieted, became eerily silent. About two minutes into his eulogy, the *Toreador March* blasted from my purse and a hundred heads swiveled my way. Eyes wide, the minister paused. He stared in my direction. So did all the mourners, every last one of them. I rummaged in my sack of a purse for the cell as tinny march music filled the room. I used to be organized. What happened? I came to Maine is what happened. Where was that damn phone?

Behind me, Nick sighed. "Maybe I should take a picture of this," he whispered.

I finally found the cell, and turned it off.

I saw Hannah roll her eyes, and Ida shake her head. Aunt Agnes probably hadn't heard.

"Lori calling," I whispered over my shoulder when the minister resumed his talk.

At the grave site I stood back by the cars. Good thing I had a four-gigabyte disk in my camera. More people here than at the funeral parlor.

For the most part Nick ignored me, but I saw him glance my way off and on, a faux-threatening look on his face. I smiled back.

Before it was over, Mary Fran grabbed my arm. "I can't stand this. Knowing Percy'll see his slut this afternoon . . . I want to say something, tell him I'm on to him." She shook her head. "No. Let me be totally frank. I want to mash his freaking head with a hammer."

"That sounds worse than cutting off his body parts."

This was the Mary Fran I remembered, the violent Mary Fran of my childhood.

"Don't," I cautioned. "You'd never get the money and that's the best revenge. Hang in there. Go back to work and let me do my job. I'll bring you the pictures."

I wondered about the possibility of ticks as I hid in the woods alongside Kendall's driveway, waiting for Marla the slut to make an appearance. A person could get a disease being in these woods. Bugs could crawl up a person's leg. You had to be careful. I swatted at a swarm of gnats and hunkered down. I checked my watch. It was almost three. Marla was late. Naughty Marla.

I waved my hand to disperse the cloud of gnats, but they continued to swarm back. I think they liked the spot I was occupying. Maybe it was their spot and I was the intruder.

Low-hanging, dark clouds had replaced the beautiful morning weather. If it got any darker the pictures might not come out well at this distance, but moving closer would be risky. I had my big camera this time, the one with the new high-powered lens that cost more than the camera. I tested it. Took a few shots of the house. Okey-doke. Not too dark yet. I turned off the automatic flash. Couldn't have that lighting up.

The gnats were a nuisance. I waved my hand through the swarm again. They disappeared, but were back seconds later circling my head.

I wore a huge old green and brown mottled army fatigue shirt that I'd found in the closet, so I blended in nicely with my surroundings. Ten minutes later I heard the front door bang and I looked through the lens. Percy stormed out wearing . . . what on earth? It looked like an old-fashioned, little-boy outfit with short pants, a bow tie, knee socks. Geez.

The whole getup made me want to yell, Where's your pinwheel hat? Oh, I needed a shot of this. I waved the gnats away, and snapped a few shots.

Percy paraded to the end of the driveway and scanned the road. The impatient lover? A guy's got to be pretty brave to come out of the house looking like that. It didn't take imagination to figure out what sex game was slated for today. I couldn't help wondering whether he played these games with Mary Fran, too.

Percy stomped back, stopped directly opposite me, and placed a call on his cell. Great spot. Perfect.

"Where are you?" he demanded.

A pause.

One of his socks slipped down when he stamped his foot.

I wished he were on a speaker phone so I could hear her side of the conversation. Percy turned away and I missed what he said. I crawled closer. More gnats.

"You've never been late. You playing games?" Percy hollered.

If he'd continue to talk this loud, I'd hear just fine.

But, no. I missed the next thing he said and was forced to inch closer. Then it happened.

Ohgod, ohgod, ohgod! A gnat flew up my nose.

I leaned forward, exhaled sharply with my mouth closed. No good. Still there. Damn gnat. I sat down and stuck my finger in my nose, probing. Had it gone to my lungs? Where were all the cilia I learned about in biology class? They were supposed to prevent this sort of thing. I blew my nose into the sleeve of the shirt.

"Yes, I saw you at the funeral, sitting with those—" Percy turned away and I didn't catch the rest of what he said. Did he mean when he nodded toward the women? Was one of them Marla? But Amy, Vivian, Margaret and Aunt Ellie were together. Not a Marla in the bunch.

The gnat was still in place and his buddies were swarming around looking for him.

"Since when does the likes of you hang around with—" He

turned again and I missed the name.

Percy listened, his face reddening.

Sticking my head in my blouse to muffle the sound, I blew my nose again.

"You can keep your fucking buyers' list." he yelled. "I don't intend to meet those guys. I told you that. I'm not getting involved in this shit. I've done enough. Look at Collins."

Look at Collins?

Was that Percy's involvement? Murdering his partner?

My mouth dropped open and my hands began to shake. These two were definitely involved in something that Collins had been shot over.

The buyer's list? Was that the list I'd seen in his office?

I inched closer, exhaling sharply through my nose.

"Is this why you came on to me? Through Al to me?" Percy demanded, pacing like an angry bull.

I missed the next thing he said.

The gnat seemed to have shifted. It was still in there. I made snorting sounds into my camera bag to muffle the sound. My lungs demanded air, and I inhaled reflexively. The gnat zipped through the canals and caught in my throat

"Yaaah." Disgusting. I spit it out. "Te-eew, te-eew, eeuck." I wiped my tongue on my sleeve.

Percy stopped suddenly, facing me. I flattened myself on the ground, lying in twigs and leaves and heaven only knows what else. I am not a woods' person, and that's an absolute. I shivered just thinking about the creatures that were probably crawling over me. The gnat had been bad enough.

"Who's there?" Percy bellowed in my direction. He slipped his phone into his pocket, and I put my head to the ground, trembling beneath the leafy underbrush, hoping his eyesight was poor, hoping I was well hidden, hoping I would miraculously think of some way to escape if he came looking.

Small branches crackled and popped as Percy stepped into the underbrush. I had a flash of Collins with a bullet hole in his head, and wondered whether Percy had a gun. I had to make a run for it.

I jumped up, scraped my cheek on a branch and felt my shirt rip. The need for self-preservation propelled me forward. I bounded like a deer, hopping over dead trees, shoving branches aside, stepping into who-knows-what.

Coming to Maine was a big mistake.

Behind me, I heard Percy crashing through brush, hot on my trail. He was a big man. I didn't take the time to look back, even when I heard a really big crash.

I think he fell.

I hoped he fell.

TWENTY

By the time I pulled up in front of the sheriff's office, I had finger-combed most of the forest debris from my hair, plastered tissue to the scrape on my cheek, and brushed something suspicious, maybe moose caca, off these ridiculous camouflage pants. I didn't care about my appearance, a first for me, not counting the Dumpster episode, of course. The other first, almost being attacked by a killer, overshadowed everything. I have my priorities.

"Where's Nick?" I asked deputy Miller as I approached the big desk.

To his credit he didn't comment on my appearance. I suppose he was getting used to it. Last night chocolate mousse, this afternoon forest debris. And I used to be so careful. I didn't like what was happening to me. I had to get back to the old me. The neat me. The fashion-conscious, New York City me.

"What the hell happened? Who did this?" Nick demanded as he strode from his office, his expression stony as he studied my face. "You're bleeding."

He took my arm and led me toward his office. Over his shoulder he ordered, "Miller, earthquakes or murders only."

"Yes, sir."

"I was in the woods by Kendall's," I told him as soon as he closed the door.

"And?" he asked tightly.

"Percy was supposed to meet Marla and I was on hand with my camera."

"Percy did this?"

"No. I was hiding. Then a gnat flew up my nose and I tried to dislodge it and Percy heard me, so I ran. He didn't see who I was. I'm almost sure of that."

"Damnit all, Nora."

He went into a small lavatory and came out with a damp cloth, some Band-Aids and a bottle of hydrogen peroxide. "Sit up here." He patted the edge of his desk. With a gentleness that almost made me cry, he removed the tissue that was stuck to the dried blood. As I sat there inhaling the spicy scent of his aftershave, he wiped my face.

"It's not too bad," he said as he cleansed it. He kissed my forehead. "Anything else?"

I lifted my shirt and he dabbed at the scratches on my midriff.

"Do I have to lock you up to keep you from getting yourself killed?"

"He knows something about the Collins murder," I said.

Nick stood back and stared at me. "And you know this how?"

I recounted Percy's side of the phone conversation.

Nick repeated my words slowly, as if he were weighing every one. "I'm not getting involved in this shit. I've done enough. Look at Collins."

"I think he killed Collins," I said.

"This Marla's into more than sex. I wonder who she is. Don't know anyone by that name around here." He paused, then said, "So Collins was involved in something that got him killed, and now Marla wants Percy involved in the same thing. She's the link between the two."

"You're going to check Percy out, right?"

"It might surprise you to learn I'm already doing that. After all, he was Al's partner."

I nodded my approval.

"Marla's one of the women who sat with Aunt Ellie at the funeral." I told him about Percy's nod to one of the women.

"I'm going to pretend you didn't say that."

"Sure. What do I know? I'm telling you he made contact with

a nod. But don't listen."

He shook his head. "That doesn't prove a thing. He could have been saying hello. Nora, you jump to conclusions."

"Like Aunt Ida?" I asked, a superior edge to my voice.

"There was that carpet-in-the-creek episode," he said, almost to himself.

"What are you talking about?"

"It's why I wasn't so quick to pay attention to your aunt's claim about a coming murder." He paused and gave a deep sigh. "I know it's no excuse, but it is a reason. A while back she called me, hysterical about a body rolled in a carpet that was tossed into the creek. I wasted hours hunting for it. Tied up half my force. Turned out to be a section of carpet old man Gardener was throwing away. The body inside was a rusty pole lamp."

I wanted to defend my aunt, but was hard pressed to think of much. She watched a lot of crime shows.

Finally, I said, "She was being a good citizen. The trouble with the world today is that most people don't want to get involved. They want to look the other way, mind their own business. Aunt Ida isn't like that, to her credit."

"Yes, there is that."

"Getting back to Percy's lady friend . . . Are any of those four women on the library list I retrieved?"

He went through some papers on his desk, and pulled out the library list. "All of them," he said, "except Margaret the librarian, but we know she was at the library."

"See." I hopped down from the desk.

"See what? None are named Marla."

"I know. Maybe it's a sex thing."

"Come again?" he said, his brows lifting a notch.

Nick smiled at me. I loved the way he smiled.

"Maybe it was a name in a story they were acting out. Who knows? They play games. I think it was part of the game."

"Games? You never mentioned games."

"I guess I left that part out." I gave a casual shrug. "Percy wore Gestapo boots, I think. Talked with a German accent. He carried a riding crop. At least I think it was a riding crop. He said that she was very naughty for coming late. His exact words were, 'When I hired you as my maid I warned you not to be late, didn't I?'"

"You remember the exact words?" Grinning, Nick shook his head.

I smirked in reply, then asked, "You ever do stuff like that?"

"No."

I laughed. "Glad to hear it."

He said, "I'm not much for playing games of any kind."

I wasn't about to comment on that. "I'll find out who Marla is," I said with great enthusiasm. "You concentrate on finding the killer."

He looked around the room, a puzzled frown creasing his brow. Slowly, the frown lines eased, and were replaced by an expression of sudden awareness.

"Yes, this is my office. There's my hat, my computer, my jacket, the dead plant my mother gave me." He turned to me. "Ay-uh. My office. I know without looking that the sign on the door says Sheriff, Nicholas Renzo, which is another way of saying Head Honcho, Chief, or Guy In Charge. Take your pick. Now, Ms. Nora Lassiter, which one of those titles don't you understand?"

"I think you missed something."

"Did I?"

"Yes. The subheading that says Mulish: Unwilling to Utilize Skills of Helpful Lady."

"That's because duty compels me to protect the Helpful Lady."

He was right, of course, yet I pressed. "Duty? Is that what motivates you to protect me?"

As soon as the words were out of my big mouth, I wanted to snatch them back. What was wrong with me?

"Let's not go there," he said immediately, gathering his first aid supplies and carrying them back to the lavatory.

"You're right."

Nick Renzo was forbidden territory. That was part of his allure, I suppose. We are all drawn to those things we cannot, or should not, have.

Switching the topic quicker than you could say moose crossing, I said, "I was scared in the woods. Only Percy's clumsiness saved me from whatever might have happened if he'd caught me. So I guess you're right."

"I am."

I heard him close a cabinet door in the lavatory.

"Percy knows who these people are. You going to arrest him?"

"On what charge?" he asked when he reappeared.

"Can't you at least bring him in and ask him about this information?" I nodded at the paper with the names and numbers on it that was tacked to his bulletin board.

"You stole that information. Shall I mention that to him when he asks about it?"

I let out a puff of air. "Your hands are tied?"

"Somewhat. But I can still ask around."

I thought about that. "I'll leave you to the investigation," I said as I headed for the door. "I have a few more things to do before I leave town and I'd better get hopping."

"I'm relieved."

At the door, he lifted my chin with his finger, and gave me a quick kiss on the lips. I was not prepared. As usual. Mmm. He tasted good.

"And honored," he continued, "that you trust me to finish the investigation."

We left his office together and headed for the front door.

A man in a sharp gray suit and red tie entered as we were leaving. He held the door and nodded at us.

"Who's he?" I whispered.

Nick had a puzzled look on his face.

"Jay Neddleson, a high-powered lawyer. I don't know him personally, but I've seen him around the courthouse. I'm surprised he's here for such a small case."

"Case? You mean the guys you arrested last night?" I asked as we walked down the station house steps.

He nodded. "Ay-uh. Drunken disorderly, marijuana possession, resisting arrest."

We stopped at my truck.

"I still haven't taken this for a test run," he said as he went around to the driver's side and hopped in. I got in beside him. He pulled out and drove down the street, putting Ce-Ce to the test. When we arrived back, he said, "Not too bad. But definitely get the radiator fixed, or you'll end up getting stuck with a seized engine block."

"That doesn't sound good."

"It's not."

He started to explain and I put my hand up. "Stop. I don't want to know. I don't care."

He got out, and I moved behind the wheel.

"Thanks for the information, Nora. You've been helpful."

I shouldn't have felt as pleased as I did.

I said, "One more thing. Percy said he's done enough, so that means he's done something already. That something could be that he killed Collins."

Nick placed his hands on the door and leaned toward me.

"You said that before. You want it to be so because you don't want your Uncle JT to be guilty, but JT is a prime suspect, and I can't change that. He ran, Nora. Took off two days after the murder. If Ellie's heard from him since that first call, she hasn't told me. She could be lying to protect him."

I knew we only had her word about his phone call and his reason for leaving.

"Do you know something else about JT that I don't?" I asked.

Nick hesitated, and I knew there was something .

"What? Tell me. I'm a battered and bleeding woman."

"Battered by a gnat? And you're not bleeding any more."

"Nick."

He sighed. "JT and Al Collins had a disagreement a while back, maybe a year or so ago. JT gave Al a black eye."

"Doesn't mean he killed him."

"Correct. But it goes to bad blood between them."

"Still, I think it's Percy. Marla may be involved, too. I think she's one of the three I mentioned. You have anyone else in mind?"

"I'm checking out the salesmen from the lot and two other guys who work at JT's auto repair place. So far, nothing."

"How do you find this killer?" I asked, discouragement evident in my voice. "What do you do?"

"I think motive first. What could be gained by his death? Money is usually the key. Money from insurance. Business. Crime. Maybe he didn't pay a gambling debt, or perhaps he knew something someone wanted kept quiet. Could be a lot of things. The sooner we find out what it was, the sooner we can find the killer."

"What does Percy stand to gain? Or Collins' wife?"

"Percy gains the business, and Collins' wife gets a share. It's a possibility, but I don't think that's it."

"Percy said Collins was into something."

Nick looked at me. "And that's the key. I have to find out what that something was."

"So you have to trace his contacts. Maybe they're on the sheet I gave you. Marla's part of it. She has to be. And maybe it's going down on the twentieth."

"I've run those two names, Michelle Gray and Phil Clinton, through the database and nothing much has come up. They're probably aliases.

On Saturday morning I got up to the scent of good things

wafting from the kitchen. Ida was preparing one her specialties, shrimp creole, with the secret family recipe sauce.

"We having this tonight?" I asked, getting a spoon so I could take a taste.

"No, it's for the bean-hole supper we'll be having during Silver Stream Days. I'll freeze it up. I like to have everything ready ahead of time so I don't have to rush."

"I remember Silver Stream days. Sort of. And if I didn't remember, all the signs around town would clue me in. I vaguely recall the bean hole, but no details."

"They dig a huge hole," Ida said, "and bake the beans in it for hours. Oh, they're wicked good. We all bring a covered dish to the celebration. I'm going to bring two."

CSI Miami was playing on the kitchen television as I dipped into the sauce. "Mmm. Delicious. The second dish is supposed to be my contribution?"

Nodding, she smiled. "Just in case you're still here. Wouldn't want you to go empty-handed. I'll give you the recipe so you can tell folks what's in it."

"I can cook a few things. Tacos, hard boiled eggs, burgers." I took another mouthful of sauce. "I'm not very good at soft boiled eggs. I also do a mean tuna casserole with potato chips."

Ida made a face. "Few is right. I can help, you know. Wouldn't want to push, of course. Hannah's the pushy one in the family. Not me." She paused and looked at me. "You and Nick get in late last night?"

"Sort of."

"Have a good time?"

"Very good."

I knew she wanted details. I put some wheat bread in the toaster and poured a cup of coffee, holding off. I was used to keeping my private life to myself.

"Humph."

Ida stirred with renewed vigor.

Again, "Humph."

"All right." I smiled, relenting. "I had a good time with him. Nick's a nice guy and if I were staying . . . well, I'm not. Besides, I'm not ready for another relationship.

"The food was excellent, but we never did finish," I went on. "Nick got into a scuffle, and arrested two guys for drunken-disorderly in the restaurant. Turns out they were having a little marijuana with their wine."

"Oh, that marijuana's been a problem in these parts for a long time. I thought that was a thing of the past. Haven't heard much about it lately."

"Really? Folks around here are big on marijuana?"

"Used to be that more adults in Maine used marijuana than in any other state, not a statistic to be proud of. Don't know if that's still true. Used to grow the stuff in the woods because it was hard to detect from the air. Grow it under-ground, too."

"That must be some feat."

Ida stirred shrimp into her pot. "Nick didn't get hurt, did he?"

I pulled my thoughts away from underground marijuana farms. "No, he wasn't hurt." I studied her expression. "I think you like him. The first time you mentioned him, you called him a nitwit."

"Did I? I don't recall." She added a dash of cayenne pepper to the pot, and stirred. "Must be my age. I forget a lot."

"Oh, really? I think not." I gave her a side hug. "You interested in details?"

"It's not nice to tease an old lady."

I smiled. "I got involved in the fight. On the side of law and order."

"Oh, my word. Tell me about it." She put the spoon in the ceramic spoon rest and gave me her full attention.

"I threw some spaghetti at one of the bad guys. Chocolate mousse, too."

Her hand went to her heart. "Oh, I'm so proud of you." She stopped the *CSI Miami* episode. "What else? What happened next?"

I gave her a blow by blow, leaving out only the kiss at the end of the evening.

"Hannah will love this," she said when I finished. "Now tell me what's new in the murder investigation."

I gave her a few details.

After breakfast, I headed for the Auto Mart. The problems Nick had mentioned with Ce-Ce required attention. Snooping was not my number one priority. If I happened to learn something worthwhile, all well and good. I didn't have Head Honcho written on my door.

I was almost positive Percy hadn't seen me yesterday. Not only had I not turned to face him, but the light wasn't good because of the dark clouds and trees. When I pulled into the Auto Mart, Percy was standing next to a red Honda Civic talking to a woman. I hesitated a nanosecond, then drove right up to them and the woman turned.

Margaret the librarian.

TWENTY-ONE

I hid my surprise, and lowered the window.

"Hello, Margaret. Percy. You buying a new car, Margaret? That Lexus over there looks like a fine one." Expensive. Unless one is a special friend of the boss, on intimate terms, so to speak, and will get a big discount?

Dressed in her working clothes, a brown A-line skirt, white blouse, gold jacket and sensible brown oxfords, Margaret smiled, at least as much as her tightly bunned hair allowed.

Could Margaret be Marla? Mar and Mar. Both names started the same way. Coincidence?

"I'm thinking about one, but just looking around at the moment," Margaret said, not a shred of warmth in her voice.

Percy's phone conversation with the mystery woman ran through my head at warp speed, and I wondered what she wanted him to do that he didn't want to do. Was that the reason Margaret was here? Was she Marla, here to pressure him? Mary Fran's rival might have a dual motive. Sex might be the bonus as well as the motivating factor.

I studied Percy a moment. How could any woman be attracted to him? What woman would want to play sex games with him? No accounting for taste.

Percy wasn't exactly fat, but he probably would be in a few years. Heavyset applied now. He had a crew-cut. But the crew was bailing out. Not on his legs though. I'd seen the mat of fur on those gorillas.

I knew from the book she had been reading that Margaret was into erotica. It was possible that behind her conservative clothing lurked an accomplished slut who broke free whenever the spirit or the opportunity prompted her. In which case, any man who could satisfy her might do. Was Margaret a closet *Lascivious Lucinda*, hiding behind boring clothing and the name Marla? Maybe it was a name in a book she'd read? One they both read?

I didn't know.

I got out of my truck. Prolonging the official reason for my visit might make them suspicious. "Percy, I've got a small problem with the truck."

I told him about the leaky radiator and the bald tires, looking him in the eye the whole time, hoping to pick up some hint about yesterday in his expression. Nothing. He had not seen me, I was sure.

Margaret listened without moving. What a woman. Such control. I wondered what her high, squeaky voice sounded like. The Marla voice? No way to find out at the moment.

"I don't take care of repairs. That was Al's bailiwick," Percy said, trying for a mournful look, but failing. Or, was that just me being too hard on the guy? "I'll have to hire someone else. In the meantime, you'll have to wait. Go talk to Pete. He'll put you on the list."

I nodded, my expression appropriately somber. "I understand. I'll make an appointment."

I got back in my truck. "So long, Mar. See you in the library." I nodded to Percy, aware of Margaret in my peripheral vision, watching for a reaction to the Mar. No reaction. Mar was a cool lady. I wondered how cool she was when she read her books.

I looped around to the main building, parked in back, out of sight of Percy, why, I'm not sure, but it seemed like a good idea, and went inside.

Pete, the young guy who sold me the truck, came over, a wary look in his face. "Hi there. Everything all right?"

"Almost. Small radiator problem." I figured he might have known that when he sold it to me.

"Oh. I could check that out for you."

We walked to the car, and he lifted the hood.

"Ay-uh. Radiator leak. Small one. A little sealer will hold it, if you don't do too much driving. You need a new radiator. I'll see that it's ordered."

"I'm so glad. I thought I might have to wait because Collins was in charge of repairs."

Without commenting, he removed the radiator cap. "I'll put the sealer in for you."

I tried again. "I guess Collins will be hard to replace."

Still nothing from him. I decided to try a lie.

"I met his wife at the funeral. Poor woman. But she seemed to be handling it well."

He made an odd sound. I pretended he'd said something I hadn't heard and moved closer. "Excuse me?"

"Nothing."

Typical man-answer. A grunt.

I tried a different tack. "Must be nice working here. Lots of benefits. Bet you get a car for personal use."

He pulled his head from beneath the hood. "Yeah. I drive that Ford Expedition over there," he said, pointing to a black SUV. It's one of the perks."

"What a car." I gave him my best, most admiring smile. "You must have a great boss to let you drive that."

"Al Collins set me up with that baby."

"Oh? I thought Mr. Kendall was the big boss."

"He is."

I said, "Maybe Mrs. Collins will want to get involved in the business. You know, to replace her husband."

He shook his head as he wiped his hands on a rag. "Hope not."

"Don't want a woman boss, hunh?"

"Not that one."

"Why not?"

"She's got a cash register for a heart. If it weren't for her driving him . . ." He shook his head and tossed the rag aside.

"Water under the bridge. You need anything else?"

"Driving him? To do what?"

Pete busied himself with the empty sealer container.

"Aren't you related to JT Lassiter?" he asked, sidestepping my question.

"He's my father's brother."

"We work with his company. Maybe you could get the radiator sooner if you talked to him."

"I'll try that. Have you seen him lately?"

He shook his head. "Can't say as I have."

Disappointed, I got into my truck, and called Nick on his cell. No answer. I decided not to call him at the station. I was making contact with him way too much. Getting close when I should be pulling back.

I had a big problem, a serious problem that required action right now. It had gone on long enough. My fault.

I had nothing to wear.

I sat in Ida's driveway mulling over the situation. I couldn't keep rifling closets and borrowing Salvation Army-style clothing worn by my relatives a generation or more ago. Old furniture might have value as antiques, but old clothes were fodder for the ragbag. Ida'd never thrown them out because she was a saver. Not that I was complaining. In a few instances, her collection saved me. But I'm not, by nature, a ragbag kind of woman. I need decent clothes, even if they are only woods walking clothes.

God, I'd looked a sight yesterday in that army fatigue shirt. The memory made me shiver. The dark olive color with the blotchy brown spots was all wrong. The shirt fit like a tent, and the material . . . well, what can I say? It was a little softer than plywood and smelled stale enough to attract gnats.

A few years back I'd had my colors done. Some discerning fashion consultant told me I was a summer, which meant I looked best in warm colors, especially near my face, muted pinks, mauves, yellows, off-whites, certain greens and blues. I carry color swatches in my purse—the Girl Scouts 'Be Prepared' motto applies to lots of things—and I haven't deviated from my palate since. I'm partial to certain blues that match the color of my eyes, my Viola blues as Agnes calls them. I wear a lot of off-whites and light blues next to my face, too.

Today I wore a light blue Jones of NY tee shirt with khaki slacks and a stylish pair of tan sling-back sandals. I felt normal. But soon I'd have to return to the damn woods to get the damn photos, and the damn buried treasure box.

Damn.

The bottom line was I needed clothes, even if I was going back to New York shortly.

Resigned to my fate, I went inside. Ida was knitting, and watching one of her DVDs, *Homicide: Life on the Street*, a show I'd never seen before.

I took a deep breath. For courage. For strength.

"Ida," I said, my voice trembling, "where's the L.L. Bean catalogue?"

On Sunday I went to see Vivian the Pomeranian Lady. I hadn't planned to see her, but since there was a slight, very slight, possibility that she might be Marla, I figured a short visit couldn't hurt. It wasn't like I was interfering in the murder investigation or anything.

I called to tell her I was coming.

As I drove, I wondered if anything had happened yesterday. Although he never said much about it, I knew Nick was alert because of Percy's list. Something was going down on the twentieth. We both knew it. Maybe Nick suspected something specific. If so, he was unwilling to share. And if that were so and I found out, well, I wouldn't share with him again either.

Petty of me, I decided, as I drove past the sheriff's office.

Once outside of town, the road narrowed and trees were the

main scenery. Trees and some fast-churning brooks. It was a gorgeous day, pure sunny September with a blue sky above and a light breeze ruffling the leaves.

Maybe I was naive, but I figured if I could find Marla babe, everything would fall into place.

Percy's words to Marla played in my head again, like a mantra.

I'm not getting involved in this shit . . . I've done enough . . . look at Collins.

What shit? Something to do with the car business? That would make sense since Collins and Percy were familiar with that. They knew the ins and outs, how to scam, how to cheat.

Was JT involved in that, too? Scamming people? Ripping them off. Could they all be ripping off companies. Let's see. Companies. Insurance companies? Suppliers? Who else was involved with them on a business level? I'd have to find out.

And Collins? Had Percy been forced to kill him for some reason? Maybe to shut him up?

Then I had a mental flash that almost caused me to crash into a tree. Marla might work for one of the companies associated with the Auto Mart. I hadn't considered that. Maybe someone should be checking those women out, too. She could be their connection to inside information. I straightened Chevy Charlene and concentrated on the road.

But it still came down to one woman, and she went by the name of Marla, at least on one occasion. I decided to concentrate on the women Percy had nodded at. Three possibilities in Silver Stream: Margaret the librarian, Vivian the Pomeranian lady and Amy the waitress. Not Aunt Ellie. Couldn't be her.

TWENTY-TWO

Vivian lived in a wooded section at the outskirts of Silver Stream. A U2 CD blared from my speakers as I cruised the winding road toward her house. I had a Silver Stream town map on the seat beside me. No sense getting lost any more.

Windows open to the beautiful day, I sang along. It's amazing how when I sing by myself, I hardly ever miss a note. I should record myself at times like these.

As I pulled to a stop in the driveway, I heard a screechy racket that rivaled the sound of pneumatic drills skidding across chalkboard. My God. Several little furry dogs, curly tails bobbing, yapped at me. With an early-warning system like that, it was no surprise that Vivian opened her front door before I turned off the engine.

So these were the Pomeranians. The name was bigger than the dog.

"Sugar Bottom. Button Nose. You quiet down." Vivian yelled.

Sugar Bottom and Button Nose were obviously obedience school dropouts. They did not quiet down on command.

Vivian's blond streaked hair looked better than the last time I had seen it in the holey cap. She was a stocky woman, in her late forties, dressed in jeans and a dark green tee shirt that proclaimed her a Pom Mom. I had an awful thought about that. Weren't female dogs called bitches? Vivian must know that. Yet she still wore the shirt. People were a puzzle sometimes.

Enough. The question was, Could she also be Marla?

"Muffy. Coco Puff. Lovey Poo. Quiet. Into your pen." To me she called, "I'm so glad you came. I really want to nail that Buster

Verney. Throw his sorry ass in the slammer."

She signaled me out of the truck. All the dogs weren't in the pen yet. Two bounced and barked, probably communicating with each other: attack, attack, attack. These little pups had teeth, didn't they? Needle teeth, like piranhas. I remembered a movie I saw once where piranhas got loose in a river and chewed up a bunch of kids swimming at a summer camp and left arms, legs and other body parts floating all over the place. A bloody mess. Gave me nightmares for weeks.

Finally, Vivian locked her piranhas in the pen and invited me in for coffee.

"I'm trying to socialize them," she informed me, leading the way into a kitchen that hadn't been updated since Nixon, or maybe Kennedy, was president. "Pomeranians need extensive exposure to people. They're naturally cautious dogs and we don't want that natural caution to evolve into suspiciousness, do we?"

"No, of course not." To my credit, this came out as sincere.

"They get along fine with the cats now."

Cats? She had cats, too?

Vivian dusted animal hairs off the gray Formica-topped kitchen table with a dirty rag. In the rays of light beaming though the window, I watched them float back to earth and resettle. I sneezed. At least this time I wasn't trapped under a bed with a cat.

"So Vivian, who's this Buster Verney you mentioned and why do you think he poisoned your dog?"

She jerked her head toward the window with the ruffled café curtain. "Lives just down the road. I've known him for years. We don't get along. His wife died a little over a year ago and since then he's worse than ever. Thinks he can go around killing my poms and get away with it. I'm a new dog owner. Got these poms last winter because I wanted to fill the house with life again. The two cats weren't enough. My Jake's been dead going on two years now and we never could have kids."

"Sorry for your loss." I paused. "How did the dogs annoy Verney?"

"Once in a while one of the dogs runs off. Dora was a runner."

Vivian swallowed hard and despite my feelings about Dora's friends, I felt empathy for her. All loss is hard on those who survive.

"Dora would race down to the road and bark at cars. One day she raced after Buster's truck and he swerved and hit a tree."

I sneezed twice in a row and Vivian handed me a tissue. I wondered whether it had dog or cat hair on it but didn't bother with a thorough inspection. Throwing caution to the winds, I blew my nose. At least there weren't any gnats around. A thought about fleas flashed through my head, but I pushed it aside.

"He could have hit the dog," I pointed out, bunching the tissue. "But he cared enough to swerve."

"He threatened to kill them all." she said, her voice going up an octave. "Came right to my door. 'Good-for-nothing mutts.' he said to me. 'Someone should do the world a favor and wipe out the entire breed.'"

The change in voice had me picturing Vivian as Marla, moaning in ecstasy, saying, *Oh, Percy* in that phony, high-pitched, squeaky voice. *There's no one like you. No one, my love.*

Were the voices the same? Hard to tell.

I tried to think of something else to get her riled so I could hear it again. Like a replay.

"Verney had just had an accident," I said. "Maybe he loved his car or truck or whatever." I paused, then decided to go for it. "Did you apologize for your dog causing him an accident?"

"What? I should apologize to that creep? That dog killer. If that's what you think, maybe I don't want you looking into this."

Well, her voice went up all right, even squeaked, but it lacked the Marla quality I remembered. Of course, the circumstances were different. One has to make allowances.

I could have pointed out that Verney hadn't killed the dog at that point, if, in fact, he did kill the dog, but I could see no point and tried to calm her enough to keep me on the case.

"Vivian, I know that seemed harsh, but I have to say these things if I'm to get all the facts."

"Well," she said, sounding mollified.

"Sometimes people say things when they're angry, make threats they don't really mean. My mother's a prime example. She used to say, 'I could kill you, Nora.' She never meant it, of course because here I am."

Vivian put an instant coffee bag into a cup of water and set it in the microwave without commenting, but I could see she was calming down. She moved a pile of newspapers from a chair and sat on the cracked, yellow vinyl cushion opposite me.

"I suppose I can understand that."

"Good. What did the sheriff say when you told him about this?"

"Renzo sent that deputy of his, the skinny one, to investigate. That guy couldn't find his di—"

"Trimble?" I interrupted.

"Right. He said unless I had concrete proof, he couldn't do a thing. Is there a way you could prove Buster's guilty?"

I was in over my head. I had no idea how to prove who killed her dog. I tried to think of similar episodes on *Murder, She Wrote* or *CSI Miami* or *NCIS*, but nothing came. I'd have to watch more of Ida's DVDs.

Finally, I asked, "Why didn't you get along with Buster?"

Vivian placed a cup of steaming coffee in front of me. An animal hair floated on the top.

"It's a long story," she said.

As she set the microwave timer for her tea water, I fished the hair from my cup. Hot, hot, hot. I burned my finger. I breathed in sharply through clenched teeth, consoling myself with the thought that all major germs must have been annihilated.

"Tell me about it," I said, blowing on my seared finger.

I sneezed again.

"The man's fifty-five going on fifteen. He drives a Chevy Camaro, for heaven sakes, one of them sporty cars. Besides, I think he's into a few things, if you know what I mean."

I didn't know. "Things?"

Vivian shrugged. "Smoking. But I don't care about that. I'm just interested in the big stuff, like murdering my Dora."

"Smoking? You mean pot?"

"What else?" The microwave dinged and she removed her tea water. "This is a small town. You hear things. He gets together with his little group."

"Do you think he was smoking when he hit the tree?"

"Don't think so, but I don't know."

"I'll go see Verney later."

I added milk to my coffee. Tiny white chunks curdled on the surface.

"Drink up," Vivian said as she grabbed a bag from the shelf. "Have a cookie with it."

Gingersnaps. I didn't like gingersnaps. To me, they fell into the same category as raisin cookies. They're a why-bother kind of cookie. To be polite I took one and forced myself to nibble. That way I didn't have to drink the coffee with the hair and the sour milk chunks.

Back to probing. Gently.

"Vivian, do you get into town much?"

"Once a week, sometimes more."

"That's good. It must be lonely living out here."

"Sometimes. But I've got my dogs and cats for company. And friends. And I go to dog shows now, too."

"You must miss your husband. I know I still miss my father, and he died over three years ago."

She nodded and set her tea on the table. "Sure, I miss him, but that's life. Maybe one of these days I'll meet someone else, get married again."

Meet someone else. The magic words. Had she met Percy?

"Not too many places to meet someone around here, Vivian, but I guess there are a few."

"Umm. Gotta go where the men are. That's what my friend

Margaret always says."

"The librarian?" I asked just to be sure we were talking about the same woman. Ms. Erotica.

"Yes. You've met her?"

"I have," I said. "You must read a lot. Go to the library a lot?"

"That's for sure. Too much."

I couldn't help the flurry of excitement that set my heart racing. I wondered if Aunt Ida had heard Vivian's voice in the library. She'd made the Returns' List. I might actually be talking to a murderer. Or the accomplice.

"Meet any nice men yet?" I asked, going for the direct approach.

She looked at me strangely, her mouth slightly open. What did I expect her to say? Oh, yes, I know Percy Kendall very well. Had wild sex with him just last week.

Nora, Nora.

Vivian just shook her head.

I'm not good at this detective business. I should turn in my badge. If I owned a badge, I might turn it in.

"Well, Vivian, I'll look into this for you."

"What's your fee?" she asked, picking up her checkbook.

"You can pay me after I've uncovered some information for you."

"Mary Fran said I should give you a retainer." She wrote a figure on the check and handed it to me. "Please take it. I insist."

"Thank you," I said, glancing at the generous check. "But it's really not necessary."

She handed me a few doggie treats. "Here, give them a bite to eat. It'll help your relationship with them."

I did not want a relationship with her Pomeranians, but I tossed the treats in Sugar Bottom's direction as a diversion. It worked and I made a quick get-away.

I drove to Buster's house and knocked on the door. No one

answered. A truck was parked in the driveway, so I knocked a few more times. If Buster had poisoned Dora, I wanted to nab him. Although I had no great affection for animals due to my body's adverse reaction to most of them, I would never harm one, and I detested anyone who would sink so low.

Vivian loved her Poms. I understood love. And loss.

I left without seeing Buster Verney.

But I thought I saw a curtain flutter as I was leaving.

TWENTY-THREE

With a sinking feeling, I laid out my recently delivered L.L. Bean order on the bed Monday morning, wondering whether I'd lost some part of myself by doing this. A six-pack of white socks, two pairs of jeans, a blue sweatshirt, a natural Irish fisherman crewneck sweater, a second red-patterned sweater, several plain blouses, and—a mental drum roll here—Gore-Tex waterproof hiking boots with soles thick enough to walk through fire, protect from snake bites, and grip the snow like tires with chains.

There was also a Swiss Army knife. Can't say what compelled me to add this to my purchases. I needed a weapon? A tool? I was letting Maine things go to my head?

All of the above.

I hefted it in my hand. Well, I could use this. It had a can opener and I ate lots of canned stuff. I opened all the little sections. How useful was this. Everyone should have a Swiss Army knife, a nice red one like I had. Besides the can opener, there was a bottle opener, screwdrivers, a saw, a key ring, tweezers and a toothpick. I wondered about the tiny saw. I closed the sections, then flipped them open again. Amazing. Maybe for Christmas I'd buy my friends a knife like this. But not shiny apple-red like mine. I'd get them New York black.

I set the knife on the dresser where I could look at it, and selected a pair of stonewashed jeans and a dark denim blouse. They were comfortable clothes. I had to admit that. The jeans fit well. I put on the socks. With a grimace, I pulled on the Gore-Tex hikers. I'd selected the light gray, a good choice, I thought. Everyone else probably chose the darker charcoal so they wouldn't show the dirt. I would keep mine clean. I turned them this way and that. How different from my great-grandfather's dumpy boots. I walked around.

"Testing, one-two-three-four."

Not bad. Comfortable. They wouldn't aggravate the blister on my heel caused by the clodhopper boots. I was good to go. I picked up my knife. If I wanted, I could hook it onto the belt loop at my waist. For now, I slipped it into my pocket. Later, I'd try it hooked to my loop, something to look forward to.

I found Aunt Ida reading a mystery in the front room. Ignoring the tantalizing aroma of freshly baked bread wafting from the kitchen, I asked, "Did you ever notice that Grandma Evie spent time in the woods?"

She put her book down. "My-oh-my!" Her eyes lit. "Don't you look the one today. I like the boots. And the jeans. And the blouse."

I looked like I was on my way to a hoedown or something, but I acknowledged her praise with a simple, "Thank you." Then, "About Grandma Evie?"

Ida wrinkled her forehead. "I wouldn't say she spent a lot of time in the woods. 'Course, every now and again she'd go berry picking and would be gone a while. It always seemed she should have found more berries considering how long she was at it. In her last year, of course, she didn't go at all."

I sat on the hassock in front of Ida.

"She buried a box. I didn't tell you about it before because I thought she wanted me to keep it secret, but I've decided there've been enough secrets in this family."

I handed her the letter and the map. "Here, read this."

I wandered out to the kitchen to investigate the aroma. Bless this woman. She'd made fresh berry scones. I took one, added a bit of raspberry jelly she'd set out, poured a cup of coffee into a violet-flowered, bone china mug, and carried my treasure to the front room.

Ida looked up. "I don't suppose you found the box?" she asked, surprising me by not commenting on the sexual harassment business. That was the important part of the letter. I shouldn't be surprised. Why was I surprised? What was wrong with me that I couldn't understand her reluctance to discuss sex, or the problems that made my father run to a place where no one knew him and he could get lost in a crowd?

I shook my head. "No. I tried to find the box. No luck. I'm going to get Nick to help me today."

I took another nibble of the scone, and closed my eyes in pure ecstasy.

"No need. I know trees as well as Evie did."

Oh, no.

My mouth full of scone, I rasped, "Yes, but—"

"This should stay in the family."

I swallowed quickly. "You can't go tramping through the woods, Ida. I don't want that."

"Sure I can. I still walk in the woods."

"Not a good idea. The box could be a distance from the house."

Fortunately, she stopped arguing and accepted. "Family," was all she said as she reached for the phone. "You need family."

"Okay. I guess I could do that instead of having Nick."

I wasn't sure who she intended to call. One of the cousins? Uncles? Resigned to having a relative accompany me, I sighed, more for dramatic effect than anything else, and went back to the kitchen for another scone. Maybe I'd try the blueberry jam with this one.

"Who's coming?" I asked when I saw her going up the stairs a little later.

"Hannah and Agnes. This will be great fun. They weren't doing anything today either."

"Ida," I said as she bustled up the stairs. "I thought you were calling one of the uncles. I am definitely not going to traipse into the woods with you, Agnes and Hannah. Absolutely not. Someone will fall and break their neck."

She waved her hand, dismissing my concern.

"Nonsense. We'll manage just fine." She disappeared at the top of the stairs.

"Agnes has trouble getting out of a car," I called up.

"Luckily, we won't be using a car," Ida called back.

Half an hour later Hannah and Agnes drove up in the big teal GTO. Ida had the front screen door open before they knocked.

"We have our work cut out for us today. I hope you're both up to it. Nora's concerned we won't be able to manage the woods."

"Pshaw." Hannah said, showing me her work gloves. "We may be slow, but we're fit. Let's get on with this before it's time for my nap. Or Agnes's potty visit." Chuckling, she winked at Ida.

Cute. Very cute. I was crazy to go out with this trio. I should have my head examined.

Agnes bagged two scones on the way to the back door. Her jeans, which were probably size super-jumbo, stretched tightly across her lumpy rear end. I followed the trio at a snail's pace, out the back door, map in hand.

"I thought we could all use a bit of adventure," Ida remarked as I handed the map to Hannah and opened the shed door. "There's a mystery here and we shall solve it."

"Do you think we should bring a thermos?" Agnes asked. "We didn't bring a thermos, you know."

"A shovel would be better," I suggested as I passed one out. Not that I expected the aunts to dig. I would handle that.

Hannah studied the map. "Trust Evie to make a treasure map. That woman loved pirate stories."

"Doesn't our Nora look wonderful today?" Ida asked as we inched through the high grass toward the stream. It was ten-fifteen in the morning. The box was probably a few hundred yards from the house. If we made it back before dark, I'd consider myself lucky. Agnes had the right idea bringing rations. I should have considered a picnic lunch, at the very least.

"I did notice," Hannah remarked. "Lovely. Not that she

doesn't look lovely in her city togs, but . . . Oh, down this way." She pointed toward the stream. "There's the red pine. We cross here and go past the grove of white pine."

Fortunately, the stream was barely a trickle at this point, and there were big flat stepping stones. We crossed easily. Agnes made me nervous, but she waddled across without mishap. Slowly. Very slowly.

"Maine is the Pine Tree State because of the abundance of these white pines," Hannah informed me.

"Interesting," I said, not interested at all.

We moseyed along at a tortoise pace for about half an hour.

"Sunlight ahead," Hannah called over her shoulder. "That's probably where the quaking aspens are. "Oh, yes. Here we go. North for a bit."

"I hope we're almost there," Agnes boomed. "I'm ready for a break."

"Don't complain," Ida admonished. "You wanted to come."

"I do not want gum. It sticks to my false teeth," Agnes said loudly.

"*Come*, not gum," Ida clarified.

"Come where?" Agnes asked.

"West at the poplar tree," Hannah directed in an officious voice. "Step lively everyone."

Lively, I had come to understand, was one notch above pause.

Ida fell back and walked next to me. Smiling, she said, "Hannah always has to be in charge. It's her way. Her Henry used to call her Queen of the World."

"Good title. It fits."

We moved onto a narrow path and hiked along single file.

"What are we looking for next?" Agnes asked as we approached the aspens.

"Should be a hawthorn a short ways northwest of the aspen grove. That's our final destination."

There was a trace of fall in the air today, no mistaking it. It was past the middle of September, still summer in New York.

Here, the air was brisk, pure, with a hint of things to come. I breathed deeply. No exhaust fumes. No city buses. No loud noises. No pollution. Some of the leaves were touched with gold and bits of red. In another week, this area would be spectacular. Too bad I'd miss it. I'd do more photography and take the beauty home.

When we reached the hawthorn, Agnes, breathing heavily, plopped down on the trunk of a fallen tree. I paced off ten steps from the hawthorn in the direction Hannah indicated, and found the spot beneath the leaves where some rocks had been arranged in a circle. I began to dig. Hannah pulled on her gloves and offered to dig.

"I'll start. You can dig once I loosen this up," I told her.

She joined Agnes and Ida on the downed tree trunk, and watched the show. I was glad I had heavy boots on. It made shoveling easier.

In short order the shovel connected with the metal box. It wasn't buried too deeply. Grandma Evie didn't want to spend much time digging, I guess. Smart woman. When I pulled the box out, Hannah and Ida eased off the tree trunk and came over. Agnes remained behind.

I pried the cover off with my L.L. Bean Swiss Army knife.

Opposite me, the aunts waited as I opened the box. There were two envelopes inside. I opened the top one.

"Hey." Agnes called from the tree trunk. "What is it?"

"Money," Ida yelled, staring at the bills in my hand. "And a paper."

"It names my father, then Mom, then Howie and finally me, as co-owners of this money," I said.

Astounded, I stared at the money in my hand. How had Grandma Evie managed this?

"I'm stuck," Agnes called, breaking into my thoughts. "I can't get off this tree trunk."

We walked back and I helped Agnes up.

I decided not to open the sealed envelope right away. I had a strong feeling it contained something important, more important than the money or even the land.

Back at the house, I set the box on the kitchen table and we all read the short note again.

"Thought her savings account was low," Ida commented. "This is where the money went. I wondered about that."

"I was surprised in the lawyer's office when there wasn't more inheritance money," Hannah said. "Now we know why."

These women amazed me. "Why didn't you say something then?"

Rubbing her butt, Agnes shrugged. "No need."

Ida and Hannah looked at me blankly and Hannah said, "It was Evie's business," in a tone that implied I should have known that.

How easily they accepted this. No rancor, no anger. These three Lassiters were not a greedy group, that was for sure. Maybe it had something to do with their age. Maybe not. But I did wonder about JT.

Then I opened the second envelope and took out an old yellowed newspaper clipping encased in Saran Wrap.

"What on earth?"

I held the clipping gently in my palms. The front page headline jumped off the page and slammed into my chest.

Percy Kendall Murdered.

The breath snagged in my throat. Why had Great-grandma Evie included this? Please, God, it wasn't what I thought. I had to force myself to drag air into my lungs. Inhale. Exhale. Inhale. Exhale.

The article was dated twenty years ago.

Hit in the head with a baseball bat . . .

My hands began to shake. Did this relate to my father? I knew it did. Knew it without reading another word. Knew it as sure as I knew I was standing here.

I looked to the aunts and they looked away, even Hannah, stalwart Hannah, couldn't look me in the eye. I raced through the story, glancing at details, looking for a name. There, near the end of the article I found it:

Thomas Lassiter, who'd had a fight with Kendall that was witnessed by several employees at Kendall's Auto Mart two days prior to the murder, was brought in for questioning, but released when his alibi checked out.

Dad had been a suspect.

"You knew this and you didn't tell me? How could you?"

"Nora, honey," Hannah began. "We knew. Yes. I didn't think it would help you, help anyone, to rehash this. It's over. No amount of talking about it will undo what's been done. Your father is at peace now. Let it stay that way."

I had one more question to ask them all and I dreaded asking, because I dreaded hearing the answer. I prayed it wasn't as bad as I thought it was. But Great-grandmother Evie had included this clipping for a reason and it had something to do with the money. She was giving me, actually she had wanted my father to have, eight thousand dollars. She was paying for more than money lost when dad sold his home and business and fled Maine.

This was guilt money.

The reason went beyond her feelings about the sexual harassment incident. She was paying for a bigger mistake.

I thought I understood.

TWENTY-FOUR

My father didn't leave because his family didn't back him up when he wanted to press sexual harassment charges. He might have been pissed, as he used to say, but that wouldn't have made him pull up stakes and haul his own family to New York.

I closed my eyes briefly, then finally asked what I needed to ask.

"Did you all think he was guilty of killing Percy Kendall?"

Ida started to cry. I wanted to run to her and take her in my arms. Agnes sniffed. I loved both of them and wanted my arms around them, but I couldn't make myself budge. This revelation had the quality of a physical blow.

Hannah said, her voice low, cracking with emotion, "I am ashamed to say that we didn't think he was innocent. There was such anger in him back then. Anger at Percy. At us, too, for not immediately believing him.

"Maybe we should have lied and told him we thought he was innocent, but that night when he came to the family, I'm sad to say we let him know how we felt."

Anger flaring, I fought back. "How could you? You knew him. Knew what kind of a person he was." My throat clogged. My eyes filled with tears. "He was a good man, the most ethical man I ever knew. Not perfect, but moral. Honorable. He never would have done such a thing. If I know that, why didn't you?"

Her face a mask of sorrow, Hannah's hands went to her cheeks. Ida wept quietly, her arm around Agnes.

Agnes said. "He hated Kendall. He'd punched him a few days before. And he had no alibi for the time of the murder."

"No alibi? It says here he was released because he had an alibi."

Hannah said quietly, "I supplied it. Without an alibi he would have been arrested for sure, then tried and possibly convicted. He told us he was out walking by the lake, looking at the stars. I offered to supply an alibi. He was angry that we didn't believe him. He wanted to tell the truth, but we convinced him that would have been suicide. I'd lie. Tell the sheriff he was visiting me. He reluctantly agreed because the alternative was jail, a trial, a lawyer. He had his wife and children to consider. So, I told the sheriff he was with me.

"What we really thought was that there might be extenuating circumstances, things none of us understood that made him do what he did. All he could see was that we thought he might have murdered a man. He couldn't take that. Your father never could abide disloyalty."

But he accepted the fraudulent alibi, I thought, swiping at the tears that wet my cheeks.

I was still upset when I spoke to Howie that evening.

"You're telling me they all thought he murdered someone? Bashed some guy with a baseball bat?" Howie asked when I finished telling him what I'd found out.

"They thought he might have," I corrected. "Of course, they weren't sure."

"And now?"

"I don't know, Howie. I get the feeling they still don't believe in his innocence one-hundred percent. I couldn't bring myself to ask."

After a long pause, he said, "You don't think that he did it, do you?"

"Wash your mouth out with soap. He would never do that and you know it," I said. "A baseball bat? Give me a break. The person who did that was a lowlife. Cruel, savage."

"You're right," Howie agreed. "Unless Dad was a different person back then, and I don't think he was, he sure doesn't fit the profile."

"Exactly," I said.

"It seems to me that the person who gained the most in all this was Uncle JT. He got our house and land for a lot less than it was worth."

"You're not suggesting he killed Percy, senior, are you?"

"No. But it's strange that he disappeared after that guy Collins was murdered. If I were the cop on that case, JT'd be at the top of my suspect list. He's involved."

"You have that jumping-to-conclusions gene, Howie."

"You're playing detective, trying to prove JT is innocent, aren't you, Nora?"

"Not exactly."

"Stay out of it. Leave it to the professionals."

"Oh, right. They do such a stellar job. Like catch the guy who murdered old Percy a couple of decades ago."

"What makes you think it was a guy?"

What indeed?

"I don't know. Too vicious for a woman?"

"Not if she were protecting herself and a bat was all she had handy."

Food for thought. See, that's why it's good to run this stuff by Howie. He comes up with these angles I never consider. "Never thought of that," I said.

"What are you going to do with the money and the property?" Howie asked.

"Me? You mean us. I'm up here facilitating the whole thing, but Evie left the money and the land to us, not me. Oh, and she wanted me to bring the family together again. What are you doing on your vacation this year?"

Silence.

"Come-on, Howie. I have an assignment from our great-grandmother. Her dying wish."

More silence.

I said impatiently, "You're rolling your eyes and making a face, aren't you?"

"Absolutely not," he replied.

"Your pants are on fire, liar. At least tell me what we should do about our money and our property? I'm asking for help here, and getting a big fat zero."

"I'll go along with whatever you want, Nora. The decision is in your capable hands."

"Convenient. Okay, here's my decision. I think I'll keep everything myself."

I hung up before he finished laughing.

My next call was to Lori. After asking if she'd seen any listings for computer analysts in the *Times*, and hearing the negative answer I expected, I filled her in on my expedition into the woods with the aunts, then let her vent about her breakup with her boyfriend. She went on for fifteen minutes. I listened for fifteen minutes. Sometimes, I am a saint.

When I got off the phone, I thought about Whatshisname and our breakup. It seemed like a long time ago. I realized that it had been days since I'd pictured him showering with that woman. Progress.

I needed to look at my digital funeral shots on a large computer screen. When I flipped through them on the tiny camera screen, certain figures were indistinct. Since I intended to show any incriminating results to Nick, it made sense to use a computer in the sheriff's office. Besides, I wanted to find out if he'd learned anything new.

I felt a heaviness when I thought about my father, so I pushed him from my thoughts and read the note Ida'd left on the fridge. She'd gone to another church meeting with Hannah and Agnes about the upcoming bean-hole supper. Having grown used to her breakfasts, I was a little disappointed. To make it up to me, she'd set out freshly baked blueberry muffins. Oh, it was going to be hard to leave Maine.

As a kid one of my favorite books was *Blueberries for Sal*, the attraction being the berries that were plinked into Sal's pail. I loved berry picking as a kid. This was the first batch of blueberry muffins Ida'd made. She told me she had frozen the berries she'd picked out back this summer. Good woman, Ida Lassiter.

I ate one muffin. The warm butter dribbled down my hand. I wrapped two muffins to go. Pretty soon I wouldn't be able to zip my jeans. Instead of making coffee, I'd stop at the Country Store and pick up a container before dropping into the sheriff's office. Nick only worked half a day today so I wanted to get there early. Aside from using his computer, I needed to ask him about Pom Mom Vivian and her neighbor. I also wanted to know more about the gruesome murder of Percy Kendall, senior.

Amy gave me a cheerful hello when I walked into the Country Store. She was refilling salt shakers. The place was empty.

"Taken any good pictures lately?" she asked as I slipped onto a stool at the counter.

For a moment I was taken aback, thinking she was referring to the funeral. An instant later I realized she remembered the disks and batteries I'd bought here.

"A few. But I haven't run anything off yet. I will when I get home."

I looked at Amy with different eyes today, wondering if she could be Marla. I had looked at Margaret and Vivian the same way, regardless of what Mister-Head-Honcho wanted. One of these women was likely the mystery woman, the "tramp," and the key to the Collins murder.

"I'll just take a coffee. Regular."

"Sure thing."

All I knew about Amy was that she was a widow, like Vivian, and she was either a liar, or a woman with a piss-poor memory.

No one gets murdered in Silver Stream. This here's always been a safe place to live.

That murder must have been the talk of the town for a long time. Of course, Amy recalled the event when I jogged her memory.

As she poured the coffee, I tried to picture her in a maid's outfit, playing the meek one as Percy stomped around in his boots. Or would she prefer to play the dominatrix to his little boy persona? It was too early in the morning for such images. Some things really didn't go with breakfast.

I asked, "You buy your car at Kendall's Auto Mart?"

"Sure. Most folks around here do," she said as she put the coffee pot back.

More interested in her reactions than what she had to say, I watched her carefully. "You know Percy Kendall well?"

Amy shrugged, but I thought I saw a flicker of something. Resentment? Wariness? Hard to tell. It was the kind of thing that happens so fast you're never sure what you saw. If life came with rewind-replay buttons, I'd be good to go.

"As good as anybody," Amy replied casually, wiping the counter. "Sure are full of questions today. You sound like the detective you are."

That took me by surprise.

I added cream and stirred my coffee. "No, it's just I'm new in town. . . ." I left the thought hanging.

"Ought to ask your family. They know the history of this town as well as anybody."

In other words, shut up, Nora? Had I hit a nerve?

"Maybe even the sheriff," Amy continued. "I hear you been spending a lot of time with him lately. You two got something going under the sheets? You New York City girls work that fast?"

That came out of left field. Her tone was petty, vengeful. Is that what people thought? Or was Amy trying to turn the tables on me?

Whatever.

I wanted to smack her in the head. Instead, I replied calmly, "Would it bother you if I were sleeping with Nick?"

"What the hell do I care what Renzo does?"

Bingo. One button pressed. The only thing was, I didn't know what it meant.

Why would she care about Nick and me? Was she interested in him? For some reason, I didn't think so, but maybe I should consider that.

She inhaled and the button over her breast looked like it was about to pop. Momentarily distracted, I wondered why she would wear something so tight to work.

It would be prudent to back off, not say another word, but since prudence wasn't my strong suite, I said, "Well, I'm glad it's nothing to you. That leaves the way clear for me."

I was turning into such a liar, I couldn't stand myself. This was not me. I was famous for telling the truth. I didn't believe in lying. The lofty me felt it diminished a person.

"I thought you were leaving Maine and going back to New York."

"I'm not so sure," the diminished me replied. I took a sip of coffee. "This is a nice town. Except for that murder, of course. But Nicky's really working on it. He's got several leads. Promising ones. I think he'll solve this mess soon."

Had I really called him Nicky?

She stared at me. Said nothing. Then turned on her heel and went into the kitchen.

Nick had said Amy's name was A.M. Yanetti. Could the M stand for Marla? Maybe I should check Vivian's middle name. And Margaret's.

After breakfast I went across to the sheriff's office. Nick, aka Nicky, was in his office with the door open.

"Any news?" I asked as I peeked in, going for cheerful when I felt anything but.

The sun cut through the vertical blinds on the east window, laddering his desk and his left side.

Nick shook his head. "Nothing. Quiet day so far."

"I need to download some photos from my digital," I told him. "I know you have a photo program on your computer. I noticed the icon when I was here last time. Adobe Photoshop."

"And who says you're not a crack detective?"

I hid my feelings behind the expected smile.

"What's wrong?"

"What do you mean?"

"I mean," he said, coming from behind his desk, "What's the matter with Nora Lassiter this morning? She's upset."

"No, I'm not. I'm fine."

He nodded as if accepting this, then surprised me by saying, "All right. Tell me when you're ready." He led me into the back room. "Do I need to show you how anything works on this computer?"

"I think not. Thanks." As he was walking away, I said, "If I find the murderer, I'll call you."

He chuckled and waved over his shoulder without turning.

Once I had downloaded the photos I clicked through them one at a time, enlarging each one in turn and studying it. The process got tiring. I hadn't realized I'd taken so many pictures. Then I saw something. My stomach did a flip. I hit the zoom and closed in on one section of a photo where a head was barely visible, someone peering from behind a tree.

I gasped.

The image was blurred because it was a good distance from the figures I'd focused on, but even blurred I recognized Uncle JT. Numb, I stared. I quickly clicked to the next photo, hoping for a clearer shot. Nothing. I went through the rest of the pictures, then back to the beginning of the set to check everything a second time. No other pictures with JT in the background. I blew up the photos of Ellie, thinking JT may have been looking at her, but nothing showed.

I went back to the original and studied it, wondering why he was there, why he had run, and where he was hiding.

I was studying the blowup when Nick returned. It was close to noon, time for him to leave, and he'd changed from his uniform into jeans and a gray sweatshirt. It was cool out today, but beautiful.

"It's JT," I said quietly, motioning him to come around and look at the screen.

He sat beside me and stared at the picture, his expression intense. "How did I miss him? I was looking."

"For JT?"

"For anything or anyone out of the ordinary. He certainly qualifies."

"Don't blame yourself for missing him. He was hiding."

He grunted in reply as he studied the photo on the screen. I knew he was beating himself up inside. Although I wanted to reassure him, another part of me wanted to defend my Dad's brother. Torn, I said nothing as I saved the photo of JT to the hard drive, then removed the disk.

"JT knew Collins. He did business with him, and he wanted to return for the funeral," I said, quelling the other thought rattling around in my head, which was directly connected to the reason I took the photos in the first place. No and no. Not possible. JT was not a murderer, just like my father had not been a murderer.

"Sure. Just two good buddies," Nick said, his voice laced with irony.

I closed my eyes and sighed. Life stinks sometimes.

"Do you have any hard evidence that he killed Collins?" I asked. "And don't tell me about that stupid patch again."

Nick didn't speak immediately. Finally he said, "He ran. It happened on his land." Then, "Let's go for a drive and talk. I have to get away from this place for a while."

We left my truck parked outside the Country Store and took his sheriff's SUV. I didn't bother to ask where he was going. I didn't care.

TWENTY-FIVE

Nick and I ended up at the lake, a breathtaking sight. Trees and boulders hugged the shoreline in a random pattern. Both had been here long before humans found the place. Perfect for a photo shoot. I mentally framed a few shots, but had no desire to get my camera.

It was peaceful here and so quiet I could hear the breeze dancing across the tops of the trees. Nick and I walked a well-traveled path through the meadow down to the lake. This coming weekend the whole area would be swarming with people enjoying the Silver Stream Festival, especially the bean-hole supper that started the event. I would probably be in New York City by then.

Nick pointed to a pile of wood in an area that had been cleared. "They'll bury the bean pot over there. You remember any of this from when you were a kid?"

"Sort of, and Aunt Ida told me about it."

We walked over to a pit about three feet deep and almost as wide, lined with flat rocks.

"I remember this pit," I said, stepping back from the edge. "Wouldn't want to fall in that when it was hot."

"Friday night they'll fire up half a cord of hardwoods, maple and oak, and get that going for about four hours or so until they have some real hot coals. The bean pot will be placed on top. Then they'll cover it with dirt to keep the steam and smoke from escaping. Cover that with a sheet of plywood, and leave it overnight. A fair number of folks gather 'round just to watch that part of it. The beans'll be ready by Saturday. They've got to cook at least sixteen hours. Wicked good beans. For sh-ur."

"Ida said they were wicked good, too. I hate to miss this."

"Do you have to?"

Like an arrow shot by an expert marksman, the question hit the target and stirred a deep yearning I had been unwilling to acknowledge. *Do I have to go? Do I?*

To distract myself, I sidestepped the issue. "I remember being at this festival. I was in a three-legged race with Howie. My mother insisted we do it together. I fell a few times. Howie was such a pain about it. One complaint after the other."

Why had I said that? The town fair was a fun time yet all I could think of was falling when I was a little kid. It was damn hard to shake this mood, which was unusual for me.

"Most kids fall in that race," Nick said.

"Mmm."

Pointing down the shoreline, Nick said, "Everybody skates around here. When the lake freezes up we build a fire in those barrels over there. Even the old folks come out, some to skate, some to watch. They bring folding chairs, hot chocolate, and very warm hats and boots."

"That would be me. Bundled in a down quilt, wearing earmuffs and a wool hat, sitting with the old folks so I wouldn't freeze."

"I wouldn't let you sit."

I looked up at him. He was smiling at me. Damn. I loved his smile.

"I wouldn't let you freeze either," he said.

In silence, we walked along the shoreline, over rocks, around bushes, enjoying the clean scent of autumn in Maine, the feel of the sun on our faces, the sounds of water lapping gently near our feet.

Nick didn't probe. Didn't push. I appreciated that. I knew he wanted to know what was wrong, but I needed time. I thought this might be the last time we were together, alone like this, and I found myself memorizing the moment, storing it away like a squirrel storing nuts for a long winter. Instead of helping, this made me feel worse. I tried hard not to let any emotion show on my face.

Finally, we came to a large flat-topped rock and I climbed up and spread my arms wide to the sky, then hugged myself.

Nick watched and I wondered if he saw more than I suspected. He hopped up. We sat together on the rock overlooking the calm waters of the lake where Nick Renzo swam in the summer and skated in the winter, where he had brought me as summer headed into autumn.

"One of the few things I remember my great-grandmother telling me when I was a kid was that autumn made her sad," I said. "She considered it a dying time, a time when things come to an end, leaves, flowers, all of it. At some point every autumn, I remember her telling me that."

I swallowed hard.

"You're not good at keeping things bottled up inside, Nora. Some people are very private, hold things close to the vest. Like me. You're not like that though," Nick said.

My first impulse was to deny the truth of what he'd said. I didn't want to seem weak in his eyes, wimpy, or needy. I assured myself that I was strong. Sorrow was not tantamount to weakness.

It was several minutes before I replied. "Sometimes, if I can't share, I think I'll explode."

He accepted this quietly, but didn't take the opportunity to probe.

I told him what I'd found in the box, about my relatives, about my father. I finished by saying, "I can't find the real murderer, can't clear my dad's name. It all happened too many years ago."

"Do you want this all kept secret, or are you willing to open it up? Possibly reopen old wounds?"

"What do you mean?"

"I can check into the cold case files, see if anything was overlooked. Murder cases have no statute of limitations. I can find out the name of the cop in charge and everyyone else on the case. Get their take. If I start asking around, other people will find out we're looking into it. They might wonder about your father's guilt.

Would that bother you?"

"I don't care who knows. If there's a chance. . . ."

Before I finished speaking he pulled out his cell phone and hit a number.

"Miller, everything quiet?"

He listened. "Good. Do me a favor and check out some old records on the Kendall murder. Kendall, senior." He gave Miller the information. "Find out who had the case, who took the initial call. Get back to me ASAP."

The longer I knew this man, the more he pleased me. He was a man of action, a man who got to the heart of things, minus all the fanfare.

To me he said, "Most likely, the cop would be retired now. But if we're lucky he may be able to tell us things that aren't in the file." He set the phone next to him. "Are you angry at your family?" he asked before I could thank him.

"No. What Hannah did balances it out. She lied for him, put herself in jeopardy. She could have been arrested for giving false information in a murder case." I stopped suddenly. "Maybe I shouldn't have told you that part. Could she still be arrested?"

He took my hand. "Hannah won't be arrested. You have my word."

Relieved, I continued, "About what you asked . . . if I hold a grudge, I'll be recreating the feelings that existed back then and I don't want to do that. My father threw away family relationships, and I don't intend to walk in his footsteps on that one."

"The Lassiters are good people."

"I know that."

After a while I said, "Thank you for making that call. I would never have thought of contacting the cop who handled the case."

He smiled and kissed me. "That's because you're not a cop."

I nudged his shoulder, and hopped off the rock.

We headed back.

"How's the Collins' investigation coming?" I asked as I teetered my way across a series of rocks. "You haven't told me much lately."

"I've interviewed everyone connected with him that I know of, and several people who knew him casually. Al Collins lived in Silver Stream all his life. Went to school here. Many hint at a shady side, but claim not to know much about it. For the most part, I believe them. But some are reluctant to talk because they know he was into something illegal and they don't want their names tied to it. Maybe they were involved, too. Who knows?"

"You have any idea of what the illegal part was?"

"I'm not sure, but I'll find out. Could be related to cars. Drugs are a possibility, too. Can't rule either out."

"Drugs?"

Rubbing his hand across the back of his neck, he stopped and looked at me. "Because of his involvement with cars, cars would be the logical choice. But my gut feeling tells me drugs."

"Why?"

He shrugged. "Easier to move. Big money. He wasn't hurting for money, that's for damn sure. The inside of his house looks like Donald Trump's decorator let loose."

JT's, too, I thought, but didn't say anything.

"Could marijuana be involved?" I asked, recalling what Ida had said about pot farms.

"It's a strong possibility. I'm looking into it."

We continued up the slight incline toward the parking lot.

"Miles and miles of woods to check," he commented as we crested the hill. "If that's the direction we're going, I'll need more help than I have now. The Maine DEA usually handles this, but they don't concentrate on marijuana much any more. Arrests and seizures are down. Not the supply though. They have limited resources, and have had to reallocate to investigations involving other drugs."

"You think those names with the numbers are drug contacts?"

"Could be. We've checked them out. Nothing so far. Several people with those names in the country, but no reason to suspect any of them. The names don't add up."

"You watching Percy?" I asked.

He smiled at me. "Yes, *Detective* Lassiter. We're watching Percy and a few other folks."

"Surveillance. Good. What other folks?"

"I have guys on overtime," he told me as we sidestepped a fallen branch. "They're watching the Auto Mart and JT's Auto Repair. If I had more help, I'd also watch the women."

"The Marla maybes?

"Yup."

"Want me to watch?"

"Nope."

"I should have known better than to ask," I said. I should just do, not say. Mentioning the ladies, made me remember something I wanted to ask.

"I went to see Vivian and her dogs. She hinted that her neighbor Verney was into things. Like pot parties or something."

"Yes, I know about that."

Nick took my hand as we headed for his SUV. It felt good. There was something solid about him. I felt safe, which was a mild surprise because I hadn't been aware of feeling unsafe.

"Verney's not a bad sort," he said. "Last winter things got kinda loud by his house. Bunch of his hunting buddies were high one night and they took to the clearing to skeet shoot. Florescent skeets. They'd painted them. Vivian called it in. She heard the racket and wanted Verney's ass in jail. For life, I think. She would have been okay with the death penalty, too. The woman wants him drawn and quartered, the real reason being that she thinks he poisoned one of her dogs."

"Sounds like the Vivian I met."

We got into the SUV and I said, "Did you question Verney about Collins' murder?"

"Yep. He's clear. Alibi checks out."

"And Vivian?"

"Clear, too. She was at a dog show when Collins was shot."

One down and two to go. Margaret and Amy. Three, if you

counted Ellie.

"Can you find out the middle names of Amy and Margaret?"

"Already know them."

I waited. Nothing.

"So?" I prompted. "You going to share?"

"Margaret Mary and Allison Mary."

"Or Mar. Both close to Marla," I said. "How about Vivian?" No way was I going to ask about Ellie. I could find that myself.

"Vivian's middle name's Joyce."

We were driving back to town when Nick's cell phone rang. Unlike mine, his had a nice normal ring.

He activated the speaker so I could hear.

"Chief, about that case you wanted me to check out?" Miller said. "Lieutenant Duncan was first on the scene, and he was in charge throughout."

"Thanks." He clicked off and made a U-turn. "He's retired. Lives about ten miles past Kendall's place."

We drove until the road forked, then followed a bend where it narrowed. Overhead, dense trees canopied the road, blocking the last of the late-day sun. It was like driving through a scenic version of the Queens Midtown Tunnel. Unlike this stunning view, the Tunnel, with its grungy tile, always reminded me of someone's dirty bathroom.

"Think he'll remember the case?" I asked.

"Only murder in Silver Stream on his watch."

Duncan, a ruddy-complexioned man in his late sixties, early seventies, was hanging laundry on a makeshift clothesline strung from the side of the house to a nearby tree.

He set the last clothespin on a pair of striped boxers and turned to greet us.

"Hey there. Nick." He looked to me, and Nick introduced us.

"This is Nora Lassiter. Her father was Tom Lassiter. Used to live in these parts years back."

"I remember him. This about Tom?" He was wearing a plaid work shirt and faded jeans that looked like they had been new about thirty years ago. The words *good ole boy* ran through my head like a mantra. I didn't like myself much for judging so quickly and on such shallow evidence, but there it was.

"Well, I was going to say howdy and how's it going first," Nick said, "but yes, it's about Tom."

"Sit. Have a beer." Duncan gestured toward the small deck off the back of the house.

"Sounds good," Nick said.

I didn't want a beer. I wanted to hear what he had to say about my dad, and leave, but I smiled and went along.

"Damn dryer broke," Duncan said as he tossed the bag of clothespins onto a chair.

We sat in Adirondack chairs and waited while he got the beers. Nick seemed at ease. I whispered, "Did you work for this guy?"

"Yes."

"He a good cop?"

Nick said, "Listen to him. Tell me what you think."

I smirked. "A straight answer would be good here."

The guy returned and handed us each a can of beer. He gave me a glass. It was clean. No dog hairs, a point in his favor.

Nick explained what we were interested in, and ended by saying, "I haven't read your report on the murder yet, but I was out this way and decided to stop. See if you could recall anything, get your feel for the case. I know it was a long time ago."

"Never did find the killer and I regret that. Everyone figured it was Lassiter. That was stupid. He didn't do it."

That set me back on my heels.

"A lot of people thought he was guilty," I said. "Why didn't you?"

"Two days before the murder, Tom decks Kendall. Most folks

put two and two together and come up with five. Bad blood between them, they say. He must've gone back and killed the guy. Dumbass thinking. That's the exact reason Tom wasn't guilty. He'd had his revenge. He didn't need to go back. That would've been overkill."

Duncan chuckled at his own morbid pun and so did Nick. Cop humor.

Duncan continued. "'Course, Lassiter had an alibi. Don't know how good it was. One of his aunts. Probably covering for him. If I'd thought the guy did it, that wouldn't have stopped me. Never did find anyone who knew what the hell had gone on between him and Kendall. The wife, your mother, I mean, said she didn't know. Probably had to do with her working there and leaving so quickly. My best guess? Percy fired her ass and Tom couldn't accept the reason, whatever that was. Must have been very personal. Don't suppose we'll ever know now, unless she's willing to talk." He looked at me. "Hasn't she told you?"

"No. But I don't have to ask her now," I said, relieved by what he'd told me. "I know she wasn't fired. She quit. Sexual harassment."

My opinion of the old cop had done a one-eighty. He wasn't a good ole boy, but a thinker in backwoods clothing. He suspected Hannah's alibi was trumped up, yet hadn't called her on it because he believed my father was innocent. Technically, not good police procedure. Can't tell a book by its cover.

"Kendall was after her?" he said, leaning forward.

"Yes. That's what I heard."

"That fits with your dad's reaction. That occurred to me, but since your Mom and Dad didn't press charges, I figured I was wrong. I mean, why wouldn't they press charges?"

As we were getting into the SUV, I turned and gave Nick a quick kiss, startling him. "Thanks," I said. "I feel better knowing he didn't think Dad was guilty. He was a good cop, wasn't he?"

"Kiss me again and I'll tell you."

TWENTY-SIX

All the aunts were at the house when I got back, sitting in the front room having tea. I guessed they'd been talking about me. Maybe wondering how I was holding up since they'd last seen me. Ida hopped up immediately. "I'll get you a blueberry turnover. A dollop of cream?"

"Sure."

"Coffee?" Hannah asked, following Ida.

"Okay. That would be good."

"Here, let me plump your pillow," Agnes offered, shuffling over.

"Thanks," I said, leaning forward, although I could have plumped my own pillow. Or poured my own coffee. Or gotten my own blueberry turnover.

Then it hit me. The melancholy I'd been feeling had been triggered by things about my dad, but there was another layer I had kept well hidden. From myself.

Do I have to go? Do I?

I would be leaving the family soon, the aunts in particular, people who hadn't been part of my life for a very long time, but who had become special in a very short time. Special people are rare in anyone's life. It was hard to think about walking away.

Right now they were trying to make up to me for not believing my father, for causing me unhappiness. Such kindness. It made me want to cry.

When I was all settled in, and they were all settled in, I decided to tell them what was going on with Percy and Mary Fran. I knew they would enjoy hearing about it. It would also be my way of telling them that I held no hard feelings toward them.

"I have something to share with you all. First, I must swear you to secrecy."

They looked from one to the other. "We swear."

I launched into the "case." I told them everything, including my time in the Dumpster and my time under the bed. I left nothing out. *Absolutely nothing.*

Their eyes grew wide. They leaned forward again and again, oohing, aahing, and chuckling.

"Who would have thought that nice Mary Fran was having such a time of it," Ida remarked, shaking her head. "I get my hair done at her place once a month. She's nice as can be."

"My goodness," Agnes said, her eyes wide. "All this going on in Silver Stream. How can we help?"

"I suppose if we could tell you who this Marla is, it would help," Hannah said.

"I was hoping you'd know someone named Marla."

"Roping? Somebody was *roping* somebody? Was this another one of those games?" Agnes asked.

I repeated myself for Agnes.

No one knew anyone named Marla.

"We do have a lot of contacts," Agnes said. "We'll ask around."

"No," I said vehemently. "Definitely not. I want this kept quiet. I don't want Percy to find out. If he knew, he'd hide his money, make arrangements for some of it to disappear for a while so Mary Fran couldn't get her fair share." I didn't mention her fair share would be about eighty percent. "Even Marla, whoever she is, can't know because she'd tell Percy."

"She's gotta be from out of town," Ida said.

"Maybe not." I told them my theory, based on what I'd observed at the funeral. "There was a certain look in his eye when he nodded in their direction. I think Marla may just be a name she used during sex."

They all nodded. They knew the look. Pursing her lips,

Hannah said, "Game playing," like she knew about such stuff. "Trust your gut on this, Nora."

"I do. I now think Marla might be one of two women because Vivian has been eliminated. It's down to Margaret and Amy. I'm pretty sure it wasn't Ellie."

"Oh, my word." Agnes chuckled. "A secret vamp. Amy or Margaret? Who is the real Marla?"

Ida tsk-tsked.

Hannah grinned and slapped her thigh. "Well, I'll be. Haven't heard such goings on since Viola was alive."

"The vamp in the family tree?" I asked. "The one whose blue eyes are like mine?"

"*Wine?*" Agnes asked loudly. "I don't usually drink during the day, but if you're serving. . . ."

"Eyes like *mine*," I said.

Next, I told them about the photo I'd taken at the funeral with JT in the background.

After the gasps, Agnes asked, "Are you sure it was JT?"

Ida's hand went to her heart. "Thank the Lord. I didn't want to say it, but I was beginning to think he might be dead."

Hannah said, "I wonder if Ellie knows. Do you suppose he's been in contact with her and she hasn't told us because she's protecting him?"

That seemed unlikely, but you never knew.

The following day, I drove out to JT's auto repair place to see about the radiator for my car. I was only going because of my car. Period. No snooping planned. Since the salesman had put in a purchase order, taking over Collins' job without being asked, I simply wanted to hurry things along.

The place was busier than it had been the last time I'd been here. I could see at least five men working as I stepped from my truck. No boss, but they were working. Interesting. JT must have put someone in charge.

I went into the office, wrinkled my nose at the stink of smoke, and told a guy with a cigarette dangling from his mouth about my radiator. He didn't bother to remove the cigarette when he said he had to check something and left me standing there.

Several pads of business forms on the cracked linoleum counter caught my attention. I glanced around, didn't see the smoker, opened a book of invoices and flipped through, just passing the time of day, nothing more. I should have brought a book to read. Dull stuff in this invoice book. I glanced around, but the smoker was nowhere in sight. There was a second book on the counter, this one labeled Purchase Orders. I flipped it open.

Omigod.

My heart raced as I quickly leafed through the pages. Without reading details, I ripped one out, stuffed it in my pocket and continued looking. My heart was still doing double time as I turned to see the cigarette guy staring at me from the doorway. When had he returned?

"Looking for something?" His voice was harsh, accusing. I drew a momentary blank. Nothing came.

Be calm, Nora. Be calm.

I took a breath, which I needed, and smiled. When in doubt, smile. Then inspiration struck.

"I was looking to see whether Kendall's Auto Mart had sent you an order for my radiator. The guy said he did, but you never know. I'm from New York. Skeptical is my middle name. I'm sorry, really. It was nosy of me."

I laid it on, hoping he hadn't seen me rip a page out. "I need that radiator. I'm afraid of breaking down and getting stuck around here." Poor little, incompetent me. "I was here a few days ago about a rattle. My Uncle JT fixed it."

Mentioning my relationship to the owner helped. I knew I had him. Thawing was evident around the edges. Not all that obvious. But to the trained eye . . . Nora, Nora, you are too much. Trained eye?

He took a puff on his cigarette, tipped his head and blew a

plume of blue smoke to the ceiling where is swirled into the rest of the fog.

"I'll see what I can do." He took a business card from the counter and handed it to me. "Call back later."

Chatty guy. Well, it was better than nothing.

Nick had said someone was watching JT's place. If that were so, the watcher was well hidden. I took my time starting the truck as I searched for him. Then I phoned Nick and asked, "Who's watching JT's Auto?"

He said hesitantly, "No one right now. Why?"

"I'm here."

"Damnit all, Nora. Get out of there."

"I have a bad radiator. You said so yourself. I came to see if Kendall's Auto ordered the new one. I've got a warranty, you know."

"And what else are you up to?

"You are so suspicious."

"You are so transparent."

"Nick, I give you valuable tips. You said so yourself."

"Why are you asking about surveillance if you're only interested in a radiator?"

I hesitated, more for drama than from reluctance to share what I'd found.

"JT signed the purchase orders in the book," I said.

After some silence, I said, "You still there, Sheriff?"

"How did you happen to see the purchase order book?" Nick asked, a sarcastic edge in his voice. "I can't picture anyone saying, 'Here, have a look at our Purchase Orders.'"

"The smoking guy left me alone and I had nothing to read. I flipped through a few things."

"For most people that would involve magazines."

"The thing is, I think you should have surveillance here during the day, too."

"I don't have enough men. I'm stretched thin as it is."

"I could watch for a while."

"No," he said in his no-nonsense sheriff's voice.

"Why not?"

"I won't dignify that with an answer."

"Where does the surveillance guy watch from? I don't see much around here," I said, checking the woods on either side.

Silence again.

"JT signed the purchase orders," I repeated. "*All* of them."

"I heard you the first time. But his signature could be forged."

"You won't have too much trouble checking the signature."

I heard him groan. "You snatched one?" There was a hint of despair in his voice. I imagined he closed his eyes, too.

I drove to Aunt Ellie's. When I pulled into the driveway, that same rush of nostalgia washed through me. Like the last time I was here, I remembered bits of my childhood. Running through the sprinkler on a hot summer day, catching fireflies, riding on the tractor with Dad as he plowed a trail through the woods. So many happy things. Before everything changed.

I stopped the car and took the photo from the seat beside me, wondering whether Ellie would be shocked that her husband had been so close that day. Or, had she known?

The day was warm and crystal clear, like so many September days, so many back-to-school days. I had loved going to school here.

I felt again the sadness of separation that I'd felt all those years ago, sadness at the injustice of it all. Why hadn't Great-grandma Evie just called Dad? Or other members of the family? I would never understand that. All those years, wasted.

I knocked on the door to Ellie's house. Once, I wouldn't have knocked, I'd have breezed right in.

Did I want to live in Silver Stream again?

A troubling consideration. I was a city girl.

I made a strong effort to shrug off the nostalgia. I was here on business today.

"'Morning, Nora. Come in," Ellie said as she held the door for me. She was dressed in a yellow warm-up outfit with a gray turtleneck underneath. Her hair was done up and sprayed stiff enough to resist a nor'easter. I didn't care for that shade of green eye shadow, but hey, it's a free country.

We stood in the foyer. She didn't ask me to come in for coffee. After an awkward moment, I said, "I came to show you one of the photos I took at the funeral."

She stepped back as if I had a communicable disease, her face a mask of disgust. "You took pictures at a funeral? No one takes pictures at a funeral. How ghoulish."

I held the picture out. She refused to look. I guess she needed time for the impact of my barbarism to ease. I waited, my hand still extended. Finally, with all the enthusiasm of someone looking through a mug book for a serial killer, she glanced at the photo I'd blown up.

No disgust now. Just annoyance.

"The man's a fool. Showing up there," she said as she stared at her husband's picture.

"Why did he run, Ellie?"

"I told you. Besides, what's it to you, anyway?"

The animosity in her voice took me by surprise.

"He's my father's brother," I replied.

"I think this is none of your business. You're here for a short time. Don't get involved." She looked at her watch when she spoke, not at me.

"What do you mean?"

She didn't answer.

"Did he kill Collins?" I finally asked, my voice a harsh whisper.

"You'd better leave," she said, pushing the door open for me.

TWENTY-SEVEN

Everyone I'd met in Silver Stream, plus a few hundred folks I'd never seen, were at the lake for the bean-hole supper, an event I was sure I'd miss. But I was still in Maine, still in Silver Stream.

It was close to dusk. The sun was dipping in the western sky. It was cool. In the open tent with the aunts, all the folks wore wool sweaters or light jackets. Being a cautious woman who doesn't like the cold, I wore the natural wool fisherman sweater I'd ordered from L.L. Bean, and jeans. Tied at my waist was the deep red Norwegian-inspired snowfield fleece pullover that had just arrived this morning. Not in my color palate, I admit, but necessary. Not that it was cold at the moment, but the sun was sinking in the west, there were woods all around, and we were heading into the tail end of September in Maine. Do the math.

Huge tent-tops dotted the meadow with folks milling around each one. The delicious aroma of baked beans wafted across the fairgrounds from the bean hole. I could smell the molasses they put in the beans.

Local talent livened up the place with piano, banjo, fiddle, accordion and washboard, playing music from a different era. If I were home, I wouldn't waste my time listening.

When they segued from the *Maple Leaf Rag* into *Down By the Old Mill Stream*, I sang along, my voice lost in the impromptu chorus that rose up around me. Why didn't I ever listen to this kind of music? I should. I would.

I sang along. "by the old mill stream . . . where I first met you . . . dressed in gingham, too . . . croon loves tune . . . dah-da-da-dah."

I got a few amused looks. Not sure what that was about. After all, other people were singing, too.

I did a little soft-shoe shuffle as I set out the plastic forks Ida handed me. I remembered a few steps. I wasn't bad, not that I had a career in the dance field, or anything. My mother made me take tap as a kid. That lasted two months, only because my mother said the teacher said I had no discernible sense of rhythm, which was not true at all. I had liked dance class.

Along with Hannah, Agnes and Ida, I helped set up the section for the church's pot luck supper. We arranged bowls of clam chowder, corn & pumpkin chowder, baked wild duck breasts, lobster salad, brandied pumpkin soufflé, fiddlehead ferns, strawberry-rhubarb pie and blueberry pie, those last two baked and frozen this past spring and summer for this occasion.

As the song ended, Mary Fran walked into the tent. "Someone around here was singing off key. Did you hear it?" She shuddered. "Enough to send chills up my spine."

I looked around. "No, I didn't hear anyone singing off-key."

The aunts barely glanced at Mary Fran. I guess they didn't want to appear too interested in her business.

"I have to check his computer," I told her quietly. "See when they plan to meet again."

"It's getting harder and harder to be civil to him," Mary Fran whispered as I watched Nick approach. "Last night I lost my temper and tipped a bowl of hot chowder into his lap. Ruined his new pants. Too bad I didn't ruin anything else. Next time I'll make sure it's scalding hot."

When Nick entered the tent, many women, young and old, swarmed around him, sort of like teens around a rock star. It was ridiculous. They wanted him to try their specialty? I had a feeling a few were offering more than food. Tastefully, of course, no pun intended.

I raised my brows and gave him a tight smile.

"It's not amusing," Mary Fran said, misinterpreting the direction of my thoughts. "I want to murder Percy. Really, I do."

"I know," I replied, pulling my attention back to her instead of Himself and the infatuated ladies of Silver Stream. "I understand how you feel, Mary Fran, and I'm working on it. Is Percy here now?"

Who cared what women were nuts about Nick? Didn't matter to me. I wished them all well. I was leaving in a few days.

"He's over by the bean hole with our daughter," Mary Fran said as she gestured with her head in that general direction.

At the same time, Nick laughed at something one of the women said. Then they all laughed at something he said. They were having a wonderful time. Good. People should have fun at the festival.

"I had to get away," Mary Fran was saying. "It was either that, or get arrested for sending him ass over teakettle into the damn bean hole. The temptation was strong, Nora. Very strong."

"I'm glad you showed restraint," I said. "Remember your objective."

"Right. By the way, he's going to a car auction this weekend. Leaving tomorrow morning. Do you suppose he'll meet her there?"

"Could be. I'll check his email. Where's the auction?" I wasn't really interested, but I felt it was only polite to ask.

"Gray."

Gray? Gray.

Michelle Gray, 8011a0920. Phil Clinton, 401p0925.

My heartbeat kicked into overdrive. Tomorrow was September twentieth. Gray, 0920.

Normal as you please, I asked, "Gray is a place in Maine, right?"

She looked at me as if I were not the brightest bulb in the chandelier. "It's just about half an hour west of Freeport. Years back, Percy would take me to the outlets in Freeport and drop me off and travel to Gray. Then Lard Ass took over the job."

My heart started palpitating with such gusto I thought it might show. I put a hand to my chest to cover my excitement. Gray was a place, not a person. Omigod. I had to tell Nick. Wait till he heard this. It could be the breakthrough we needed. We?

Two of the women I'd seen at Hot Heads Heaven interrupted to talk to Mary Fran. I went back to setting up the plastic flatware, ignoring the stupid scene with the sheriff and the ladies of Silver Stream, annoying though that was.

The aunts surrounded me like so many mother hens, eager to hear the latest on the Mary Fran case.

"Has Mary Fran found out anything new?" Hannah asked.

"Has Marla met with Percy again?" Ida whispered.

Nick shot me a wide grin over the heads of his fan club. I smiled back politely and bumped into a stack of paper cups. About five-hundred cups went rolling. So graceful. My mother should have insisted on ballet instead of tap.

"Told you," Ida said quietly, watching the commotion as I gathered up the cups. "All ga-ga over him, the lot of them. 'Course he is wicked good looking and such a manly man, if you know what I mean."

"They call it sexy today, Aunt Ida," I snapped, blowing the dirt off one of the cups and putting it back in the pile.

"A rose by any other name," she said.

"About Mary Fran?" Hannah persisted.

"Nothing new," I said, deciding it was high time I investigated the damn bean pot. It was an interesting process, right? I should learn about it. When I got back to New York and my friends asked me what I did in Maine, I would describe this bean-hole business. Besides, it would give me a chance to chat with Percy.

I passed the folk art tent with only the briefest glance. Same for the quilt tent. My thoughts cut back and forth between Nick and a place called Gray. A group stood around the bean hole listening to the bean-hole maker. Margaret was standing next to Percy. His head was bent toward her, listening. On the opposite side, his daughter tried to get his attention. His face stern, he spoke to the child and she ran off looking unhappy. Margaret looked up at him. Touched his arm. A lovers touch? I wished I could hear their conversation. Nick should be watching this. But no. He was busy wallowing in the adulation of the Silver Stream singles.

I circled around and came up in back of Percy. Margaret turned immediately. It was enough to make me believe the woman had ESP.

"Margaret. Percy. Hello."

". . . use about twenty-five pounds of yellow-eyed beans," the bean-hole maker was saying, "and the onions and molasses. . ."

Percy gave a reluctant hello. Margaret smiled and said hi.

"This is wonderful, isn't it?" I said, with a wave of my arm to encompass the whole area.

"Umm."

"Will you be back tomorrow for the games?" I asked them.

"No," Percy said.

"No," Margaret said, glancing at Percy, then back at me.

"Oh?"

"Car auction," Percy supplied.

"Business," Margaret said. "And you?"

"Getting ready to go back to New York." I thought of my Abraham Lincoln library book, but decided, again, not to mention it.

To see what he'd say, I asked, "Where's the car auction?"

Instead of replying, he said, "Heard you were over to JT's, nosing around."

"Well, I–"

"And taking pictures at Al's funeral?"

I controlled the gasp. How had Percy seen me? I had been so careful.

"Pictures?" Margaret looked at me as if she were looking at something smelly stuck to her shoe.

"There are worse things," I fired back. "Let's see. Like lying or stealing, murdering, cheating, philandering, blackmailing, selling drugs. The list goes on. Funeral shots are down near the bottom."

Several other people joined the bean-hole watchers, and we shifted to give them room. During the shift, Margaret and Percy swung around quickly to leave. I took a step, and felt a sharp pain in my right ankle. I was not sure how it happened, or even what happened. Next thing I knew, my arms were pin-wheeling, grabbing at air to keep from falling into the smoldering bean hole. I didn't even have time to yell.

Two men grabbed at me, one got hold of my L.L. Bean natural wool fisherman sweater, the other grabbed at the deep red Norwegian-inspired snowfield fleece pullover tied at my waist. The pullover came off in his hand, and I dipped to the side, stretching the wool sweater to its fullest. I was like ammunition in a slingshot. In my peripheral vision I saw Percy and Margaret walking away, not even looking my way.

One foot slid over the edge and knocked loose one of the rocks that lined the hole.

"Hold her, man. Those rocks are heavy enough to crack the cover."

The man's grip held. Two guys grabbed hold of him to keep us both from falling onto the cover below and crashing into the pot.

"Get her up, quick!"

"She'll get dirt in the beans!" someone shouted.

Dirt in the beans? The heat was curling around my legs, for God sakes.

The sweater slipped, looped under my arms and dug into my chin. Slipped to my neck. I could see tomorrow's headlines: Woman hung by L.L. Bean sweater.

I dangled over the bean hole. I was a coat hanging on a peg. I was a side of beef swinging from a hook. I was a woman being choked by her sweater.

Omigod, omigod, omigod! Get me outta here!

Hands snatched at me. Caught my hair, my collar.

"Ow!"

"Get her before she ruins the beans!" Same guy yelling as before. The self-appointed bean protector.

When I got out of here, I was going to smack him good.

My feet scrambled for purchase. Knocked another rock loose.

Would they tar and feather me if I ruined the damn beans?

"The pot's still covered! The beans are protected."

My arms flailed wildly in the air.

"Hold still," someone ordered.

"Grab her arm!"

"Watch out!"

Someone caught my arm.

"Get her feet up. She's knocking more rocks down."

Someone caught my other arm. Seconds later I was on solid ground, Nick in front of me.

"You okay?" he asked, taking hold of my hand.

"Yes. Fine. Never better." I brushed hair from my eyes as I stepped away from the bean hole. Straightened my natural wool fisherman sweater, which was now stretched large enough to accommodate a whole other person. I took a few deep breaths. Stuck my shaking hands in my jean pockets.

"You sure?"

Someone held out my red sweater. Nick took it and that was fine with me since I couldn't steady my hands enough to get them out of my pockets. I looked around, listening for the bean protector.

All eyes were focused on me.

"You all right, lady?"

"I don't think she's from around here," someone whispered.

"I'm fine. Thank you all for your help."

"Take care, dear," an older woman said, patting my shoulder. "It could happen to anyone."

Chin high, I walked away, hands still jammed in my pockets.

"Hey, that lady almost fell in the bean hole," some dopey kid announced, pointing.

"Yeah. Did you see that?"

". . . the mustard is every bit as important as the onions," the bean man continued as if a person hadn't almost died a horrible death in his stupid bean hole.

"What happened?" Nick asked as we walked toward the tent

where the three aunts and other members of the Lassiter clan had gathered.

I shook my head. "I don't know. One minute I was talking to Percy and Margaret, the next I felt pain in my ankle and it gave way. I don't know whether someone kicked me, or not. Next thing, I'm swinging over the damn bean hole."

"You think Percy or Margaret did this?"

"I don't know. He said he saw me taking pictures at the funeral, and he also knew I'd been to JT's repair place. I felt threatened." I paused, biting my lower lip. "But he didn't actually say anything threatening. Maybe it was all in my head because I spied on him. Maybe I feel guilty. Anyway, when he walked away . . . all of a sudden, there I was. Swinging in the breeze. I don't know what happened. I really don't. But I have strong suspicions."

"And Margaret?"

"She doesn't like me." I stopped before we reached the tent. "I have to get presentable."

I headed to the porta-potty, Nick beside me.

"Did Percy trip you? Kick you?" he asked again.

I shrugged. "I told you, I can't say for sure. Peculiar, but true."

I flipped the light switch in the porta-potty several times. Nothing. "Wonderful. The light doesn't work," I called out.

"You won't need it. The top is open."

"I see that," I said as I looked up. "No ceiling. Was this a cost-cutting measure?"

"We're thrifty folks."

"You are not going to stand guard next to the door."

"Ay-uh. I am," Nick said. "So don't bother your head trying to convince me to leave."

"At least step away from the door."

"I'm taking two steps back."

I gagged a bit on the smell, even though the top was open. I wasn't sure which was worse the sweet scented air deodorizer, or the stink it was meant to mask.

I did what I had to do, telling myself I didn't care whether

Nick heard or not, telling myself I didn't care that I could hardly move in this confined space.

When I finished, I squinted into a small mirror to see my hair. The sun was low in the sky allowing very little light into this small space, but it was enough to see I was a mess. Big hair jutted every which way. My face was worse. Smoke smudge city. My nose, my cheeks, my chin. This is what I got for coming to Maine. This kind of thing never happened in New York. People had seen me looking like this.

All right. No time to bemoan my fate. Serious damage control was called for. I needed a shower. That wasn't possible. A damp paper towel would have to do. I dabbed at the soot. It smeared. A dozen paper towels later most of my makeup was off, but the soot was gone. Good thing I carried replacement supplies.

"What's going on in there? Are you okay?"

"I'm not talking to you."

"I didn't want you to feel self-conscious. That's why I didn't say anything."

Just then I remembered what I had to tell him. "Oh, you'll never guess what I found out. When I spoke to Mary Fran."

"Sheriff. Sheriff. There's a fight behind the quilting booth. Come quick."

"Have to run," he told me, hurrying off.

I sighed. My news about the Gray auction would have to wait. He'd be amazed when I told him about the solution to the puzzle. Right now, I figured I could get Mary Fran's key and check Percy's computer for the latest email from Marla babe while they were all here.

I found Mary Fran in the church tent talking to Hannah. As soon as she spotted me, she came over. "You want to go to my house, right? While Percy's here?" She looked me over. "You look awful. What happened?"

I closed my eyes briefly. "Good thing you live so close to here. Just give me the key and call me on my cell phone if he leaves early."

"He won't. He never leaves before the beans are served. He's a bean man," she said as she slipped me her key. "This is my extra key. You don't have to return it right away."

"This won't take long. I'll be back in less than half an hour."

I saw Hannah watching, wondering what was going on. I nodded to her to confirm her suspicions, and headed to the parking lot.

TWENTY-EIGHT

This couldn't be. It just couldn't, I thought, as I sat in front of Percy's computer. I'd never get the photos now. And if Mary Fran really needed them to get her eighty percent, she was out of luck.

I wanted her to have the money so badly, wanted it as much as I had wanted to throw Whatshisname's Big Berthas out the window. As much as I'd wanted that part of my fiancé's bank account that I'd foolishly allowed him to keep in his name because I'd trusted him. His checks were our savings. I'd given that man my heart, my whole self, my money, and he'd cheated on me, in my own apartment, no less. Like Percy had cheated on Mary Fran, in her own bed, no less. Brothers under the skin, both of them. This kind of hurt cut layers deep. It was physical, emotional, financial.

I couldn't let Percy get away with this. Mary Fran had more of an "investment" in him than I ever had in Whatshisname. Years, more. And there was a child to consider. This had become personal.

If I told Nick about the Gray auction, chances were good that Percy would be arrested before he had a chance to meet up with Marla. He might be persuaded to give her up as an accomplice, but there would never be photos of them that proved they were having an affair.

I reread the last few lines of Marla's email:

After business, comes pleasure. Since this will be our last time together, we'll make it special.

The words *last time* seemed to shout from the page. She was ending the affair. If it was their last time, it was my last chance to get photos of them together.

I pulled out my cell phone and hit Mary Fran's number.

"Is there any chance you can get the eighty percent with just the emails?" I asked without preamble.

"You can't get the pictures?" she asked, a frantic note in her voice.

"I'm not sure," I hedged. "Answer my question."

"Hold on." She paused, then said, "I had to find a private spot. I'm in the porta-potty now. Stinks in here. Anyway, I have to tell you, I just reread the prenup yesterday and it says I need irrefutable proof, like photos. It mentions photos. I even spoke to my lawyer about this. It seems since the emails between them never mention a time or place, Percy could claim he never got together with her, was never actually unfaithful, except in his fantasy life. Do you believe it?"

That sinking feeling was back again. "All right, Mary Fran. "I'll get the photos."

How? I wondered, as I clicked off. How could I do this?

Would it hamper police business in a big way if I withheld? It would. But what if I took photos and video to cover whatever the sheriff might miss? What if I called Nick from Gray?

No, I could not do any of that. I had to tell him tonight.

Twenty-five minutes later, I was back at the bean-hole supper. I hurried to the church tent and joined the aunts. I got Hannah aside, told her what had happened, and told her to tell Ida and Agnes on their way home. No one else.

"You're going to Gray?" she asked.

I sighed heavily. "I'm not sure. I have to tell Nick about this. Once I do, my involvement might end."

"It's a shame. Don't feel bad, though," she consoled, patting my hand. "It's the sensible way of it. If you went down there, it could be dangerous."

I saw Nick heading toward me. He passed Percy and his daughter. My gaze was drawn to the little girl tugging at her father's sweater to get his attention. He brushed her hand away and continued talking with some man. No time for his little girl. He was scum.

That sealed it. I had to get him. Had to.

"Hi," Nick said. "Sorry to go running off before. Not much of a fight. A couple of kids."

We chatted about the goings on, then he said, "What were you about to tell me when I left? Something about Mary Fran and Percy?"

There might be a way, I thought, steeling myself.

I stared up at Nick, swallowed hard. I liked this man. He was good and honorable. Men like him were a fading breed. For a brief moment, I found it impossible to speak. He cocked his head, a question in his upraised brows.

"Mary Fran is getting antsy," I finally said, taking a giant step I was ambivalent about, to say the least. "She dumped a bowl of hot chowder on Percy. Last night, I think."

"Good for her."

The guilt washed over me. In waves. My stomach churned. My heart hammered.

On Saturday morning I awoke in the dark. I'd set the alarm for three, an ungodly hour for anyone, especially me. I needed an early start to get down to Gray in plenty of time. Percy had given in to whatever it was Marla wanted him to do. Afterwards, Marla planned to meet him at some place "where we had our first time," she had written. Since I had no idea what place she referred to, I'd have to follow him there from the auction.

If possible, I'd take photos of things the sheriff would need. If I wasn't able to do that, they could always go to the auction the following week in Clinton. That would be a repeat performance.

It occurred to me that Percy might recognize my truck, so I had spoken to Hannah. When she realized she couldn't talk me out of it, she agreed to let me take her other car, a silver Toyota

Highlander she seldom used. The agreement was that I tell the aunts everything when I returned, every last detail. I made her promise not to talk to Nick before I called him. Reluctantly, she agreed.

I showered faster than I'd ever showered in my life. A record breaker. The hot water was non-existent today. The damn burner was either off or broken. Equally fast, I dressed in one of my Maine outfits, jeans and a warm navy wool sweater. This way, I'd blend in at the auction. I took one of Ida's hats that had a brim, in case I had to hide my face. I had no definite plan. I'd play it by ear. How hard could it be to find Percy at the auction and follow him?

Piece of cake.

Before going to bed, I'd loaded the SUV with supplies, essentials first—make-up mirror, make-up, three combs, two brushes, mousse, hairspray, perfume, toothbrush, toothpaste, dental floss, mouthwash and dental mirror. Then I added chocolate chip cookies from Ida's cookie jar, a few cans of soda, several bottles of water, two bags of chips. I checked to make sure I had the Maine map, mace, binoculars that I found in the closet, my trusty Swiss Army knife, camera, extra batteries, and camcorder.

For nourishment, I made a tuna on seedless rye. I hate the seeds that get stuck in your teeth. I took some Swiss cheese wedges, too. When I arrived in Gray, I'd stop for coffee and donuts as a special treat, something to look forward to. I was a woman prepared for the day. I left a note for Ida telling her I'd call when I arrived. She did not approve of my plans. She had told me she was worried.

I was worried too, but I tried not to focus on the negative.

It was dark when I pulled out of the driveway for the long haul down to Gray. My driving had improved since I'd come up here, and I wasn't as nervous as I had been. Once on the highways, I intended to push it up to fifty miles per hour. Risky, I know, but I felt I was ready. Since I wasn't used to this SUV, I'd wait awhile before shifting into daredevil mode. The trip took several hours. I played my new Shania CD, singing along full blast. I'd found a few

CDs in the glove compartment, *Oh What A Night* by the Four Seasons and *Duets* by Kenny Rogers. Unfamiliar stuff. I played both. And sang along, making up lyrics as the need arose. No law says you have to sing the exact words.

I finally hit Route 95 and took it to 202. I got it up to fifty-two miles per hour. Once in Gray, I stopped at Dunkin Donuts. The two cops ahead of me on line took forever, loading up with so many donuts I thought there'd be none left for me.

I treated myself to a small coffee and a creme-filled donut, the white creme kind that I love but seldom allow myself. I got directions to the auction from the guy behind the counter and drove the short distance. Nothing much going on that I could see. Too early.

I passed the auction entrance, made a U-turn and headed back. No one around. I had my choice of parking spots along the street. Good. I could just pull alongside the curb. I wasn't good at parking yet. Parallel parking especially. What a horror. But this was easy.

Instead of parking exactly opposite the entrance, I drove down a ways so I wouldn't be easily spotted but still had a prime view of the entrance. I am getting the hang of this detective business.

No telling when Percy would arrive. It was after nine when I settled in. Wished I had a good book to read.

Michelle Gray 8011a0920.

If the **a** indicated A.M., then around eleven something should happen. Of course, I expected Percy to arrive earlier than that.

I wondered who Michelle was, or even if there was a Michelle. I was about ninety-nine percent sure the Gray part referred to this Gray, Maine auto auction. If it didn't, I'd made the long trip for nothing.

It was safe to assume the other name on the list, Phil Clinton, referred to an auction in Clinton, which is why I knew the cops could nab these guys there. It helped with the guilt. I was conflicted about this. I decided to call Nick when I had the photos. He'd call the Gray Police. Maybe they would still be able to make arrests.

By ten o'clock, no one I recognized had come to the auction. My mind started to wander. Nothing too intellectual. I started thinking about Oreo cookies. Maybe I should have gotten those instead of the donut. Except that I didn't have any milk. I needed milk with my Oreos. Oreos are for dunking. There's an art to it. You can't just dunk. The cookie has to be submerged for exactly the right amount of time. Too long and you get mush, too little and you still have crispy. Re-dunking doesn't work. You can lose the cookie that way. Then there's another problem. You must make sure you don't run out of milk before you've finished your cookies. It's an art.

By ten-thirty, I'd finished the donut and one bag of chips, and was seriously considering the tuna sandwich. I held off.

This was an interesting spot. Lots of action at the auction now. People and cars coming and going. Gray Road was busy. A woman wearing jeans and a dark gray sweatshirt placed orange road cones on one side of the entrance to prevent cars from parking too close. The color reminded me of Nick's slippers. Because I had little else to do, I wondered why she didn't cone off the other side. Well, what did I know about coning.

By ten-fifty, I no longer cared about how interesting Gray Road was, or about the cones. I was getting bored, and naturally I had to pee. One of those horrible porta-potties sat across the street nestled among the trees. Since I didn't want to chance missing Percy, I decided to stay put and suffer. This decision was like a signal for the clock to move more slowly, and my bladder to feel fuller. I was about ready to give up and make a quick dash when an approaching black Ford Expedition slowed at the entrance area, almost coming to a complete stop. The driver was looking for someone. A white van came up behind the Expedition. In response, the Expedition continued on.

Percy.

My heart jack-hammered in my chest. I was glad I was on the opposite side of the street in Hannah's SUV, and there were cars parked at both bumpers, shielding me. I yanked the brim of Aunt Ida's hat down and turned my head aside as Percy passed.

I started the engine, intending to make a U-turn and follow him, but hesitated, waiting to see if he was doing what I had done. Case the place. I followed his progress in the rearview mirror. Sure enough, he turned and slowly made his way back on my side of the street. I turned away again. Once past me, he paused at the entrance. The cone lady suddenly materialized, this time wearing sunglasses and a baseball cap. Incognito? She had to be Percy's contact. Michelle? Tense, I grabbed my binoculars, sunk down in the seat and focused.

The woman inclined her head slightly at Percy, or at least I thought she did. It could be that she was just being friendly. I watched with sinking heart as she went back to the auction lot and Percy drove on by.

Several minutes passed with nothing happening. I was breathing hard. I was nervous. A green Subaru Outback came out of the lot and edged into the space set off by the road cones. That was nervy.

Then the cone lady herself got out, picked up the cones, tossed them into the back of the car, and it began to make sense.

Minutes later, Percy pulled into the space left in front of the Outback. How smooth. I marveled at the simplicity.

He popped the back of his Expedition and began unloading boxes labeled Air Filter. I reached for my camera, slumped down, and started snapping. At least the sheriff would have this for evidence. I hoped I could get a shot of them opening one of the boxes, and a shot of the contents, which I knew had nothing to do with air filters.

Together, Percy and the woman put them all in the back of the Outback. I checked my watch. It was eleven o'clock. I was right about the number eleven in the code. Nick was right about the date. We made a good team.

I switched to the camcorder, keeping only the lens above the window. I got a clear shot of her license plate. Nick would want that.

It was time to call him. I grabbed my cell phone and hit his number.

"Nick, Percy's involved in a drug buy. I'm almost positive it's drugs."

"What? How do you know this?"

I hesitated, knowing the reaction I'd get.

"Last night Mary Fran told me Percy was driving to a car auction in Gray today. Gray. The name we thought was a last name. Michelle Gray 8011a0920. What it means is: Meet Michelle at the Gray auction at eleven in the A.M. on September twentieth. Don't know what the eight-zero means. Eighty something? Maybe pounds."

"You're just telling me now!" he yelled. "Why didn't you tell me last night?"

Even though I expected this, I still winced at his tone and his words.

"I couldn't. I had to be here."

"Here? You're there now?'"

Before closing the trunk the cone lady, who had to be Michelle, checked each box.

"I'm in Gray. I can see Michelle from here. I think it's Michelle."

"What!" he exploded. "Get out of there. Fast."

"I knew you'd say that. Hold on." I put the phone down.

I tried to see what she was checking, snapped pictures like crazy. I could hear Nick yelling on the phone. I picked it up and interrupted him. "Michelle just finished looking inside the boxes that Percy gave her. She's handing him a shoe box tied with a red ribbon. Hold it again. I'll tape this."

I turned on the camcorder again, and aimed it at Michelle and Percy.

"Where are you? Exactly," Nick asked, his voice booming.

Even without the phone to my ear, I could hear him.

"Across from the auction entrance and down a ways," I said. "Percy's opening the shoe box. I can't see what's in it, but a ten-year old would know it was money. They're both returning to their cars."

"What in the hell possessed you to do this?"

"I needed the shots of Percy and Marla. You would have stopped me from coming."

"Damn straight, I would have stopped you."

"I'm sorry. But Percy would have been arrested, and Mary Fran would have no case. This was to be their last time together, my last chance to shoot photos. Don't worry," I risked saying, "if you don't get him today, you can get him in Clinton next week."

I heard Nick talking to someone in his office, issuing orders to get ready to move out.

"They're getting ready to leave. Percy's meeting Marla at some motel or hotel or bed and breakfast. I'm not sure. I'll call you when I know."

"I can't believe you're doing this. Stay away, Nora. This is way too dangerous."

I started the engine and took off after Percy, clicking the phone on speaker phone, and setting it on the console next to me.

"What the hell are you doing now?"

"Following Percy."

"You do, and I'll lock you up for withholding evidence."

"I got pictures of everything." I gave him the license plate number of the Outback and a description of Michelle.

"A New Hampshire plate. Hold on." I heard him say something to someone about putting out an APB on the car. "Nora, where are you now?"

"Still in Gray. There are two cars between Percy and me so he won't make me."

"Make you? Get out of your damn cop mode, Nora. My God. I can't believe this. I thought you had more sense."

I shot through a red light to keep up with Percy. So did the huge white van in back of me. I heard Nick issuing orders to someone.

The cars ahead turned off on a side road and I fell back a bit more.

Percy took a sharp turn. I slowed and the van almost plowed into my back bumper. I hate it when people tailgate. Well, evidently I had taught that driver a lesson. He dropped back.

"These people play for keeps, Nora. Collins got killed because of what they're up to. Don't think they won't kill you, too, if they find out you're on to them. In a heartbeat, babe. In a heartbeat."

Okay. So now I was scared. More scared, that is. "I'll be careful. I'll leave after–"

"Back off right now. I'm notifying the Gray Police. Tell me what road you're on."

"Don't. I'll never get the pictures."

"Pictures? The hell with the pictures. What's the matter with you?"

"I promised her I'd get them."

"If you need money that badly, I'll give it to you."

"It's not the money, Nick."

"Then what?"

"I promised."

"And what else?"

"He's been cheating on her. In her own bed."

I heard his door slam, his engine start, his police scanner crackle to life.

"Like your fiancé cheated on you?"

I felt a sob work its way up and I forced it down. "Yes," I admitted on a wobbly breath. "Yes. He has to pay."

"I don't know what to say to you that I haven't already said. I can't remember being this worried about another person in a long time. Or being this angry."

"I won't let them see me," I assured him. "I've been super careful so far. I'll continue to be. I wish I had a gun. I do have mace."

"Mace? You have to be within eight to ten feet to use that stuff. They use guns."

"I know." I slowed a little more, keeping a good distance between Percy and me. "I have Hannah's Highlander, not my truck. I'm being careful. Percy's way ahead of me."

I heard him giving more orders to someone.

Another bend in the road. I lost sight of Percy's Expedition, but I didn't speed up. I slowed and moved to the right. The white van slowed, then passed me. Good, I now had another buffer.

When the road straightened, I saw Percy signal a turn, and pull into a driveway. I kept going.

TWENTY-NINE

The bed and breakfast was a two-story white contemporary set back from the road and surrounded by woods. A well-kept lawn, and a garden with dead flowers, fanned out around the front. When I'd passed it, Percy's Ford Expedition hadn't been there. He must have pulled around back. Only a small pickup, and a red Honda Civic were parked in the driveway.

The Civic set off bells in my head. I'd seen one like it in the library parking lot. Seen it beside Margaret at Kendall's Auto Mall. Margaret must be Marla.

About a half mile past the house, I came to a cleared section just wide enough for the Highlander. I pulled off, got as far into the woods as I could, and parked. No one would see the SUV from here.

I wasn't sure what to do next. The only thing I could think of was to walk down by the bed and breakfast, hide in the woods and wait for Percy and Margaret to emerge. Except, there was a possibility they could both come out separately. No, that was unlikely in a place they didn't expect to be recognized.

I had to get closer. I wasn't crazy about going into the woods, home of the animal kingdom, and my least favorite place to be, but I couldn't see any other way.

I loaded up my saddlebag pocketbook with cell phone, camera, mace, Swiss Army knife, corn chips, ginger ale, napkins. With a light jacket tied at the waist, I set off, my thoughts still on Margaret. Ida hadn't thought the voice in the library was Margaret's, but she had been wrong about that. An angry woman can sound a lot different than a sweet-as-sugar woman or a game-playing sex machine. Even I couldn't identify Marla from her voice, and how long had I listened to that from my post under the bed?

I circled around back of the house, keeping to the security of the trees. After being cramped in the truck for so many hours, it was good to be moving. From here, I spotted two other vehicles in the upper part of the driveway behind the house. One was Percy's. I figured the other, the white van, belonged to the owner. Maybe he was the one behind me on the road. I came back to the side of the house. Better view. From here, I could see the front and back door. Perfect.

I had to pee, so I moved deeper into the woods to handle that need. Gee, how I hated doing this, but what a relief. I hoped I wasn't squatting in poison ivy or something just as nasty. Wouldn't that be a hoot? I chuckled and almost fell over before I finished. Nerves.

I wondered how long Percy and Marla, no, no, I meant Margaret, would stay in the bed and breakfast. I certainly hoped it wouldn't be overnight. The thought of spending the night in the woods made me shiver. Well, I wouldn't spend it here. If they didn't appear before dark, I'd go looking for them. Many of the rooms were on the first floor, and the windows were low. Convenient, but risky. I could shoot pictures through the window. That might be better.

If necessary, I was prepared to go inside. Ask for a room for myself. As soon as I got the shots, I'd run like the devil was at my heels.

I dug into my pocketbook and pulled out the tuna sandwich, hoping I wouldn't get ptomaine, or worse, when I ate it. I dug out the can of warm ginger ale and dropped it. Great. It hit a broken limb, bounced and rolled down a few feet before it lodged between two protruding roots.

I grabbed it, then froze when I heard a rustling sound. In the next instant, I was scanning the area, my head swiveling and bobbing like one of those bouncy dolls that people with no sense of the appropriate put in the back window of their cars. I didn't see a thing. But I'd heard something. An animal? A person?

The tree line, the lawn, the back of the house and the woods looked clear. Then I heard it again, from the woods. No mistake this time. Someone or something was near. Scared silly, I scooped up my gear, dropped the soda can in my bag and glanced around. Unsure of what direction to run, I waited, alert now in a way I had never been before.

That's when I saw it.

A moose.

He was a huge behemoth of a thing the size of King Kong, just lumbering through the woods, his antlered head swinging from side to side. Every moose story I had ever heard, horror stories the lot of them, flew through my head. He stopped about a hundred feet from me. His ears rotated. I froze. Held my breath.

I thought about the mace. No good.

I had to get away. Climb a tree. Hide behind a tree. Slowly, making no spastic moves, I adjusted my saddlebag pocketbook so it hung down my back. Even more slowly, I began to move. Inch by inch, millimeter by millimeter, I stepped toward a large tree with a low-hanging branch. Once I was close enough, I grabbed the branch and swung up. I could do this. I could. I climbed to the second branch and out of reach.

Safe, finally.

I breathed easier. I braced myself against the trunk and straddled the limb, careful not to catch my purse on any smaller branches. For the next twenty minutes, I sat there. I had a good view of the bed and breakfast, so I knew I wouldn't miss anything.

The moose munched on tree bark and leaves, not even bothering to look in my direction. But I stayed put, just in case.

I managed to open my purse, find the cell phone and call Nick, all without falling out of the tree.

"Are you all right?" he yelled as soon as he heard my voice.

"Sort of. I'm in a tree in back of the bed and breakfast." I gave him the location. "The Gray cops don't need to come racing over, so don't be calling them immediately. I want those photos.

Give me some time."

"Get out of the tree before you're spotted."

"There's a dangerous moose below. I'm waiting for him to leave.

"Oh, God, Nora."

"He's leaving now, finally. Gotta go."

Relieved, I worked my way down to the lower branch. I was about to ease to the ground when my purse strap snagged, throwing me off balance. I took a header, landing on the ground with a thud loud enough to alert the moose.

Precious seconds flew by as I took inventory of my body parts. Nothing broken, just bruised. I looked around for the monster, but couldn't see him. Gingerly, I stood, scooped my purse and leaned against the tree, still surveying the area.

Disaster averted, I fished in my purse for my cell phone.

"Drop it!"

Shocked, knowing before I turned who had spoken, I whirled around. "You?"

"Drop the phone. And the bag. Now!"

"Amy. You're Marla?"

A look of surprise flashed across her face. "Only Percy uses that name. He made it up."

"Well, I—"

"Who cares, Ms. Nora Lassiter from the big city? I said drop it."

I would rather have faced the moose. This woman wanted to kill me. The white-knuckle grip on the bat, the anger etched on her face, the combative stance . . . she wanted me dead.

Drop my saddlebag purse with the mace canister jammed in the bottom?

I think not.

It didn't take a detective to figure that for a stupid move. Run. I had to run. It was my only chance. Negotiation was not an option.

In the seconds we stood staring at each other, several things clicked through my head like photos being snapped at a fast F-stop. Green. Her lime green cotton sweater stretched tightly across her ample breasts. There was a pull in the sleeve. Loose threads. I knew where the missing thread was. In an evidence bag.

Lime. I saw her wearing that shortly after I came upon Collins' body. I would have made the connection. I know I would have. But Nick had told me they analyzed a green cotton thread. Did the man not know his colors? One doesn't say green when one means lime.

"Did you kill Al Collins?" I blurted.

She grinned as she flexed her hands on the bat. "Oh, you're the smart one, you are."

Keep her talking, I thought. Keep her talking. "Why?"

"He wanted more money. Little shit thought he could blackmail me. Nobody does that and lives to tell about it, not even Al. I told him to set up a meeting between him and JT. In the woods. Wanted him to take out JT, the chickenshit, then I intended to take him out. Surprise, surprise. No JT. Just me and my shotgun." Amy rested the bat on her shoulder like a player at home plate.

"I meant to see that JT got what he deserved, too. I set up the frame. Right there in his beautiful Maine woods I planted his patch on a branch. I'm surprised he never noticed it missing. It fell off in the Country Store one day and I kept it."

"You planned this in the library, didn't you?"

"Yes. How . . . never mind. I'm finished chatting. Drop the bag."

I wanted to take a step back, but was afraid to move, afraid she'd start swinging. I wondered how long it would be before the Gray police arrived. I knew Nick must have called them. Would they even know I was here? I'd hidden the Highlander down the road. Percy's truck wasn't visible from the road.

Please, God, send them fast, let them find me somehow. Send

someone, even the moose. I would love to see that moose again. Really, I would.

"What does JT have to do with this?" I asked to keep her talking.

"Mighty slow for a detective," she said, a touch of superiority in her voice. "His land, big city girl. His land. He's got over a hundred acres."

So my uncle was involved.

Time. I needed time. I sensed she wanted to brag so I encouraged her. "Land for what?"

"Hah. You don't know shit from Shinola. Whatever the hell Shinola is."

"I believe it used to be a brand of shoe polish," I said, shaking in my boots.

She looked at me as if I were crazy. "Who the hell cares? I needed land for weed. Pot. Marijuana. What'd you think Percy was selling? Air filters?" She snorted. "My stuff is grown underground in beds dug by my dear, departed husband. After he croaked, JT wanted to cancel everything. I made him see the light. Poor, wimpy JT. He took off when things got a little too hot." She gave a harsh laugh devoid of humor. "He musta thought he was next after Al. He was right about that."

She shifted the bat from hand to hand. I sensed her impatience.

Playing for time, scared in a way I'd never been scared before, except maybe on those first days in high school when someone tried to throw me down the stairs, I asked, "You would have killed JT? Who was next? Percy?"

"No one takes advantage of me. Never again. Hear me?"

I nodded my understanding, inched back, hoped she wouldn't notice. Perspiration formed a river between my breasts. I could feel sweat puddling under my arms.

"Who else took advantage of you, Amy?"

Watching her arc the bat back and forth, I thought I already knew the answer to that one.

"That fat slob. Percy's father. You asked me about him a few days ago. He raped me when I sixteen. I worked for him. I cleaned his damn showroom, his damn toilets, his damn offices. He considered me trash. If I told anyone, who would have believed me, a kid from the wrong side of town?"

"He harassed my mother," I said.

"Big deal. He cornered me in the storage closet. They kept baseball equipment there for the office team. Fat fool turned his back when he zipped his pants. Do you believe that? Mister Modesty. After what he'd done. Last pair of pants he ever zipped. Since then I've carried a bat in any vehicle I've ever driven. Quieter than a gun. Sometimes you need quiet. Know what I mean?" she said quietly as she stepped toward me.

Terrified, I turned and ran.

My fears ratcheted up a notch as I zigzagged through the trees, ducking branches, hopping over downed limbs. I smashed into a tree stump and went airborne, ass over teakettle, as they say. Stuff flew from my bag. In seconds she was there, the bat raised above her head.

Terror gave me strength and I rolled, avoiding the worst of the blow. But it caught the pinky on my left hand and I screamed. I rolled over the soda can and snatched it up.

As the follow-up blow descended, I held up the can to ward it off. Stupid, I know, but you go with what you have. The bat connected with the can of ginger ale, and it exploded, catching her in the eyes, giving me precious seconds. I was on my feet, running again, holding onto my pocketbook for dear life. The mace! I had to get the mace.

The pain in my pinky was excruciating. Such a little body part, such a huge pain. I knew it was broken. No X-ray needed when a person can see a little bone jutting through the skin. Every jolt, no matter how small, increased the pain. A bat to the head would put an end to pinky pain. That was a given. So I kept on running because my life depended on it.

She was gaining ground. Friendly waitress Amy with the Pam

Anderson breasts, murderer Amy with in the lime sweater, widow Amy with the weed patch. Her widow's weeds.

I should have returned to New York City where it was safe.

I didn't turn again, just focused on navigating the woods, hopping over brushes and branches, avoiding depressions, Nora the gazelle, who should have taken ballet instead of tap. Tears flowed, blurred my vision. I couldn't turn off the damn water works.

I had to get the mace from my pocketbook. Had to. Had to. Had to. I needed to reach for it with my good hand. I needed time. God, give me time.

Shoving low branches aside, I ran full out. My mind whipped and spun. The only plan I came up with was holding the next large flexible branch back a few seconds, a kid thing to do. Mary Fran had pulled that one on me when I was eight or nine. I gave it a try. It worked. Unable to avoid the fast whip-like motion, the branch connected with a solid thwack. Amy let loose with a yelp of pain and a string of curses.

Good, good, good.

Clutching the pocketbook between my left arm and my body, I reached in for the mace, dropped the pocketbook and spun around. I flipped the cap as the bat came at me again, knocking the canister out of my hand.

No.

I dove in the direction it had flown. She came at me again and I squeezed under a dense bush with a web-work of thick, gnarled branches crisscrossing the top.

"Think you'll get away?" she rasped, her cigarette voice making her sound like a female version of Freddie Krueger from the horror movies.

"You come up here for a few days from the big city and think you can ruin what took me years to build." She swung the bat, connected with branches, and I rolled to the trunk. Twigs jabbed everywhere.

I had to get the mace. Blurry-eyed, I kept my gaze on her as I routed around for the canister amid the leaves and debris. Keep her talking, I thought. Keep her talking.

"Let me go, Amy. I won't tell anyone. I promise. I'll go back to New York. No one will hear from me again."

"You see 'stupid' tattooed on this forehead? I sell thousands of pounds a year. You any idea how much that brings in?"

"No, I don't," I answered, my voice trembling. "How much?"

"A lot. I'll be able to retire and move to an island somewhere."

"I had no idea."

Another flood of tears blurred my vision. I couldn't stop the waterfall. I'm such a crybaby sometimes. I was going to die in Maine. I'd planned to spend four fun-filled days here, get to know the family and all, and here I was in the damn woods, stuffed under a bush about to die at the hands of a maniacal widow waitress in the weed business. I'd once left her a hefty tip, too. Talk about regrets.

"Don't play the innocent. You knew about this. That's why you followed us. You're on the job."

"No. Believe me. I had no idea."

I spotted the mace in the jumble of vines, but couldn't fit my hand through.

"I've been working for Mary Fran. She wants to divorce Percy. She needs photos of him with the woman he was having an affair with. Marla." While I talked, I reached into my bag for the Swiss Army knife, flipped it open, sawed through several vines. "That's it. I knew nothing about your business. I'm not interested, believe me." I eased the small canister out.

"You fool." she said. She swung the bat at the bush, breaking through one of the sections. "Working for Mary Fran."

"Marla? Why Marla? Why not your own name?" I asked, desperate.

Where on earth were the police when you needed them? Stocking up on more Dunkin' Donuts, that's where.

"Percy picked it. Some name from his favorite porn video.

And I never much liked my name." Amy started swinging hard. Cracking branches, sending pine cones flying.

The scent of pine was heavy in the air. I could think of nothing except the oldest ploy in the book, except for swinging branch, that is. I yelled, "Hey. A cop. Finally."

Distracted, she turned. I was ready. In a lightning move I didn't know I possessed, I surged between two bowed branches and rolled out, mace at the ready. Killer quick, Amy spun back and swung wildly. On the downward arc, the tip of the bat caught my foot. Like Wonder Woman, I rolled to my feet, ignoring the pain. When she raised the bat again, instead of pulling away, I lunged to the side and let go a long burst. A dead center hit, right in her face. I scudded farther to the side to avoid the back spray.

Target neutralized.

Amy dropped the bat at the same time her eyes slammed shut. She started coughing. A choking cough, music to my ears. No symphony ever sounded so beautiful. Shaking, I set the mace down, and using my good hand, tossed the bat as far as I could.

"Marla, darling. Where are you?" Percy's voice.

I grabbed the mace again.

Too bad Ms. Marla couldn't answer. She was too busy choking and gagging. Then Percy spotted us. My self-confidence leaked away as he came at me. I shifted upwind to Amy's right, the mace hidden at my side.

His eyes cut from Amy-Marla to me. "What the hell are you doing here?"

He didn't wait for an answer. Enraged, he lunged at me.

"Percy, stop. She has—"

I caught him with two bursts, a real snootful, and just for good measure, blasted slugger Amy once more, up close. Without letting go of the mace, even though I figured there was precious little left, I scooped up my pocketbook.

My pinky pained like nothing I had ever known before. I wanted to sit down and cry. Since that wasn't an option, I started back to the house, moving as quickly as I could. In the distance, I heard the welcome wail of sirens. Dunkin' Donuts must have closed.

Halfway to the house, I stopped suddenly, dug out my camera one-handed, pointed it at the maced couple emerging from the trees and clicked. I did what I had come to do. I took pictures of Mary Fran's husband with Marla the Tramp.

Click. Click. Click.

Fumbling, I set the digital on telephoto and raised it again. Amy, aka Marla, was hanging on Percy's arm as she coughed her brains out. And gagged. It was hard to make out her face though the haze of tears in my eyes. No matter. I'd see it in the pictures later.

 Click. Click. Click.

Percy's arm went around her shoulder, all lovey-dovey. Picture perfect. I couldn't have posed it better myself.

Click and double click.

She shoved him away.

Case closed.

Piece . . . of . . . effin' . . . cake!

THIRTY

Nick burst into the emergency room and shoved my privacy curtain aside while the nurse was wrapping my foot in an ace bandage. No sense of decorum. Gee, I was glad to see him. If I could have, I would have hopped off the Gurney and thrown myself into his arms. I felt like crying again. But I showed some control.

"Nora. What happened to your foot? Is it broken?" His gaze darted from ace-wrapped ankle to my splinted finger. "Oh, God. Your finger?"

"Yes," I sniffed as the doctor breezed back in. "Broken. In battle."

The doctor was a short man with huge glasses and a white flowing medical coat. "Very much so," he told Nick. "Compound fracture. Came right through the skin. Bad break, very painful. But this is a brave lady. You can be proud of her." His brows shot up in question. "You're her husband, right?"

"No. A good friend." Nick smiled at me. "A very good friend."

I felt warm inside.

The doctor nodded. "Police told me she subdued two drug dealers out back of the bed and breakfast."

The doctor yanked the blue striped privacy curtain open the rest of the way, and handed me a prescription for painkillers and an antibiotic. "You take better care of this woman. Hear?"

"I will," Nick promised, ignoring my smirk as I stuffed the prescriptions in my pocket. Looking at me, he repeated softly, "I will."

"Please call Ida for me. Let her know I'm all right. I haven't called her all day, and I know she's worried about me. Heck, I was worried about me."

"I'll call outside. Be right back," he said as the nurse secured the bandage.

When Nick returned, he scooped me up in his arms, and carried me out to his vehicle with Silver Stream Sheriff emblazoned on the side. He set me in the front seat and fastened my seat belt. "Stay put. Promise?"

"Promise. But Hannah's SUV?"

Placing his hands on either side of my face, he kissed me gently, possessively. "I'll handle it. Miller's with me, and he'll drive it back."

I fell asleep on the way home and didn't wake until we pulled in Ida's driveway.

"JT is involved," I mumbled, as he unhooked my seatbelt. "He let Amy use his woods. Marijuana."

"I know," Nick said. He turned off the engine. "A hydroponic operation. Underground tanks. An underground garden. Each tank held about a hundred plants and there are tanks all over the place."

"But he didn't kill . . ."

"Al Collins? I know that, too. Amy killed him."

"You know a lot," I said. "How'd you find out?"

"I'm a cop."

"I found out, too, Mister Head Honcho."

"And if you ever pull a stunt like this again. . . . "

Ida opened the front screen door and stepped out onto the porch, her hand over her heart. Even from here I could see she was upset. Behind her, Hannah and Agnes were no less upset. Agnes's hands went to her mouth as soon as our eyes met and I could see she was trying to hold back tears.

When was the last time anyone cried over me?

Nick by my side, I limped up the front steps, glad to be home. This place felt like home. I was hugged and led into the front room. After I was seated in the best overstuffed chair in the room,

Nick on the hassock beside me, Ida went to get me hot chocolate, Hannah tucked a plaid throw around my shoulders, and Agnes set up a tray with cookies and cakes on it.

I loved how they fussed over me. I knew they were dying to hear what had happened, so when they were all seated, I gave them a brief sketch, leaving out the most violent parts.

"The Gray cops called my cell phone on the way home, while you were asleep," Nick said. "Amy knew she was going down and opted for a deal. She talked. She had convinced Percy to meet her contacts at the auctions. JT wanted out. He was afraid. Thought the operation was getting too big, too risky."

"She was going to kill him," I said. "I think he knew that."

"Ellie found out about this several days ago. She told us this morning," Ida said.

I explained, "Amy killed old Percy. She was a scared kid. He'd raped her."

"I know. She had a lot to say once she was in custody. Evidently, after she murdered old Percy she went to Al Collins, her high school friend. He took her bloody clothes and gave her clean ones. Al said he'd burn hers. He didn't. He buried them in a plastic bag," Nick said. "Then a few weeks ago he told her unless she cut him in for a bigger profit, he was going to see that the right people found those bloody clothes."

"Blackmail," Ida said, shaking her head.

"She tricked him into the woods at the beginning of hunting season," Hannah finished. "No one hearing the shot would think much of it."

"Right," Nick said.

Ida asked, "She told Al to meet JT in the woods and instead she was there with a gun?"

"Yes, Ida. That's part of what you overheard."

"My father's name will be cleared," I said. "Finally, he can rest in peace. I'll call Howie in the morning to tell him."

The aunts were nodding.

"We're so glad," Agnes said.

"So glad," Hannah and Ida echoed.

"What's going to happen to Percy?" I asked Nick.

"They got him on selling weed. Eighty pounds. The eight and the zero are from your mystery list, Nora, the one that mentioned Gray. That minor detail you decided not to mention to me? The chief investigator? The head honcho?"

"Sorry."

"Sorry? Hmm. Another lie tumbles from your lips."

"Well, I'm sorta sorry." I held up my splinted finger and my bandaged ankle in a bid for sympathy.

"I hope this ends your detective career."

"I almost never lie, you know."

"I didn't know that."

I nodded. "It's true."

"About your detective career? It's over?"

"Ended. Absolutely." I held up my right hand as if I were taking an oath.

The aunts watched all this with great interest, but no one said a word.

The following morning I slept late. After a speedy shower in cold water—damn water heater—I went downstairs, knowing my time here had come to an end. I'd had a long visit, gotten to know some wonderful relatives, proved my father's innocence, caught a killer, helped a friend get evidence against her cheating husband. Nothing to sneeze at. I'd never accomplished half as much in a year in New York.

I heard Ida talking to someone in the front hall as I came down the stairs.

"Mary Fran?" I said, smiling, hobbling over to her. "The case is wrapped up."

Mary Fran's hand flew to her mouth. "You're hurt. I heard that and came to see. I feel responsible."

Since I'd already taken a pain pill and was feeling absolutely no pain, I brushed it off. "No problem. I feel fine." I steered her to the kitchen, the source of the wonderful aroma of blueberry pancakes and bacon.

"Percy called and wants me to get a lawyer for him." Mary Fran's face was one big smile. "I told him to get his own. I have one for myself. Then I hit him with his coming divorce. But held off mentioning the prenup. I want to spread out the bad news. Savor it. Did you get the pictures?"

"I did. Nick's having them developed."

I told her what I'd witnessed yesterday as Ida dished out pancakes. Mary Fran declined the food and said she only had time for a cup of coffee. As I was pouring, Nick arrived with the pictures. Mary Fran laid them out on the table and we all looked.

"My word," Ida commented. "Looks like those two were in pretty bad shape when you got finished with them, Nora. Aren't you the one."

"Thanks. These are perfect," Mary Fran said. "Love the one with his arm around her."

Mary Fran opened her purse and counted out a pile of twenties. "This isn't nearly enough for what you went through. You should charge more."

Behind her, Nick rolled his eyes.

The phone rang and Ida answered.

I walked Mary Fran to the front door and told her I'd try to see her before I left Maine.

"I have to be going, too," Nick said a few minutes later, his arm around my shoulder. "How's the finger today? And the foot?"

"I'm on pain medication."

"Good."

We stood at the screen door, awkwardness like a third person between us.

Ida called from the kitchen, "Nora, Vivian's on the phone. Wants to know when you'll be able to finish up her case? The Pomeranians? What shall I tell her?"

Nick grinned at me.

I wasn't one of those people who breaks her word easily. Of course, the Pomeranian problem didn't involve computers or photos, so I wouldn't know what I was doing if I took the case. At least I didn't think I would.

I said to Nick, "I have to teach you about colors."

He put his hands on my shoulders. "Colors?"

"Umm." I felt a chill shiver its way up my spine as he drew me closer. "The difference between lime green and plain old green."

His brow laddered as he thought about this. "The green fibers?"

"The fibers."

He nodded his understanding, then kissed me.

"There's lots I don't know about colors," he whispered, his mouth so close I could feel his breath on my cheek. "It may take a while."

"I realize some folks are slower than others. I make allowances," I said.

The man had a lecherous look in his eyes. I loved it.

He kissed me again, more thoroughly this time, then asked, "You willing to stay until the job is done?"

"I'm tenacious. You know that."

He brushed my lips, a light kiss that left me wanting more.

"Nora?" Ida called. "About Vivian?"

"Tell her I'll see her in a few days," I called.

"Have to go," Nick said. "Duty calls. Dinner tonight?"

"Sounds good."

Another kiss and he was out the door. As he took off down the driveway, I stepped out on the porch and breathed in the crisp morning air. September air. Maine air. The sun was coming in at a different angle now, lower, the rays more slanted as the earth tipped toward winter. Fall was settling in with all its glory. Leaves were splashed with golds and reds and purples. Of course, I didn't intend to stay forever, make Silver Stream, Maine my permanent home or anything. I was a city girl, after all.

But I had things to do here. There was the hot water heater to fix, for one. The money from Great-grandmother Evie would come in handy. Howie could put up his share. I'd tell him later how much he wanted to contribute.

And I still hadn't decided about the land. And I had to get Mom and Howie back into the fold. And . . .

Oh, I had lots to do. No way I could leave yet.

I hobbled off to get paper so I could make a list.

AUTHOR'S NOTE

Although I live in New York, I visited my cousin Madeline when she and her husband retired to Maine. I could picture myself having all sorts of adventures there, but also having a problem with the inhabitants of the woods. And so the setting for this story was born.

I'm presently working on a sequel to MURDER BY THE OLD MAINE STREAM. It has no official title, but here's a clue: it's got something to do with Vivian and her Pomeranians.

Bernadine Fagan